Jack heard the scream. Then the lights went out.

The darkness slithered down the hill. One by one, coming closer and closer, the faint orangey lamps flickered and died. Behind it, an impenetrable wall of pure black. Jack did not pause. He began walking quickly, trying to keep ahead of the slowly growing mass. The sheets of fog parted as he moved forward. He crossed from the pavement into the middle of the road, where it was the lightest. There were no cars around, and he would be completely incapacitated if he walked into a wall or a lamppost.

He stood still, listening for anything that might be coming his way. The faint fluttering of autumnal leaves in the wind. The engine of a solitary car rumbling in the distance. Other than that, complete silence.

Then there was another scream. Jack whipped around. Silhouetted against the deep sky was the hill around which the town was built. At its very peak, the topmost trees bent in gnarled shapes against the horizon. Something howled. It was like a wolf, yet at the same time it had a grinding, shrieking edge that no animal on Earth could have ever produced. It was followed by another and another and a fourth, all entering into the horrific nocturnal chorus. It was the sound of a hunt beginning.

Contents

james bartholomeusz

the white fox

The Seven Stars Trilogy

MEDALLION
P R E S S

Medallion Press, Inc.
Printed in USA

In memory of
Grandad John and Granny Pip

acknowledgments

Though it seems clichéd for a page entitled Acknowledgments, there are a lot of people I owe thanks to for the writing of this book. Alastair Jolly, Mark Pedroz, Ian Murray, Noel Cassidy, and the librarians at St. Albans School for helping me develop my interest in literature. Jonathan Stroud, my favourite young adult author, who I had the privilege of meeting at the age of twelve. Those members of the Department of English at the University of Exeter who I've been lucky enough to have been taught by and Philip Hensher for his advice on the publication process. And, though they will certainly never read this, I feel I should credit some of those writers—living and dead—who have inspired and influenced me: Neil Gaiman, Karl Marx, Friedrich Nietzsche, Garth Nix, Thomas Paine, Philip Pullman, J. K. Rowling, Edward Said, J. R. R. Tolkien, and W. B. Yeats.

I also must give my thanks to all my family and friends who've encouraged me through this and who've enabled me to be a socially functioning son/sibling/student as well as a writer. The two don't always go together.

In addition, I'd like to thank everyone at Medallion Press for helping me publish my first novel—particularly Lorie Popp for her extensive editing—and Gloria Goodman for her work representing *The White Fox* at book fairs across the world.

If all goes to plan, then Jack, Lucy, and everyone else will be returning in *The Black Rose* in December 2012. Until then, enjoy reading.

James Bartholomeusz
June 2011

Part I

"Things fall apart; the centre cannot hold;
Mere anarchy is loosed upon the world"
"The Second Coming"
W. B. Yeats

Chapter I
beyond good and evil

Jack stood on the precipice, looking into the abyss. A pit of absolute darkness, a void carved out of this place, dropping downwards forever. All the others had gone, and he was alone.

For what felt like an eternity, he seemed to exist outside himself. He saw it all: the sinuous thread of fate weaving delicately through his life from the very outset, right up until where he now stood. Everything, he realized, from that moment on top of the hill on Earth, had been part of the rhythmic march towards this point. Somehow he'd imagined it differently. He would have had others here now, his friends and companions with him, but he was alone on this boundary, this edge of stone, this edge of his future.

He glanced behind him. That rectangle of golden sky through the open door. The Light was still there, still within reach, just a single step backwards from this brink of brinks. It would be so easy to walk out that door and be free. But no. To do so would betray everything that he and others had sacrificed to reach this point. Along the way there had been many times he could have taken another course. But not now. His life had become a linear narrative, and everything had become simple. There was no room for stepping back anymore.

He turned to the frontier again. He readied himself, making sure the Seventh Shard was secured around his neck. Then he jumped, diving into the Darkness.

The silence was broken by a slight whistle of wind. Black smoke spilled over the ramparts, coiling upwards to form a tangible shape. It solidified. Where a second before there had been a bare stretch of wall, a man now stood. He was tall and skeletally thin,

so much so that he looked more like one of the surrounding gothic statues than any living creature. He
was swathed in a jet-black cloak down to his ankles,
his hands and feet encased in dark gloves and boots.
His head was completely obscured by a hood.

He was on top of a high wall, complete with cren-
ulations, made out of deep grey stone. Behind him
another wall of stone rose up, with a small window
out of which a miniscule amount of amber light illuminated the weathered barrage. From his position,
only the sky was visible—its cloudy mass seemingly
frozen, and yet in reality it shifted and churned as
roughly as a storm-ridden sea. Gargoyles clutched
the battlements—writhing forms of bats, serpents,
wolves, and many lesser-known creatures. Their
screaming expressions were frozen in the moonlight,
leering over the low courtyard.

Far below, barely touched by the light and wedged
between the square stone like an ancient crab, was a
rocky cave entrance. It struck diagonally down into
the earth, the cracks and nooks splintering the sheer
crimson light that yawned upwards from its depths.

Too red for fire and yet too natural for a mechanized light. He pondered it for a second, deep in thought at what it suggested. Then he straightened up and strode off down the rampart, the sharp cracking of his boots echoing loudly around the deep alcove.

The figure turned a corner, and the walls fell away. A narrow walkway, darkly extravagant and aesthetically impossible, stretched out before him. Either side, the view dropped a thousand feet to the city below—a jumble of thin side streets, claustrophobic alleys, and cramped buildings lost in the gloom. Dotted blue lights were everywhere, glimmering out of regimented windows. Every so often the skyline was interrupted by a skyscraper with its own surfeit of windows, but such was the height of this bridge that it rose above all of them. In the distance, from any angle, the ocean roared—the ongoing battle of sea monsters seeking to rise and engulf the airborne city. The perpetual midnight air blasted inwards from the rocky edges, speeding between the buildings like a horde of maddened ravens, then up to the fortress to spasm villainously high in the clouds.

Beyond Good and Evil

At the end of the bridge, a tower stabbed up from the rocks below. Lit windows glowed farther down, but at this height the circular overlook resolved into a steep chandelier of black magnificence. A tall, thin double door, carved with rose patterns, stood at the end of the walkway. It was towards this that the man made his way.

As always, the chamber was dark and circular, like the outside, reaching upwards into shadow. The shimmering black floor reflected the open flames in brackets above—a ghostly sapphire that seemed to not shed any light at all. Dim moonlight from a hole high in the ceiling illuminated the immediate foreground. The floor was decorated with an ornate black rose, whose extended thorny branches drew everything in the chamber inwards towards its center. The effect was hypnotic.

Glass-like tower structures, each one engraved with a similar rose, formed a wide circumference around the central flooring. All but one was filled by another black-cloaked figure. There were thirteen altogether.

The man bowed briefly to the seat directly

opposite him, which was also the tallest, and took his place at his own.

"What news, Archbishop Icarus?" the figure in the highest seat intoned. His voice was soft, yet it hung in the air seconds afterwards as if it had been shouted. It held concealed venom, like a snake waiting for a mouse in tall grass.

"It is done, Your Majesty," Icarus replied. "No one will be seeing *that* planet for the foreseeable future. No mortal, at any rate."

"Excellent. You have done well, despite your lateness."

"I apologize, my liege, for the siege was almost complete when I received your message."

"It matters not. Now to the issues of the moment."

Every figure in the room turned towards the Emperor in the highest chair. Amidst this wraithlike throng, he was the only one who could be considered short. His robes and gloves were also black but laced with swirling silver on the edges. His throne was not carved with a rose but with a spiked crown.

"Through much toil, I have uncovered the location of one of the Doors." The atmosphere in the room, already attentive, tautened.

"Two, in fact. Abject credit must go to Archbishop Iago for supplying us with our source."

Another figure, a few seats down from the Emperor, nodded.

"Where are these Doors, master?" another figure asked.

"The first one we discovered is on the planet Rauthr in the Small Magellanic Cloud. It lies within a volcanic crater at the heart of Mount Fafnir, which falls under the jurisdiction of the kingdom of Thorin Salr. I feel that in this case little regard need be given to the ruling party."

"The mining folk, Your Majesty?"

"Naturally. This is good. They are ignorant of our arts, and their stubbornness should ensure that they will not seek to learn more of them in an attempt at resistance."

There was silence as all the figures contemplated the operation at hand.

"Who is to go?" voiced one.

"I think Archbishop Iago deserves that privilege,"

the Emperor said slowly, turning towards one of the disembodied cloaks. "But you must understand the implications if you fail. It would *displease* me greatly if you were to not succeed."

"Yes, master. I shall not fail."

"And you know what must be done to release it?"

"A volcano? I have an idea already."

The Emperor nodded, his lip, the only part of his face visible, curling in satisfaction.

Iago bowed his head solemnly and held his forearm out so that the back of his hand faced the Emperor. A rose pattern, the same one as engraved on the floor, traced itself around his veins in faint violet light. Beginning at his feet, his body unravelled into black smoke. The cloud of shapeless gas swirled for a moment before shooting upwards in an arc and disappearing through the high window.

There was a pause before the Emperor continued. "As for the second Door, it is on the planet Terra in the Senso Latteo galaxy. Another easy target. Fortune has indeed smiled upon us. Icarus, you are familiar with that world. You will go there and open the Door."

"I would be honored, Your Majesty."

"The same repercussions apply to you as to Iago. Do not fail me, Icarus. You know what is at stake here."

"Of course, master. I will leave immediately." Exactly mirroring Iago, Archbishop Icarus bowed his head and gave up his form to the Darkness. The wisps of black smoke trailed upwards through the roof and out into the freezing air. He hung for a moment, then, like a gigantic bird spreading its wings, dropped diagonally downwards. Despite the stratospheric gale, he maintained his course. He circled the tower once, then dived down to the east, towards the Garrison, to collect his Chapter.

The elf staggered up the end of the slope and collapsed onto the rock face, rasping heavily. Wind sliced around the mountain like a rapier snake, cutting into his body with glacial air. His breath made clouds of steam; they were instantly sucked from his chapped lips into linear arrows of brief warmth, then lost into the blackness. All around, the mountains extended, the sublime white peaks visible miles around in the clear night. Far below, an odd rock formation jutted out of the side of a cliff, overshadowing a small valley full of mining pits. A river, enclosed on all sides by the stone monoliths, slithered down to the sea to the east and broke out into an estuary of jagged rocks.

Gathering his strength and hugging the wall, the elf, bent double against the gale, moved over to the door. It was crafted of some heavy metal set into the rock face as if to force apart the small opening like a brace. A crimson glow wafted up the passage within, and by its light he saw the carvings around the edge. The ancient dwarves of these parts had used cuneiforms rather than runes to communicate. Here, the crude markings were of wicked, licking flames, howling people, and charred corpses.

The elf gazed at these for a moment longer, then slipped into the passage. A wall of unbearable heat blasted into him, and he stumbled backwards. He raised his arms, and a barrier, only distinguishable by a slight blurring of the air, formed around him. The heat subsided. A narrow, artificial passage barely tall enough for him stretched deep into the mountainside. The glow surged up here, harshly highlighting the crevasses and crannies of the tunnel. He began down it.

He emerged at the bottom onto a small platform of rock. Hundreds of feet below him, boiling as if the basin were a gigantic wok, was a lake of magma. The bright crimson and orange mass bubbled and seethed, and here and there patches of black froth collected on the surface, dissolving in a wave of superheated liquid. Wreaths of steaming atmosphere rose hypnotically, some disappearing into the darkness above the summit to be blasted away into the midnight sky. There was apparently no way forward; on the edge of this platform, a bluestone bridge could be seen, but after a meter or so it crumbled away into nothing. The opposite end of the crater was distorted and blurred, and there too the edge of a bridge was broken off like the other one. A thick chain was slung across its diameter, high above the platform; a large,

the white fox

charred birdcage suspended from its apex.

The elf knelt down and brushed the rock below him. A trace of black powder came off onto his glove. He sniffed at it and recoiled. Not volcanic sulphur. Something else. Something that stank far worse.

He stood and lifted his arm, moving it through the air slowly and methodically. One by one, symbols flickered into life around him, oddly transparent in the steam. They hummed slightly, the full five making a strange chorus of vibrations. He flicked his arm, expecting them to flash over to the broken bridge and reconstruct a replica.

Nothing happened.

He moved his hand over them again, and again they did not respond. He reached out and touched one. It shuddered and liquefied, the droplets of black liquid splattering over the rock like melted metal. Like blood.

The elf backed away as the remaining symbols dissolved.

A column of dark fire blasted upwards from the pit with a horrific roar, the vertical streaks of flame rocketing the cage on its chain.

The elf's eyes widened in shock, he turned to run, but before he even lifted his foot, a tendril of darkness extended out of the chaotic tornado and passed through him. His eyes widened even further for a moment, then glazed over. He sagged and fell forward, hitting the rock hard. The powder and droplets sprayed over his face. A few bones crunched.

More tendrils extruded from the darkness, wrapping around him and raising him high into the air. They lifted him in a high arch and flicked him into the cage, the door bouncing off the frame after him. The tendrils retreated back into the tornado, and it swirled back into the magma, now ready to take shape.

"Fragments. Fragments in the dark."

The man was seated by the hearth, his gaze fixed into the middle distance. The last embers of the fire pulsated from under its shroud of ash and charred wood, edging one half of the man's face with an orangey glow. The wooden pieces scattered over the chessboard in front of him were half-etched with amber, half-dissolved into shadows that flickered over the black and chestnut squared board. The room was dark—the arch of soft moonlight from the window and the cold rectangle of laptop screen the only other sources of light. The only sound came from outside: the soft rustling of the evergreens in the breeze and the call of a tawny owl.

"Fragments?" the second man asked. He was using the laptop and sat at the ornate oak desk underneath the bookcase across the room. He tapped a few more keys.

"Yes," the first replied, his gaze remaining fixed upon the fire. "Loose pieces to a puzzle. What do these events have in common?"

The second man did not speak, still tapping, so the first continued. "One: in November, Isaac goes missing, presumed dead, in Chthonia. A month later we get his last letter, and it's the writings of a madman. We presume he committed suicide. Two: in February, a schoolgirl abducted in Khălese on a hiking trip. Six friends with her murdered, and the crime made to look like a rock slide in a botched cover-up. But she was taken. No sign of her since. Three: in the space of a month, four stars in completely different positions in the sky disappear. All should have been visible at this point in our orbit. All entries taken on clear nights. All gone." The man paused, now gazing into the hearth.

"What if they're unconnected?" the second ventured after a few seconds.

"You know as well as I do that they're not. We know who's behind this. But we're blind. We're seeing the edges of a master plan—only the teeth of a behemoth that's coming out of the dark to swallow us whole. Something's changing here, and it's for the worse." He fell silent again.

The second man finished typing and closed the laptop. "That's sorted. The others are asleep. We should be too." He waited a moment, then made to leave the room.

"'If you stare into the abyss long enough, the abyss stares back into you.'"

"*Thus Spake Zarathustra?*"

"*Beyond Good and Evil.*"

The second man did not reply. He paused for a moment longer to examine the chess game. Only the two kings remained in stalemate, one space apart from each other in the center of the board. Then he left the room, the door creaking shut behind him.

Chapter II
the orchard

There are several things that Jack would have liked to be awoken to—some of which are probably not suitable to write down. However, the simultaneous slamming of an extremely hefty chemistry textbook and the well-strained vocal cords of an obese middle-aged man were not amongst them.

"Lawson!" roared the obese middle-aged man.

Jack lurched off the desk, rocked back on his chair, and regained balance just in time to dodge the extremely hefty chemistry textbook. He stared up at the man with the usual mix of awkwardness and apprehension. To say that Dr. Orpheus's face was fortunate would be like saying a skunk had a mildly pleasant odor.

The textbook, a particularly tenacious volume called

The Darwinian Guide to Biochemistry and Essential Physics, had probably originated from some time around the birth of its namesake. The amount of times it had clubbed the unfortunate desks of this chemistry laboratory were uncountable, and the chance of students being hit was only measured by their reaction speed. Luckily for Jack, he had been made to sit on the end of a bench next to the window, so when something blocked the sun, it was time to move.

"What have I said about sleeping in class?"

"I wasn't sleeping, sir," Jack replied automatically. He watched Dr. Orpheus for the possible aftershock. His bloodshot, piglike eyes narrowed even more, and the crimson flush in his face, brought on by decades of heavy drinking, intensified. His stomach, already barely contained in his tweed jacket, expanded further.

"No backchat. See me after the lesson." He turned and marched off back to his desk. The light returned.

Jack slouched in his chair, trying not to doze off. Shafts of golden sunlight fell through the first floor wall of windows, scorching the students within its range. The burnt-out atmosphere of August had extended well into October, gilting the world in rusted amber. With a pang of annoyance, Jack noticed that almost every other person in the room was slumped over their desks, most likely sleeping. The inevitable drone from next to the blackboard resumed.

It had been discovered by every student early on in the year that this particular chemistry lab was not subject to the usual laws of time and space. Rather, it was a black hole that drained energy and elongated seconds into hours. In keeping with this, the remaining hour passed like days. Outside, wispy clouds lazed across the sapphire sky, seeming to brush the tops of the trees on a hill in the distance. The unattractive, factory-like block that was opposite this one leered like a portly toad over the yard below. The few withered trees that *hadn't* been pulled up to make way for tarmac blew gently in the wind, almost audibly gasping for rain.

A pigeon fluttered into the gutter above this window. A moment later something slimy and white trickled down the pane. As always, Jack didn't even bother trying to pay attention. He'd learnt long ago that whatever crucial life skills he might glean from the industrial uses of limestone he could teach to

the white fox

himself, probably at a better standard, at the end of the year.

Finally, the clock hands deigned to stretch around to the twelve and four. With almost acrobatic precision, every single person in the room sat up, stretched, and started packing everything away. Jack stood and hoisted his bag onto his shoulder, waiting for everyone to pass him. Then he made his way up to the desk.

"Exercise 18B and the summary questions on page 164," Dr. Orpheus called to the students disappearing out the door. He bent down and began packing away his books and papers.

Jack waited, the room stifling him. The flush of cool air from the door was beckoning him outside. He scratched his neck uncomfortably. "Sir?" he prompted when the teacher completely ignored him.

Dr. Orpheus strapped his satchel and stood up straight to face him. This had very little effect, Jack being several inches taller than him. "Why were you sleeping in my lesson?"

"I wasn't, sir. I promise."

"Don't give me that tripe," he snapped. "Whatever were you doing, draped across my desks like a throw rug, then?"

Several answers immediately jumped into his head. Quick-fire comebacks had never come easily to him, but the use of the same simile by the same person for several months tends to prepare you. He chose the safest option. "I wasn't the only one."

"Just because everyone else was doing it doesn't mean you have to. If all your friends jumped off cliffs, would you?"

Of course, Jack thought, if all the people who considered him a friend did in fact jump off a cliff, he doubted the peer pressure of two-to-one would be enough. But he wasn't about to let that on.

"I didn't mean to cause any insult, sir," he said, employing the obedient, sincere voice used when dealing with patronizing teachers. It was infuriating watching the look of satisfaction cross the man's face.

"I know you didn't, but just to make sure it doesn't happen again, I'm giving you a detention."

"But—"

"No buts. Wednesday night, my office. Be there, or it won't be just a few lines you'll be worrying

the white fox

about." Muttering something about how he'd never have these problems with nice, rich private-school children, Dr. Orpheus picked up his satchel and stalked out of the classroom.

Jack followed sullenly. In the doorway, he jammed the door open with a rubbish bin. Maybe with three days' air the room would return to the atmospheric state expected of a southern English building.

He turned and walked straight into someone. She moved back. "Again?"

He looked up. In front of him was a very pretty girl, slightly taller than him, with reddish-brown hair and bright, hazel eyes. He loosened his collar and pulled his tie down. "Yeah, again," he said, exaggerating his annoyance slightly for effect. He checked to see whether Dr. Orpheus was in range before continuing. "And he was happy about it as well. Everyone else was asleep—everyone always is—but he picks on me. I haven't done anything out of the ordinary, but—"

"I hate to interrupt your ranting, but I need to get home. We've got the Camerons over tonight, and Mum needs some help in the kitchen. Can we walk and talk?"

The Orchard

"I thought you hated Megan Cameron," Jack said, momentarily distracted from his predicament as they reached the bottom of the stairwell.

"I do." Lucy opened the door, and they both walked through. "But our mums went to school together. We still have to see each other every so often."

"What's actually wrong with her?"

Lucy took a moment to answer. "She's just . . . she's just a bitch. A massive snob. She's at that fancy boarding school in Darlington, and I'm not sure she owns anything that isn't Jack Wills. She takes after her mum."

"But if your mum and hers are best friends, doesn't that mean she's a bitch too?"

"I'm not denying anything," Lucy replied, without catching his eye.

"I should tell her that."

Both smirking, they continued out of the open door into the Upper Yard. The sun burnt brightly above them, a slight heat haze rising from the few cars left in the car park. The trees, dyed all hues of red and gold, whispered in the light breeze, some shining, some cast into long shadows by the buildings. Across the road, a small green was intersected by the main road and a smaller path. They followed the main road, turning left at the gate and continuing down the hill.

"So what are you doing this weekend?" Lucy asked as an ancient car rumbled by, spouting smoke. She was walking on the pavement and he on the road so he got a faceful of it.

"Not much *this* weekend, no," spluttered Jack, trying not to sound too bitter. He glanced at her sidelong for her reaction. Her hair shone in the intense sunlight, contrasted strongly with her pale, unblemished skin. She was wearing the usual girl's school uniform: a white shirt with a blue tie, navy skirt, dark tights, and black shoes. Still, she could customize anything, and this was no exception. The tie was undone at just the right angle to be stylish but not scruffy, the skirt a touch higher than it should have been, and the sleeves of the shirt were rolled up to reveal several bracelets and a Topshop watch.

"You really need to get out more," she commented a little too seriously.

Jack shrugged. It was alright for Lucy; she was confident and almost universally liked in their year *and* the ones above and below. She was always being invited to parties, and she was famously popular with the football team. He was much less welcome to other people.

"What about you?"

"Nothing much, really. Greg's house party was cancelled because his parents postponed their weekend away. Want to do something tomorrow?"

The words were barely out of her mouth before a Lady Gaga ringtone sounded from somewhere in the depths of her massive bag. After several seconds pulling out books, lipstick, and a diary, she retrieved a luridly pink mobile phone and clicked the green button. She laughed as the person on the other end said something Jack couldn't interpret.

He rolled his eyes. This was typical Lucy.

A few minutes later they turned the corner and the path opened up. They were now walking along the edge of the orchard—the rolling green descending into a cloud-shadowed valley and then rising into a thickly wooded hill. As explained by a worn tourist signpost outside the Apple Grove pub, the town, Birchford, had grown up in Roman times around this

the white fox

hill, Sirona Beacon, because of its supposed sacred significance to the invading soldiers. On the other side of the road, flowery lawns lined the pavement in front of cottages, with various cul-de-sacs spreading off.

As they passed under a pair of outlying trees, a glint of white, like something caught in bright sunlight, drew Jack's eye. There on the opposite side of the valley was a small fox. Jack stopped and turned his head slightly in contemplation. The fox *was* bright ivory white, the color of a water lily, but that wasn't the oddest part. It was sitting in a shadow on the edge of the line of trees, yet each individual hair seemed to catch the sun brilliantly, as though it were illuminated from within. And it was looking right at him.

He nudged Lucy, not wanting to make too sudden a movement.

She appeared not to have noticed and continued striding down the pavement.

"Lucy," Jack hissed quietly, snatching another glance at the fox. It hadn't moved.

". . . but yeah, that's true. Ollie's been seeing Kat—"

"Lucy."

"... and Rob is with Sophie ... Yeah, uh-huh ... Ooh, I didn't know that—"

"Lucy!"

"What, Jack?" she finally responded, holding the phone away from her ear.

"Look!" He pointed to the trees, searching for the fox. For a moment he'd thought he'd lost it, but then there it was, scurrying into the undergrowth.

"What?"

"There. Just there. Did you see that glowing fox?"

"No," she said slowly, then looked at the phone screen. "Damn, out of battery." She dropped it into her bag lightly. "Sorry about that. Where were we?"

At the end of the road, a cluster of birches split the route. One path continued along the edge of the orchard, over the stream, and down the road into the richer residential area. The other swerved off the left and was picked up by a line of semidetached houses, heading into the center of town.

"Bye, then. I'll text you tomorrow morning if I'm not doing anything, and we can maybe go out somewhere?"

"Okay," said Jack, nodding.

Lucy smiled at him and set off over the small bridge.

A few minutes later, Jack arrived at home, just as the blue dome above began to fade into orange. His route had become steadily less lined with green until trees were replaced by lampposts and patches of grass by uneven concrete slabs. This building wasn't particularly pleasant, framed as it was by an austerely spiked wrought-iron fence. Old, faded yellowish bricks made up the walls, with moss clinging in the gaps and ivy snaking up from the bottom. Rows of blackened and perpetually grubby windows showed that there were four floors, but its real nature was suggested by the complete lack of parking space or greenery. A worn sign just behind the fence proclaimed it to be a former overflow debtor's prison from the nineteenth century. The people who worked there had petitioned for the lettering to be covered up, but it was now apparently some site of historical interest, so it had to stay.

Jack headed round the side to the gate. He passed through the sun-baked garden, more rock-hard earth than grass and almost completely filled up by a rusting metal slide and a single tire swing.

The utility room was lined with shoes of the inhabitants, piles of washing, and a small, grubby sink. He continued through the door into the kitchen, something that had not changed since its prison days. It was a cavernous, neo-Gothic, redbrick chamber, in which everything was made of black metal. A massive gas stove seemed to leer out of the middle of the largest wall, the bricks above it charred black. Modern instruments such as a microwave, a sink, a fridge, and budget lightbulbs shone bright white in comparison. A huge slab of ancient oak—allegedly a table—dominated the center of the room but was no longer in use. Only the need to exhibit the kitchen as a local site of historical interest to help balance the orphanage budget kept it there. Jack thought it was hideous.

From the next room came the loud clangs, shouts, and cries that clearly meant dinner was in progress. Jack searched the cupboards and eventually found a can of baked beans, a couple of slices of bread, and a plate. After opening the can, he emptied the contents on to the plate and shoved it inside the microwave. In two minutes, it pinged.

He climbed the stairs quietly. Several misfit

paintings covered the grotesque wallpaper. These were the kind which are slightly too precise for a child but terrible for an adult. Jack had no idea why they were still on the walls. Most people weren't around at the moment, as dinner was likely to be the only time they got a good meal. However, on the first-floor landing a girl, only about five, poked her head around the door and blew a raspberry at him. Ignoring her, he continued up the stairs.

Jack reached the top floor and shunted his swollen door inwards, staggering into his room. It was not at all large, with only space for a cabinet, a wardrobe, and a bed, and it had an awkward slanted ceiling to compensate for the roof. Still, it was better than sharing. Everyone had to sleep in a dormitory until they were eleven when they got their own room on the fourth floor. The thinking behind that was most of the children had been adopted by then. Some were. Some weren't.

He tasted his beans on toast and cringed. It wasn't supposed to be hard to make, but somehow he'd burnt the beans and picked two stale pieces of bread.

He put the plate down and leaned on the

windowsill. Outside, the street was darkening, and only a couple of cars passed every few minutes. Beyond the row of town houses opposite, Sirona Beacon rose, a trunk-embellished mound set against the purple-streaked sky. The tin roof of his school, glinting artificially in the last rays of the sun, was just visible on the skyline.

Sighing, Jack slumped onto his bed. It sagged under his weight. It wasn't even evening, but there was nothing else to do here.

Wind twisted down the street as the light faded. A gang with matching tracksuits and haircuts skulked down the concrete in a pack. There was no one else around. No cars passed. A few loose bits of litter and fallen leaves swirled aimlessly around, scraping along the tarmac before being caught in the updraft once more.

The boys moved to the corner, where a lamppost was pasted with barely legible adverts for a few different clubs and parties. Across the road, they saw a figure gazing up and down the street. He was clothed in a black cloak and boots, and a hood extended over his head so that his features were completely obscured. Deciding they could get some fun out of this, one of the boys crossed the road, and his companions followed.

The man did not heed their arrival. The boys began jeering at him, and he still took no notice. He seemed to be fixed on another plane, something which they could not see. Only when one of the boys hit him on the shoulder did he pay attention. He turned his head slowly to look at the offender.

The boy felt himself shake slightly. The blackness of the hood was hypnotic. It seemed to numb everything—the noise of the wind, the light from the swiftly escaping day, and the ground beneath his trainers.

Another of the boys whipped out a short knife and grabbed the man's arm. He instantly regretted it. His shadow seemed to congeal around his feet, anchoring him to the ground. With a start, all the boys realized they could not move. They struggled, but the air was becoming heavier, sapping their strength, their lungs protesting against the slowly encroaching pressure. Time seemed to thicken, clotting from water to rancid syrup.

The man removed his arm from the boy's grip and snapped his fingers. The shadows leapt.

A minute later the man walked up the street, his spectral cloak rippling around him. In an alley, near to where he had been standing, the last of the bodies slumped to the ground. The shadow turned and slunk back into the gloom.

Chapter III
a phone call

"... but then George is really funny, so I'm not sure," Lucy finished breathlessly.

"Have you thought about which one's actually the nicest person?" Jack replied teasingly.

"You girl." She laughed, pushing him playfully on the shoulder.

He grinned.

"How's your love life, then?"

"Nothing at the moment, no," he said resignedly.

"I was pretty sure you thought Karris was fit."

"She's *fit* definitely, but she's in with all the rugby players. I've barely spoken to her."

"That's no excuse. You just need to talk to her. Attract her attention. Come on. Once she knows you, she

can't say no."

Jack shrugged and looked away in embarrassment.

It was Saturday morning, and the two of them were sitting in comfortable armchairs in Costa's, overlooking the shopping center. A large section of the first floor was cut out, so that the overcast sky pressed on the glass ceiling and down onto the tiled pattern and escalators on the ground floor. An ornate, Victorian-style clock hung from the glass ceiling a few feet away from them, its many spikes making it look like an overgrown spider. Beyond the clock, on the other side of the first floor, was the train station, and galleries of shops ran down the north and south malls to the left and right. This time on a Saturday, the whole place was bursting with shoppers.

They sat in silence for a while, watching the world drift by. The train times flicked across the electronic board above the ticket offices. People milled around, talking and carrying shopping bags. A group of teenagers they recognized from school hung around the JD on BMXs, a couple on guard for security officers. An exhausted-looking mother passed with a pushchair, her two children shrieking about the lack of chocolate currently present in their lives. A man in an Abercrombie & Fitch jumper marched past, his Doberman imprinting the tiles with perfectly formed muddy paw prints, which themselves seemed to ooze of high society. He was swiftly followed by a woman stooped with a threadbare mop, scouring the floor for something else to have the privilege of dirtying it.

Jack found it incredible sometimes that people could pass in the street and walk on by, never to see each other again. Every single person had their own life, their own problems and aspirations, and yet you looked at someone in passing as just another obstacle on your way to the bank. He kept this feeling to himself. The last time he'd tried to explain it to Lucy they had ended up in an argument about stalkers.

He gazed absently at the other side of the upper level. A moment later he registered something on the edge of his vision. "You see that?" He pointed, determined not to be misunderstood again.

Lucy followed his gesture to the platform exit.

People were queuing in front of the ticket

office. A newspaper vendor was selling *The Birchford Chronicler*. His sandwich board declared Youths Killed in Mysterious Twilight Murder on one side and Excavation Begins for Roman Remains on the other. Nearby someone was standing, surveying the ground floor below.

"Yeah," Lucy said. "You know, those guys are popping up everywhere."

"Really? She looks a bit strange." The figure, a woman judging by her stature, was dressed from head to foot in a hooded black cloak. Her hands were clad in shiny dark gloves, her feet in similar boots, and her face was indiscernible. She could have been a Halloween costume enthusiast, but there was something in the way she held herself that was more professional. She was looking down, but as Jack and Lucy watched she looked up at them. They quickly averted their eyes.

"Yeah. There was one down my road last night leaning against a signpost. Then there was another one—a man—sitting on a park bench. They don't seem to do anything. Just hang around."

A Phone Call

"So there's more than one?"

"Yep."

"Maybe it's something to do with religion," Jack suggested, stealing another glance at the strange figure in black. She was still staring at them.

"Maybe," Lucy said thoughtfully, "like some of those Wicca groups?"

"Could be," Jack admitted. There was something else about the figure that his brain was telling him he didn't want to see. It was slightly unnerving. He checked his watch. "We'd better go. The train's leaving any minute."

Lucy nodded, and, taking their coffees with them, they left.

The sky was showered with stars, a thick ribbon of smoke wound its way to the east with the wind. Its source was a crude fire—a few dried logs and loose pieces of coal—glimmering like a greedy firefly in the middle of the small plateau. Buffeted by the wind, its glow flickered off the rock faces, dancing in between the shadows of the many watchers. Humanoid shaped but shorter than humans, skinny and bow-legged. Their heads more like lizards or trouts than mammals, with the same aquatic-reptilian sheen, they clustered around the affair with mingled fear and fascination.

The chief goblin dropped to the ground, breathing heavily. Sweat rolled excruciatingly over every inch of his body. His armor suffocated him, even in the freezing night breeze. He lifted his arms and removed his helmet, an effort in itself. He now had a better view of the scene before him. His elven adversary stood above, the remnants of their battle swirling around him. Two scepter-like lances were held in his hands, the rest of him covered completely in spectral black. The only bit of skin visible was his face, mostly obscured by a mane of wind-ruffled, feral hair. His emerald-green eyes shone with an evil triumph, the scar that disfigured his features twisted slightly with a smile.

Surrounding them were the rest of the goblin's

A Phone Call

tribe, holding on to any armor they could lay their claws on. Several banners depicting his many totem spiked symbols fluttered feebly in the wind, yet none of their bearers stepped forward to assist him. Beyond them, the mountains rose up, pitch black against the deep blue sky. A sea of stars blinked down at him, and the moon's wide grin seemed to mock his defeat.

"You see, he is a weak leader." The adversary spoke slowly in the local dialect, more scratchy hissing than actual syllables. "All he has to offer you is the pillaging of a couple of villages, a few captives, some pathetic, gristly meat. Admittedly, he was the best you could muster. But you now have the opportunity to *really* sink your teeth into something."

The reflection of the flames danced in the bulbous eyes of the assembled goblins, all fully attentive and listening with the unmistakable scrutiny of a crowd that knows it is about to get a better deal.

"As we speak, my associates are being accepted as envoys to the other tribes. You, as a race, have been wronged. Supplanted in your homes by those considering themselves better than you, you have been driven out of the west into these wastelands. Your very cultural heritage is one of shame and denial. The legacy of your ancestry is for you all to be condemned as nomads. We offer you the chance to change that. If you are brave enough to undo your forefathers' mistakes, then we shall meet again in the valley of Sitzung in one week's time. If not, then you will remain hungry whilst your fellow tribes gorge themselves on the lion's share of the winnings."

There was silence for a long moment. Then a few mutterings.

"But, my lord," ventured one of the goblins in his high, scratchy voice, "our army ain't big enough. Even with all the tribes in the Wastelands we still can't stand against them."

"We will swell your armies with some military acquisitions of our own. You need not worry about that. Furthermore, there will, of course, be alchemy involved."

Instantly, the crowd erupted, jumping and cheering their approval. One overzealous goblin leapt and accidentally speared another's ear. In a flash, the

A Phone Call

second was on him, beating his pointed face to a pulp, and the cheering euphoria dissolved into a punch-up.

Rolling his eyes slightly, the stranger let his lance hover for a moment as he raised his right hand. He clenched his fist, and it burst into sickly emerald flame. He made a punching motion to the side. With a small boom, the fireball burst from his forearm and clouted a nearby goblin in the chest. He shrieked, and a moment later the metal parts of his armor clattered to the ground, the ash that was once scaly flesh slipping away on the wind.

Silence fell immediately. The chieftain was still kneeling, his head raised. The adversary lowered his weapon, so that the two prongs arched around either side of his neck, the shorter central one making a slight indent into his throat.

The goblin decided to speak. "You filthy, traitorous bunch of—"

The spear was thrust forward. Dark blood spurted everywhere, and the goblin's head rolled onto the ground, coming to rest somewhere behind the body. The corpse flopped backwards pathetically, loosing

the white fox

its crimson bounty to the rocks.

The elf knelt down. It was common tradition amongst these tribes to take a prize from the loser of a challenge. He slid the spiked gauntlets off the ex-chieftain's arms and onto his own. They were far too elegant weapons for a greenskin.

He stood up and turned, stepping around the campfire. As he passed, he kicked the dismembered head into the hearth. The flames intensified, gorging themselves on the newest meal. He marched away from the fire, the harshly highlighted folds of his cloak fading into shadow. The ranks of empowered goblins parted to let him through. He slid his hood over his face and smiled to himself. These imbecilic creatures willingly lent themselves to use as raw tools. Not for one moment had it occurred to them what *he* would get out of this arrangement. Everything was going as planned.

A Phone Call

Jack and Lucy spent the day in London. They took the train from Birchford to King's Cross and then the Underground on to Oxford Circus. On the pocket money the orphanage gave him it would have taken an age to save up for a phone, and as they were both too young to work, Lucy had bought him one. This was a fair trade-off, however, as Jack had to accompany her whenever she wanted to go shopping. He had asked her that morning and had instantly regretted it. He had been carted around Topshop, H&M, Primark, Debenhams, John Lewis, and Selfridges. They had caught the train at quarter past eleven. By six, Jack was completely exhausted and quite short fused.

"Anywhere else?" he asked, pausing to pick up a Primark bag he had just dropped for the third time.

"Nothing in particular today." Lucy shrugged. "But Claire's is having a sale."

"I am *not* going in there again," he replied, scowling. The memories of their last excursion still burned painfully. A very camp male shop assistant, thinking Jack was on his own, had tried to press-gang him into getting a flesh tunnel to "impress the ladies." As soon as he had explained that Lucy was with him, he was taken aside and given a tutorial about how to buy jewelry for his girlfriend.

"Fair enough." Lucy laughed. "Should we head back, then?"

They caught the 6:06 train to Birchford. Lucy eventually located the week's *Grazia* in one of the many shopping bags and began leafing through it feverishly.

Jack lay back in the seat and watched out the window. The scenery became steadily less industrial and more leafy as they made their way out into the countryside. Reddish-orange leaves and bare branches flashed by in some places and seemed to slow in others. At one point they crossed a viaduct. Both sides of the track gave way to rolling green fields and woods in the distance. A few horses, no bigger than matchsticks, grazed around and about, oblivious to the lanky shadows they were shedding. An old wooden stable rested in the corner of the field.

The train ground to a halt at the junction. Jack didn't mind; he took a moment to survey the landscape again. Then he did a double take. Something darted across the grass, its shadow a flickering, thin form on the blades of amber green. He tried to focus on it, but it was moving too quickly. It looked like a small cat or dog, with four limbs and a tail. Then it shifted direction slightly and caught the light, the diamond-white spark flashing brighter than the early stars. Jack straightened up in shock, craning his neck. He searched for it frantically, but by the time he caught sight of it, it was vanishing around the end of a hedgerow.

"What?" Lucy asked, finally looking up from her article on the Beckhams' new fragrance.

"Nothing, nothing . . ."

They arrived in town at quarter to seven. It was still quite light, and so the two of them made their way down past the orchard. They crossed the small humpbacked bridge and slid down into the valley, settling under an outlying oak tree at the bottom of the hill. Farther up, under cover of the first line of birches, orange tape fluttered lightly in the breeze, with a sign displaying the yellow letters *Excavation in*

Progress in front of it. The small valley was a patch-work of light and shadow, the twilight-hued grass sending elaborate cross-hatching patterns across the hillside. The lampposts marking the edge of the road were lit.

Lucy dumped her shopping bags and lay down on the dry grass, her hair spreading out like a halo around her head. Jack did the same, but one of the bags toppled over, and he had to recover it. Lying down next to her, he placed his hands on his stomach and tried to ease the aching in his feet. They lay silent for a few moments, taking in the soft owl cry and scuffling of small animals in the trees behind them.

"What's on your mind?"

Jack pondered all possible interpretations of the question before he answered. "What do you mean?"

"Anything. You seem distracted."

Jack thought for a moment. "Do you ever feel," he began, trying to make sense of his thoughts, "we could just be done with all of this? Like we could just move on?"

"Where? To university? Work?"

A Phone Call

"No, I mean . . . something big. Like there's more than what's here now. Like you're meant for something more."

Lucy turned her head slightly, her gaze fixed just above him on the warm light that still highlighted the line of trees. "I think sometimes that we should be doing something *useful* . . . It sounds stupid, but you're right—there's got to be more than life right now. More than just a day-to-day routine that goes on forever . . . Why do you ask?"

Jack smirked. "Don't worry." He was pleased with the response, though. "So what's on *your* mind?"

"Well, Amelia said that George . . ."

Jack arrived back at the orphanage half an hour later, by which time it was completely dark. As if they had overheard that morning's conversation, the black-cloaked figures had made no more appearances since the one at the train station. Lucy had dismissed it, but Jack, whose every waking and sleeping thought was not occupied by George, Matthew, and whoever the other one was, was less inclined to let the matter lie.

Slipping through the back door, he took off his trainers and entered the hallway. It was deserted and completely silent, all the other children being put to bed at least an hour ago. Jack had never really enjoyed their company. They were much younger than him and into completely different things like football and the latest brand craze. Plus, they seemed to not think much of him, either, being the only one at a secondary school. Having already spent several years here, Jack had largely given up trying to socialize with them and spent as much time as possible out or with Lucy. Preferably both.

He walked up to his room quietly and opened the door with the least amount of noise possible. Depositing his small bag of the day's purchases on the bed (his new hoodie and shoes, though quite adventurous for his normal spending, had been as always dwarfed by Lucy's near worship of Philip Green), he slumped into the aging plastic chair. In a pseudomystical way, the soft drift of light from the moonlit window fell upon his schoolbag and the unfinished English homework inside.

Sighing the sigh of someone who knows they can't get away with avoiding something for much longer, he pulled out his English books and cleared the desk. "The Second Coming" by William Butler Yeats was printed in cold black ink in the middle of the page.

How does Yeats create the sense of impending darkness in this poem?

Jack opened the desk drawer, feeling for his Biro. His hand fell on something else, a small card. He pulled it out and held it up to the lamp. It was a business card, printed in a generic Microsoft design layout. It read *Apollo Hill Mental Institute*, with a single telephone number underneath.

Jack breathed out heavily. He knew it must be a coincidence or a cruel joke. How much gratification could he really expect from this? But he thought there was always a chance, no matter how miniscule it might be. He paused for a moment longer. Then he got out his mobile and keyed in the number.

The ringing stopped, and there was a crackling noise.

"Hello, Apollo Hill Mental Institute," said a female voice.

Jack's mouth seemed to crack with dryness. He managed to force the words out after a few seconds. "Hi, can I see if I can visit a patient, please?"

"I'll need your name and the patient's."

"Jack Lawson, and the patient is Alex Steele."

There was a tapping sound of a keyboard and a mouse clicking.

He suddenly felt very aware of himself—the feel of the chair, the brushing of his clothes, the silence of all else but the background noise from the phone, and the vibrations of his quickening heartbeat. He didn't dare move in case he lost the signal.

"I'm sorry, but we don't have anyone by that name on file. Is there anything else I can help you with?"

"No, don't worry . . . Thanks." Jack hung up and let out the breath he'd been holding. He felt very hot. He ducked over to the window, creaking it open. The

A Phone Call

cold air was like icy water on his skin, and he gulped it down. He had *known* it couldn't have been real. And yet, through his insistence on trying, he seemed to have lost his friend all over again.

Chapter IV
excavation

In another Victorian building many miles away, a phone clicked onto its hook. Gaby glanced up at the others.

"Jack?" Vince asked.

Gaby nodded. Her face was flushed, and she looked a little scared.

Charles looked up from his game of chess, his finger poised on a white pawn.

They were in the mansion's expansive and extremely run-down kitchen. Brass pots and pans were hung above the rusty black stove, and cupboards, most with missing handles, lined the walls. The Regency wallpaper, categorized as classical rococo or baroque by the battalion of property developers expelled from the site upon their arrival, was peeling and completely gone in some places.

The ceiling was only partially plastered. The wooden floorboards were loose and uneven, giving the room the bizarre atmosphere of a Lewis Carroll novel. A silver minibar looked extremely out of place next to the flaking water pump.

"Well, if I'm honest, I'm surprised it took him this long," said Charles, leaving the chessboard and rolling over in his wheelchair. "Those business cards weren't one of your cleverest ideas, Vincent." He winced as a loose floorboard creaked and a wheel slipped into the groove, jolting him.

Vince grunted something that sounded like "Don't call me Vincent."

"I've been researching this," Gaby said, "and we don't seem to be putting on a very realistic image anyway. We're listed as 'abandoned mansion,' 'site of historical interest,' and 'asylum' by the three companies that have kept our details, and none of our supposed patients are available to visit. No one's ever heard of our establishment. We have no address, e-mail, fax, or website. And it doesn't help that the locals are convinced this place is haunted. We slipped up badly with those business cards—*that* cipher was only meant to be used as a last resort. I'm just not sure how much longer we can keep this up."

There was a loud creak and a bang.

They all turned towards the door.

There was another creak and bang. There was a pause and the sounds of retreating footsteps. Then running.

The swollen door crashed open against the wall, and Linda staggered in. "Can we please keep that door open? I'm bloody *sick* of this place. I've stayed in mansions, and that hovel in the mountains was better than this place."

Everyone looked away.

Charles replied, "It's only until the Cult are rooted out. That shouldn't be long now."

"That's bad, not good," said Linda. "I still think we need a plan B. We have no idea what they're up to, and it doesn't hurt to be over prepared."

"We *do* have a plan B. Alex is on standby to pull him out if the going gets tough." Gaby glanced from Charles to Linda. The latter looked disdainful.

Linda muttered something under her breath.

Vince glowered at her from his corner, apparently

judging whether it was worth pursuing the argument. "I'm going for a smoke." He left the room.

"Linda," Charles said, "if this is going to work, you have to trust Alex."

"But he's just . . . dangerous."

"And so are you when you want to be." He wheeled over to Linda and placed a comforting hand on her shoulder. He smiled, though she did not return it. "He *has* had an unfortunate past, but give him a chance, won't you?"

"Besides," put in Gaby, "what's the worst that can happen?"

No one answered her. Even with Vince gone, there was the implicit recognition of everyone in the room of just how bad things could get.

"Anyway, does anyone want a cup of tea?"

A shower of plaster cascaded down from a crack in the ceiling and landed in the open kettle.

Linda grimaced.

Jack had to walk to school on his own on Monday morning; Lucy had got a lift in. As he passed by her road and stepped onto the pavement bordering the orchard, he began wondering (or continued wondering, since nothing else had occupied his thoughts for the last twenty-four hours) about the significance of the phone call. Yeats, however good a poet he might have been, had lost all meaning for Jack since Saturday. He had spent the night lying awake, contemplating it, and Sunday had not been much better. Alex's situation was something of an enigma.

He glanced at his watch. Through the scratched glass surface the hands pointed to eight thirty. He still had quite a bit of time before registration at nine and no one to talk to. Shouldering his bag, he turned into the orchard, slipping down the hill into the valley. He was hit by a wave of ultra-fresh scent, something so blissfully different to the synthetic clean of school and the orphanage and the routine industry of the rest of the town. The grass was soaked with dew under his feet, quickly seeping through to his too-large polyester school trousers. He made his way over to the rough-hewn dirt track that wound

the white fox

around the first few trees, past where he and Lucy had been sitting on Saturday night, and continued.

Yes, Alex's predicament was extremely strange. Around eighteen months ago, he had just disappeared. There had been only a brief good-bye, just the casual "see you tomorrow" sort, and then he hadn't come back. For a while speculation had been rife about what might have happened to him and not all amongst the younger generation. Alex, to those who had known him, had been a quiet, relaxed, collected sixth former, and although his grades weren't fantastic, he had earned the respect of most of the staff and students.

When the gossip had almost died away completely, the head teacher reported that Alex had taken an extended leave of absence. This only told people that he wasn't dead, and although the head teacher had been pestered constantly, she apparently didn't know any more of the story than anyone else. It had surfaced a few weeks ago—from, according to Lucy, a fairly reliable source—that Alex was now boxed up in Apollo Hill. Jack had initially taken it to be someone's idea of a funny joke and dismissed it immediately. He had forgotten about it completely until finding the business card.

Jack found a drier spot and sat down, leaning his schoolbag against the tree next to him. Breathing in slowly, he enjoyed the cool feel of the morning. A couple of birds called to one another somewhere over his head. The trees forming the edge of the wood were apple, their oval leaves brushing lightly against each other. The sky was a drab greyish white, but dark clouds sweeping across the horizon promised rain soon. For as long as he could remember, this was where he'd come whenever he wanted to get away— either from the teachers' disapproval or the noise and bustle of the orphanage. Still, there was nothing like a Monday morning to set a damper on things.

Things *had* been different, he reflected, looking up at the basalt sky. He and Alex went way back, and Jack suspected that he was the only one who had the right inkling about what might have happened to Alex.

Alex had arrived at the orphanage when Jack was eight. To begin with, he was like Jack, an outcast, and that was how they'd got to know each other. At school, Alex, being several years older than Jack, would stick up for him in front of the other children, and that deterred bullying to some extent, even if it only meant they left Jack alone and made no effort to get to know him. Jack, being much more academic than Alex, would often help with his homework. It could have been more of a rivalry than a relationship, and they had had their rough moments, but the two of them had remained the closest of friends.

The other orphans treated both of them as outsiders, but where Alex found friends seemingly wherever he looked at school, Jack only encountered enmity. However, where someone else might have abandoned the less popular companion, Alex stayed as close to Jack as ever. That was the great thing about Alex; you could always count on him to make the right choices.

Yet there was something more than a simple orphan story. Most of them at the orphanage knew each other's predicaments, and it was treated as normal to have had a house fire or a car crash. (There was even someone whose parents had been caught up in a roadside bomb whilst working for a charitable organization in the Middle East.) Alex's story was never told, and Jack doubted whether any of the staff knew much more than he did. He had found anything that alluded to Alex's history only once, when one of the orphans had succeeded in getting to him. All that had been known then was that he had not been an orphan from birth; his loss had been relatively recent and this was the latest in a string of care homes.

Something caught Jack's attention out of the corner of his eye. He glanced to his left. Farther round the hill, the orange tape could be seen more clearly, and it looked as if the excavation had begun. A mound of sodden brown earth was piled next to the cordoned-off area, some slipping down the slope onto the grass.

More of the black-cloaked people were crowding around the area, looking down into whatever was being dug up. They were all hooded like the others, but by the movements of their heads, they appeared to be conversing quietly. Jack watched them for a moment and realized they seemed to be arguing. There was something a little unnerving about a group of people dressed in complete black in pure daylight. He had been to Camden Market only once and had found the alternative culture slightly intimidating, but this was different somehow. Again, he got the impression that his eyes were registering something his brain was telling him he didn't want to see.

One of them straightened up and turned to look directly at him.

Jack turned away quickly. After a pause, he snatched another glance back. The figure was still gazing at him, and now more of them were staring in his direction. He was acutely aware that there was no one else in sight except him, not even any cars passing on the stretch of road above him. Standing and wiping grass from his trousers, he seized his schoolbag and clambered up the slope. They didn't appear at all friendly, and he didn't want to be around when they came looking for him.

"Who was he?" the woman hissed as they moved back under cover of the trees.

"Just some kid," the man replied in his thuggish voice. "He won't know what he saw."

"You're sure?" put in a third.

"He'd better be," said a fourth disembodied voice close by, "or it's his head on the line."

The group stopped suddenly and stood back. They had only just avoided walking into another black-cloaked figure, sitting with one foot up on a tree stump. Under the thick tree cover, it was a lot darker. Other scatterings of colorless light here and there betrayed the time of day; all else was gnarled, grey trunks and scraggly grass.

"Archbishop, when can we do it?"

"Tonight."

There was a sharp intake of breath all around, and more figures stepped out of the shadows.

"You're sure we're ready? Can it be done on such short notice?"

"If my source is correct, the Shard will be arriving today. If all goes to plan, and we have picked our hostage correctly"—he eyed one of the figures to his right—"we shall be gone before sunrise tomorrow. Not that there will be anything to leave behind, of course."

There were some snorts of amusement around the circle.

"I'm glad," said one of the women. "I can't wait to get off this archaic dung heap." She spat on the ground before her, the white bubbles saturating the fallen, bone-dry leaves.

"We all want to be on our way as soon as possible," acknowledged the figure, "but we must proceed with the utmost caution. I don't have to remind you what awaits us if we squander this opportunity."

There was a slight rustle.

Instantly, all of them turned to the direction of the noise.

There was a pause. Then another movement in the trees.

At superhuman speed, the leading figure extended his arm and let loose a bolt of black lightning from his gloved fingertip.

Something tumbled from one of the trees onto the forest floor.

He glided over and rolled it with his boot. "Just a bird," he said disdainfully. "Come. We will make camp on the hilltop." He marched up the hill, followed one by one by the other black cloaks. The last one did a single sweep of the area, then followed.

Unseen by any of them, an ivory-white fox was lying inside a hollow tree trunk, its pearly tail squashed flat against the wood. The isabelline gleam that it usually held was dimmed to nothing, so that now it looked like a slightly strangely colored scavenger. Clawing at the end, it wriggled out of the organic tube and shook the leaves and dirt off its fur. Its tail bobbing with the movement, it stalked through the trees, beyond the tree line, and onto the edge of the orchard. As it passed the orange tape, it paused to gaze intently at the large stone circle that had been uncovered.

The tape fluttered noisily in the wind. There was a slight rustle, and a breeze whipped up, not out of the air but from the depths of the pit. The grass around the edge wilted and blackened.

The fox scarpered off down the hill.

Chapter V
the fox and the hounds

Monday was terrible.

The storm had overtaken Jack on the way to school. Casting itself completely over the town, its arms curling around to embrace it, the clouds had broken loose. Hail had thundered down everywhere, and by the time he reached the reception, he was drenched from head to toe in freezing water. He had to sit through double maths, physics, and French before he could get cleaned up, and even then he couldn't find a change of clothes. Lucy had had an away netball fixture all day, so he sat at the back on his own in his classes. He spent lunch by himself, sitting in the corner out of the way of the main crowds of full tables. No one even made an attempt to

come over and talk to him. The afternoon was hardly better; the titanic struggle of double chemistry awaited him. By the end of it he was extremely downtrodden, still soaked, and very tired.

For once, he just wanted to get back to the orphanage as quickly as possible. He was considering skipping that evening's detention, but he almost immediately decided against it. Making Dr. Orpheus angry once was about as wise as taunting a bleeding rhino. Making him angry twice was shooting it in the mouth with a harpoon gun. So, at four o'clock after an extremely dull media studies lesson on the analysis of a news article, he went up to the chemistry department and knocked on Dr. Orpheus's office door.

The door opened and a woman answered. "Yes?"

"I've got a detention with Dr. Orpheus tonight. Is he here?"

The woman looked behind her distractedly. "No. He left this afternoon with an urgent call home."

"Why? What happened?"

"Oh, his wife was sick or something. I assume you can just go home?"

Jack nodded at her as she closed the door in his face.

He left the school and headed down the road. The clouds had dissipated around two, typically just as lunch break had finished. The sun was once again a glazed gold, but it was lower in the sky now, hovering over the rooftops of the town. No one was around. All the students had gone home, and the teachers were either running after school activities or in their offices. He was on his own.

There was a quicker way back to the orphanage, which Jack rarely took because Lucy's house was down the other route. A car went by as he crossed the road and passed down a side street. A few cars were parked around and about, and on his right a small Methodist church interrupted the regular pattern of terraced houses. He reached a crossroads, and up ahead, surrounded by a high wooden fence, was a private ground. A notice bolted to it proclaimed it to be private property, with the threat of prosecution if trespassed upon. Someone had scribbled their tag in purple over the letters. He didn't stop to read the notice again. He slipped behind a bollard designed to stop cars and cut down an alley.

The road continued, and a second alleyway led off to the right, which he turned into. Brown and orange leaves were clustered at each end. On one side, the fence of someone's house. On the other, high evergreens spread their rough fingers through a wire mesh. Both sides blocked the fading sunlight, casting the path into the purplish-grey shadow of the sunset.

Jack began down it. Someone, probably in imitation of Banksy, had sprayed hearts in the steadily darkening colors down the fence, each about a meter apart. He passed white, yellow, orange, pink, red.

There was a rattling behind him. He looked back, but the alley was just as empty as it had been before.

Turquoise. Green. Blue. Indigo.

There was a shimmer of light to his left. The last heart was black, then below that a stylized man in a tracksuit and trainers, holding out a lighter. The word *ignite* was scrawled next to it in white paint.

There was a flapping noise from above, and a pigeon cleared the treetops. Jack watched it over the

The Fox and the Hounds

rooftop, then dropped his gaze, looking behind him. Still nothing was there. Slowly, he turned back to the front. And jumped.

A fox was sitting in the middle of the path. It was undoubtedly the same fox he had seen twice in the last three days. It shone out of the dull brown, each miniscule strand of its fur catching the sunlight perfectly, again despite it sitting in shadow. Up close, there were more details that made it seem even less fox-like. It had dark markings around the eyes, but the eyes themselves, far from being beady and black, were pearly and pupil-less. Its tail waved slightly behind it, like a bushy paintbrush, the tips dipped in ebony.

Jack stepped forward tentatively. He'd read somewhere that foxes were scared of humans and any sudden movement would make them run away.

The fox did not move. It continued staring at him through those pupil-less white eyes.

Jack waved wildly.

the white fox

No response.

Hugging the fence, he edged around the animal and kept walking.

"I wouldn't do that if I were you."

Jack spun around. The fox was facing him once more, but there was no one else there.

"They'll be coming soon."

Jack started again, but again no one was within eyesight. The fox was still staring at him. Slowly, he approached it. "Was that you?"

"Who else?" It inclined its head slightly.

Jack staggered backwards in shock. No one else was about . . . but it *couldn't* be a talking fox. Most people learnt to leave talking animals with melon-sized eyes, along with people spontaneously breaking into song, in Disney cartoons from the age of about two.

"What?" the fox asked, examining its paws and looking itself up and down. *"What did I get wrong?"*

"Well, generally, foxes don't speak," Jack replied breathlessly.

"I'm not speaking," the fox said.

Jack listened for a moment, but as soon as he did he became distracted from what the creature was

The Fox and the Hounds

saying. He did not seem to be *hearing* the noise. It was as if it were talking directly into his brain, rather than going through his ears first.

"Okay, okay," Jack said, trying to straighten it out in his head, "so you can talk. What are you? What are you doing here?"

"What I am is of little importance. And there's no time to explain . . . Hold out your hand."

Wondering where sarcasm had entered the equation, Jack hesitantly held out his hand, palm up. The fox's eyes flared with white light for a second, and something dropped into Jack's hand. He lifted it into the sunlight for a closer look. It was some sort of crystal shard, about the size of a bean pod, and completely clear. It sparkled on the edges in the golden rays, and as he looked closer, Jack could just make out a tiny star symbol carved in gold into one of the sides.

Jack looked up, his mouth forming the words to ask what it was. But there was no sign of the fox creature. He glanced around and in front of him again, but there was no glint of white. He stood for a moment, his brain turning over what he had just seen. He studied the pendant in his hand, then slipped it around his neck, making sure to hide it under his shirt. He wasn't really sure why—and it sounded crazy in his mind—but if the fox had needed him to take it so badly, then it couldn't do any harm to keep it. He wondered whether it had been some kind of animatronics with a microphone. But then he hadn't exactly *heard* the thing speak. It had been inside his head, and it was absurd to think of a *mental* microphone.

He set off again and emerged out of the other side of the alley onto the pavement beside a road. It was deserted. The sun had sunk behind the houses across from him, the silhouetted shadows casting cliffs of darkness on either side of him and all down the street. The pink-orange sunset was receding, and encroaching from behind was the infinite veil of deep blue, tinted amber from the light pollution. A few downstairs lights glimmered, and a cat meowed in a garden somewhere to the left. Adjusting his bag on his shoulder, he followed the road on the leafy side, the pendant bobbing slightly against his chest.

The Fox and the Hounds

On the other side of town, where the houses were built high and close together, darkness was falling fast. The twilight amber blue was giving way to the third and final stage of the evening—the absolute sheet that was the night sky. The temperature had dropped like a hawk, and out of the condensation fog had begun to rise. Immaterial yet solid, it swept over the streets, snaking between the buildings and through gardens, covering everything in an opaque veil. A cat shrieked and darted inside. The tendrils slithered up the steps behind it.

Dr. Orpheus strode down the road, his long frock coat pulled tight around his body. The fog was rising higher, and now thin sheets of it hung at head height and beyond, so he could barely see his feet in front of him. The buildings were only faint outlines, and the occasional light here and there did nothing to penetrate the pallid gloom. The sound of his footsteps was completely masked, which meant that so were anyone else's.

He reached a bridge and stopped. It was a small,

curved one, the kind in any village built around a stream. Now, in the dense darkness, he thought, it was the kind that a troll might live under in a fairy tale. But of course, this was no fairy tale. He pulled his coat a little tighter and glanced around.

Dr. Orpheus never heard the man coming. He was only aware of him when he reached the other side of the bridge, by which point he was sure he had already been seen. The figure was shady, but he seemed to be wearing an old-fashioned black cloak, the hood completely concealing his face. Being unable to see his feet gave it a spectral look. Dr. Orpheus forced his mind away from such thoughts. He was a man of science and rationalism, and no Homo sapien dressed in the style of the popular subculture popularly referred to as goth was going to scare *him*.

The figure made to move. He did not speak.

Orpheus stood his ground. The seconds moved agonizingly on.

The figure did not even turn its head. The blackness of the hood stayed firmly fixed upon him.

Orpheus's hand twitched in his pocket. "Well?

The Fox and the Hounds

What do you want?"

The figure remained silent.

Orpheus could not control himself. "I've given you all the information I have," he said, not entirely successful in keeping the pleading out of his voice. "I don't have anything more. I've told you where the girl lives, and I've got no idea what happened to the boy. Now, where's my wife?"

The figure still did nothing.

"Where is she?"

"She is in use."

"What do you mean? We had a deal. I want her back."

"You cannot have her back."

"But you said—"

"We became bored waiting for our plans to ripen. She provided . . . *entertainment* for us."

Orpheus's nostrils flared and he grunted in anger. Rage seethed out of him in flecks of spittle, and he made ready to jump at the man. But he steadied himself. He could hear a slight sweeping sound. He looked down. On the apex of the bridge, in the gap between himself and the figure, something was changing. The fog, though not discernibly moving, seemed to tense, as if put under some spatial pressure. Below, shadows began to collect, flowing inwards like dark fluid from all around. Then, slowly, something began to rise out of it. A hulking figure clinging low to the ground, its rough silhouette just visible below the fog.

Orpheus stumbled backwards, his jaw slackening and his eyes widening. From what he could see, the shadow was moving, weaving hypnotically from side to side as if waiting to strike. It reminded him of biology documentaries about the hunting patterns of wolves. Except this was much, much worse.

"You made a promise," he shouted, gazing up at the figure.

The cloak was still hanging motionlessly, watching him intently. "We do not make pacts with the Mass Ignorant."

The shadow tautened suddenly. Orpheus stood stock-still. Then he turned and tried to run. He could hear the shadow lurching behind him. He reached the nearest lamppost and slipped on the wet tarmac. He rolled over, shielding his face, but couldn't help

The Fox and the Hounds

seeing what was looming over him, its eyes glowing a deep, bloody crimson in the dark.

He screamed.

The shadow leapt at him.

Jack heard the scream.

It echoed over the rooftops, absorbed by every corner and gap. He froze, standing outside a disused pub. The windows were boarded up, and graffiti had been scrawled onto the wood. The sign, a faded painting of a woman in ghostly Victorian dress, creaked in the low wind. Jack's feet were submerged in a sluggish tide of murky grey fog, flowing down from the hill to submerge the town. The houses were now just dim shapes in the gloom. The lampposts, placed every ten meters, only served to illuminate the sheets of dismal mist. The last echoes of the scream died away.

Then the lights went out.

The darkness slithered down the hill. One by one, coming closer and closer, the faint orangey lamps flickered and died. Behind it, an impenetrable wall of pure black. Jack did not pause. He began walking quickly, trying to keep ahead of the slowly growing mass. The sheets of fog parted as he moved forward. He crossed from the pavement into the middle of the road, where it was the lightest. There were no cars around, and he would be completely incapacitated if he walked into a wall or a lamppost.

On the edge of his brain, his nerves started gnashing. He knew there was nothing that could hurt him out here. This was a civilized suburban area, not a medieval forest. And yet . . . he remembered going on a trip in primary school to look at a forest in autumn. At the end of the day, it was getting dark, and he'd lost the group. He'd only been separated for ten minutes, but, in the deepening gloom, that had been enough to lose his nerve completely.

He stood still, listening for anything that might be coming his way. The faint fluttering of autumnal leaves in the wind. The engine of a solitary car rumbling in the distance. Other than that, complete silence.

Then there was another scream. Jack whipped

The Fox and the Hounds

around. Silhouetted against the deep sky was the hill around which the town was built. At its very peak, the topmost trees bent in gnarled shapes against the horizon. Something howled. It was like a wolf, yet at the same time it had a grinding, shrieking edge that no animal on Earth could have ever produced. It was followed by another and another and a fourth, all entering into the horrific nocturnal chorus. It was the sound of a hunt beginning.

Jack ran. He fumbled in his bag as he went, pulling out a small metal torch he had been given as a mass-produced Christmas present. He turned the end frantically, and it flickered on, shedding a sparse beam of light into the fog below. He sprinted down a side road, between parked cars and lightless houses. His footsteps were covered by the fog, but the juddering of the torch betrayed his movement. Blood pounded in his ears, and he kept glancing over his shoulder to check that nothing was behind him.

At a crossroads, he ground to a halt, breathing heavily and bent over. This was stupid, he told himself. He was running from nothing.

the white fox

Then another howl rent the air like a knife.

It came from his left, down the shadowy road into the dark. He didn't dare shine his torch there. Forcing himself on again, he dashed down the right path, not daring to look back. He reached a corner and continued, and the road narrowed. There were no houses here. He could hear growling and the rough grunt and guttural noises of some inhuman pounding after him. He willed himself even faster. The torchlight jerked ahead of him in time with his gasps.

Then, out of the mist, a brick wall loomed. He skidded and fell, the torch dropping out of his hand and shattering on the concrete. He steadied himself and looked around wildly. It was a dead end, and he was trapped.

The creature was nearing him, its slobbering growls becoming ever louder.

An arm grabbed him roughly. He twisted and cried out, but a hand gripped his face and clamped over his mouth. He struggled, but he was being pulled backwards into the dark. Into an alcove in the wall out of direct sight of the road.

The Fox and the Hounds

Chapter VI
the demon

Jack tried to kick his captor, but he held firm. The hand around his mouth tightened, and the elbow dug into his ribs. His breath caught in his throat, and he couldn't cry out, or even turn his head. Meanwhile, the creature was drawing closer.

A shadow passed across the narrow gap that was his window out of the alcove. In the almost absolute darkness and cloaked by the mist, it was virtually invisible. Out of the black chasm, irregular rasps of sucking air were the only sound. Terrified to move, Jack frantically scanned the obsidian wall before him, but it was completely impassable; the thing could have been anywhere. Then a gap in the clouds slid across the moon, and its

rays penetrated the fog. The silvery light glinted off the rain-washed gutters and tiles of the surrounding roofs, and the darkness was compressed into the ground. The shadow became visible.

If Jack could have screamed, his vocal cords would have snapped.

The thing that was emerging out of the depths was absolutely hideous. It vaguely resembled a wolf or hyena but was much bigger—the size of a small horse. How it had remained hidden under the fog was inexplicable. Its fur was a ragged, discolored greyish brown, which in places looked as if it had been ripped out to expose rotting, gory flesh underneath. In other places, spikes the size of carving knives tore through the surface, like curved bone, but stained with the innards of its victims. The head was either encased inside something like a pig's skull—or maybe it *was* a pig's skull—he couldn't tell.

The eyes, though, were the most petrifying. It had no eyeballs but instead ghostly will-o'-the-wisp orbs that hovered within the deep black of the sockets, shining crimson and darting all over, mercilessly raking

The Demon

the area. The rasps came from its bare nostrils, sweeping in and out of bone rather than flesh. The stench—a blackened, scorched smell like a meteoric eruption—was enough to make bile rise in Jack's throat.

"Don't move a muscle," a voice hissed in his ear.

Too stricken to do anything else, Jack complied.

The monster slowly turned on the spot, as if following an invisible scent. Jack noticed how all its legs didn't seem to bend in the right way. It swung like a grotesque scarecrow in the wind, as if it weren't used to the pull of gravity. The creature turned its back on them, searching the far corner of the wall.

A few moments passed, tautened and lengthened by fear. Jack's foot, bent into an awkward position, began to ache. Quietly as he could, he slid it backwards along the concrete and stepped straight into a stagnant puddle.

The noise seemed to echo a hundred times longer and louder than usual, as the milliseconds slipped by maliciously.

The monster had moved into the shadow cast by the opposite wall. Its head whipped around to look

the white fox

directly into their hiding place; now all that was visible were those two glimmering crimson lights.

Jack froze, incredibly conscious of the miniscule sounds the ripples of water made under his feet.

The monster turned its haggard form towards them. Jack stared, transfixed, at the will-o'-the-wisps. They stared back, the twin spheres spinning in a hypnotic chthonian whirl, and the taste of bile crept up Jack's throat another few inches.

He felt a hard push in the small of his back, and he fell forward. His arms constricted, he hit the concrete hard. Simultaneously, there was an earsplitting bang. Jack looked up at the creature that he expected to be looming over him, the twin spheres of light obscuring the silver moon. But it was feet away, weaving drunkenly, staggering on its spiked paws. A dark hole, steaming with silver, had formed between its eye sockets. It lurched away into the fog, and there was the sound of it collapsing somewhere beyond.

Jack looked back at the person behind him. He was standing in the shadow of the alcove, though Jack could tell by his silhouette that he was at least

The Demon

human. That was no guarantee, though. The man's arm was pointed out, directly at where the creature had been. In his grip, glinting metallically in the moonlight, was a gun.

Jack scrambled to his feet, extremely aware of the gun pointing directly at him. He slowly raised his arms into the air.

The figure did nothing for a moment. Then the gun was lowered into the shadows.

"Who are you?" Jack said, his voice echoing around the enclosed alleyway and alcove.

The figure stepped out of the darkness. Tall, slim, and clothed in worn jeans, a grey hoodie, and a brown jacket was a boy of eighteen or nineteen. He had a pale, knife-shaped face, with dark hair pulled over one side in an angled fringe. His eyes shone emerald green, reflecting the moon.

It was Alex.

Jack stood, frozen on the spot for several seconds.

Alex smirked and waved his hand in front of Jack's face.

He blinked. "Alex?"

"Right, you're *not* having a seizure. That's good."

"Alex," he cried at quite a high pitch and then remembered himself. He cleared his throat and offered his arm in a more masculine way.

Alex laughed and pulled him into a hug.

Jack, surprised but relieved, patted him on the back. Then they broke apart.

"Where the *hell* have you been?"

"You sound like Lucy's mum," Alex replied half-indignant, half-joking.

Jack couldn't help smiling.

"It's a long story. I can't tell you now. I will, though."

Jack noticed the gun in his hand again. He turned quickly, just in case the thing was slinking up behind him. He didn't know where to start. "How did you get a gun? *Why* have you got a gun? What the hell was that?"

Alex brushed his fringe out of his eyes and bit his lip. "I suppose I can tell you a little. It's complicated. I've been away . . . working . . . helping . . . *saving* people. I worked with this organization. They stop bad things happening . . ." He seemed as at a loss as to where to start as Jack was.

"What kind of bad things? What *was* that?"

Alex breathed out heavily. "This is going to be hard for you to believe—"

"What?"

"That was a demon. They're . . . dark creatures. They're not from this world. This organization I've been with, they protect people against demons."

"Demons?" Jack was about to snort, "They're not real," but then he remembered the rotting flesh, the bloodied spikes, the burning, fiery eyes, and the sickening feeling of it just being nearby. Even at the thought of it, the bile began to rise in his throat again. He glanced over his shoulder, but there was no movement from the cloaked darkness. Still, he didn't want to go anywhere near it. "So . . . demons?" he gasped weakly.

"Yeah. That one was a hellhound. They're not *that* dangerous on the grand scale of things, but it could easily have killed you."

Jack gulped and looked down, and something caught the moonlight. Threaded around Alex's neck was a small angular crystal, seven sided and pointed like Jack's with a different minute symbol engraved on it. "You've got one too." He reached under his school shirt and pulled the crystal from around his neck, holding it out.

Alex's eyes widened slightly, and he breathed in to speak but suddenly shifted his eyes to look back up the street. Jack followed his gaze, but through the fog he could still see nothing but the tops of buildings, rising like murky willows in a swamp.

Alex raised the gun again. Both of them listened intently. Footsteps could be heard, echoing louder and louder as they came closer. Alex reloaded the gun and motioned Jack to the wall.

A figure emerged from the darkness. Jack squinted at it slightly, then recoiled in surprise. It was wearing a dark hooded cloak that hid its entire body, including the face, just like the ones had been at the train station and in the orchard. It seemed to hover above the mist, floating like some faceless phantom towards them.

Alex had made no attempt to hide. He was standing full on, aiming the gun's barrel directly into the

The Demon

figure's hood.

"Impressive," it said in a deep, rolling voice. "You seem to have disposed of my scout. I commend you. Not many of your kind could face such a beast."

"On your knees," Alex said calmly, his voice completely at odds with what he was doing.

"What possible leverage do you think you possess? That archaic weapon is nothing—"

"I *killed* the hellhound. Just do it."

The man paused, then raised his arms. "Now, is this really wise? If I do not return, the remaining members of my Chapter will inevitably discover what has become of me. And they will find you. Do you really want to take that risk with your friend here?"

Jack flinched, but Alex did not seem perturbed. He pointed the gun more forcibly.

Slowly, the man sunk to his knees.

Cautiously, Alex stepped over to him and pushed his hood back.

Jack ventured closer and got a good look at him. He appeared about fifty, with short dark hair and a full, grey-brushed beard. He was grinning menacingly, showing one or more teeth to be blackened or missing.

"You are unwise, boy."

"Shut up." Alex's voice was poised with detectable venom, his face contorted into a snarl. "Why is the Cult here?"

The man's grin faltered. "To absorb this pitifully antique world into the Darkness, of course."

"No more games. I want the real reason. This town—this *planet*—is completely defenseless. You could have killed every living being here by now if you'd wanted to. This is easy pickings for your Darkness. No fires, no alchemy, no demons stronger than a hellhound, not even a Dark Eye. What's going on?"

The man's grin returned. "Oh, I assure you there will be an Oculatrum of sorts within the next few minutes. And as for stronger demons . . . you have no idea."

"Where?" asked Alex fiercely, shoving the gun into the man's temple. For the first time, Alex seemed a little shaken.

"At the orchard. I would hurry if I were you. The ritual is almost complete."

The Demon

"What ritual?"

"You'll no doubt find out when you get there." His smile widened and his eyes gleamed. "Not that you'll be able to prevent it."

Alex removed the gun from the man's temple and half-turned to Jack. "Come on."

"You fool. You actually believe—"

Alex whipped around and batted the man over the head with the gun. He crumpled to the ground, his body disappearing under the screen of fog, just as the hellhound's had done.

"You didn't need to do that," Jack said, taken aback. He crossed over to where Alex was waiting. "Is he . . . ?"

"No, only knocked out. He'll come round soon with one hell of a headache."

"Are we going to the orchard, then?"

Alex considered for a moment. "Yes. We'll take the bait. Oh, and that." He pointed to the crystal Jack was holding in his open palm. "Keep it safe. Put it around your neck and don't let anyone see."

Jack got a longer look at Alex's crystal. It was, as he'd thought before, slightly different to his. The

the white fox

symbol on Alex's was carved in silver, not gold, and the inscription wasn't the same. "What do these things do?"

"No time to explain," replied Alex distractedly as they hurried off.

"That's just what the fox said."

"What?"

"Nothing, nothing . . ."

They jogged off down the street. Jack noticed Alex kept the gun out—and ready—all the way. He considered what Alex had said. Under any other circumstances, he would have dismissed "working for an organization" as something like drug dealing, but now he wasn't so sure. And that wasn't something Alex would do, anyway.

What about the demon? He had been convinced such things didn't exist—everyone had—except maybe the extremely religious. But Jack had seen that thing with his own eyes, and somehow he knew that it wasn't from this world. When it had looked at him, it seemed to emanate some kind of psychic stench, which was enough to make him feel physically sick.

The Demon

And then there was the fox. He was still having trouble accepting that an animal could talk, but again, that had been no normal fox. And Alex had another one of those pendants. What did it all mean?

After an endless series of twists and turns down side streets and alleys, they came onto the main road coming down from the school. They were at the orchard. Across the tarmac and out into the sea of mist, treetops could be seen. Rising above it, silhouetted against the deep purple sky, was Sirona Beacon. Trees clustered up its sides, and right on top individual trunks were picked out against the stricken horizon.

Alex slowed, and Jack came to his pace, breathing a little harder than usual. The freezing air seared his lungs, and he had just realized how cold he was, only in a school blazer. His bag was long gone, abandoned in some alley to keep up the pace.

They crossed onto the grass and followed the path.

Jack looked at Alex, then at the gun in his hand. They hadn't said a word since the alleyway. "So one of those can kill a demon?"

"Sort of. It'll delay it long enough for us to get

away. It's only because the bullets are laced with a special chemical. Super corrosive."

"And those black cloaks?"

"They're called the Cult of Dionysus, by the way. And it depends."

"On what?"

"Who surprises who."

Gradually, light became evident before them. Alex gestured for Jack to stay quiet, and they both crept towards the source. As they got closer, they could see it was being projected in blocks from floodlights, placed in a circle around something. Closer still, and Jack could see the orange tape of the excavation site fluttering in the wind. It had been severed.

Alex moved ahead on soft footfalls, the gun outstretched. He made a circuit of the area and returned to Jack's side. They moved forward to the remnants of the orange tape.

There definitely had been an excavation here. In a circle of about fifteen feet across and six feet down, the earth had been uprooted and piled next to the hole. The floodlights had been positioned to afford maximum vision into it. They both peered over the edge.

Whatever Jack had been expecting, this was not it. His first thought was the inside of an industrial revolution–era machine—layers and layers of cogs and gears, all piled on top of each other on multiple axes, interlocking and turning slowly. They seemed to have been cast out of some rough, dark metal, and by the soil still clinging in the grooves, the whole construction could not have been exposed to the air for many hundreds of years. That, though, wasn't the strangest part. A silvery purple glow, more vapor than light, wafted up through the gaps in the inter-meshing structure. Under the thick layers of metal crisscrossing each other as far down as Jack could see, there was no discernable source.

"What is it?" Jack whispered.

Alex's gaze flicked over the gears as if it were a complicated puzzle. "I'm not sure . . ." Suddenly, he straightened up and hurried round to the opposite side of the pit. He bent down to examine something.

Jack stood and followed Alex's path around the floodlights. A few feet away, he saw what Alex was

the white fox

looking at. A curved chute, on the same level as the discs, had been dug out of the hillside. It was filled with a number of dense pipes of the same metal as the gears. The faint violet glow around them hinted at more of the vaporous light. Jack followed the path with his gaze, and it soon disappeared into the gloom hanging under the trunks. It continued through the undergrowth, onto the barren top of Sirona Beacon. "I'm guessing if we follow this pipe, we get to the top of the hill?"

"And straight to where the Cult are."

Jack looked apprehensively at the unfathomable forest and then back at Alex.

Alex stowed the gun in his jacket. "Let's go."

They climbed the slope quickly and quietly, following the path of the pipes. It took a while for Jack's eyes to become accustomed to the almost pitch-black, and then he began getting jumpy. He saw shapes in every gnarled trunk and movements in every shadow. The moon gave no illumination but just hung above, draped in grey clouds. Having seen horror films, he had thought that a full moon in this kind of situation would be an unfrightening cliché. Now he felt as if it were watching him. He forced himself to stare straight ahead.

Alex kept a few feet ahead, ducking behind fallen trunks and stumps every so often. The silence was gravely oppressive; no animal cries could be heard out of the gloom, and every snapped twig or crunched leaf seemed to echo a thousand times louder than it normally would. No sound, either, came from the hill above them. This, Jack hoped, was because there was nothing actually there. Or because whatever was up there was keeping quiet for exactly the same reason as he and Alex were. That was not a comforting thought.

They moved through the last of the trees and reached the edge of the forest. The pipe chute continued on upwards to the very top, blocked from sight from where they were. Alex gestured for Jack to get down, and the two of them began crawling on all fours up the last of the slope. The grass was sparse here, and most of the ground beneath them was painfully hard stone. They reached a jutting-out

the white fox

rock, and both crouched behind it. Alex peered over the top, and Jack followed him.

On the flat top of the beacon, now only a few feet away from them, a group of black-cloaked figures stood. Almost indiscernible against the deep sky, seven were standing with their arms outstretched in a wide circle around what seemed to be a cylindrical altar. The remainders were in a group off to the right.

Alex ducked down behind the rock and pulled the gun out of his jacket pocket, checking the rounds.

Jack continued watching, and one of the black cloaks shifted. He caught a flash of reflective reddish-brown hair and exposed skin. His eyes widened.

Another of the black-cloaks moved backwards, fully revealing the girl.

It was Lucy, still in her netball kit, her arms bound behind her back, mouth gagged, in the grip of one of the larger figures. She looked terrified.

Jack rose slowly, waving frantically at her. She saw him, and her eyes widened in surprise, then relief. Then shock, as one of the nearer black cloaks swivelled and followed her gaze. He looked directly at Jack.

Alex finished loading the gun and saw him standing up. He leapt to his feet, pushing Jack downwards, and faced the figure. He raised the gun, but, with a flick of the black cloak's hand, it was wrenched from his grip and flung sideways into the dark.

More black cloaks turned and started drifting towards them, phantomlike over the rocky ground. Alex tried to duck, but another clawlike hand motion had him lifted into the air by the throat. Jack was ripped out from behind the rock, unable to move, as the figures closed in.

Chapter VII
the ritual

"Mr. Steele," said the man. "From all I've heard, I really expected more of you."

Alex was suspended in the air by his torso, his limbs flopping uselessly by his sides. A thin trickle of blood ran down the left side of his mouth and neck and under his top, but he didn't try and wipe it away. The wind blasted in his eyes, making them sting, but he made no attempt to scratch them. He kept his gaze firmly fixed on the taunting figure before him. The figure was entirely covered in black, just like the others. The only visible skin was his pale mouth under the shadow of the hood. Currently, it was smirking.

"You come back, and yet you allow yourself to be captured instantly. Some heroic attempt to save your

friends? What is heroism without strength, but folly?"

Alex scanned the hilltop. By the sparse moonlight, he could make out nine figures dotted around him and the figure in front of him. There were several more on the other side of the pit, though he wasn't sure how many. He knew that the normal Chapter consisted of thirteen sorcerers, but this was no normal mission. There could be many more lurking beyond sight in the deep shadows of the trees. He looked behind him as far as he could. Out of the corner of his eye, he could see Jack and Lucy, their school uniform and sports kit brightly branded against the cloaks. They were held in a similar way to him, with black cloaks standing directly behind their levitating bodies.

"What are you planning?" he snarled.

The man turned his head, as if studying Alex from a different angle. He pondered him for a moment, then seemed to decide. "I don't see the harm in it. You will, after all, be playing a vital role." The man turned and walked over to the edge of the pit.

Lifted by some unseen force, Alex floated after him, still unable to operate his muscles. He reached the rim and was lowered to hover next to him.

This pit was at least thirty feet across and larger than the one at the bottom of the hill. Where below, there had been an intricate weave of gears, what had been unearthed here was much simpler. What had appeared to be a circular altar from farther down the hill was in fact the topmost of a series of rough stone discs piled on top of each other in size order to form a cylindrical stepped pyramid. Each level had chutes carved into it at seemingly random intervals and directions, all fitted with the same ancient-looking piping. The pipe chute from the lower pit ran up to the edge and dropped downwards, the end left unconnected to anything.

"Beautiful, isn't it?" The man laughed greedily.

Alex couldn't exactly see what he meant. "What is it?"

"A marker. A gateway, denoting the location of a Door into the Darkness. Its creators and custodians may have faded into extinction and myth, but this is still as fine a piece of invention as it was the day it was created."

Alex traced the patterns laid out before him,

trying to mentally assemble them. There was a small hole at the center of the highest stone slab. A hole just big enough for . . .

"How did you get here?" Jack whispered to Lucy, trying to turn his head the minimal amount for her to hear.

She continued staring straight ahead at Alex, un-blinkingly. It took Jack a moment to realize she was giving muffled whispers through her gag. "They . . . they picked me up on the way back from netball . . . They knew where I live . . . I was walking home, and a group of them were waiting for me . . . They picked me up without even touching me. How the hell is that possible? And then you show up with Alex. Where? How . . . ?" She faded into silence.

Jack glanced at her. She was unusually pale. Her clothes were torn and muddy and had leaves and twigs stuck in them, as if she'd fought through bushes trying to escape. He'd never seen her this frightened before. She didn't look as if she'd noticed the two of them were hovering several inches above the ground in the same way as Alex, and Jack wasn't about to bring it up.

The Ritual

"It has taken considerable toil and time to locate and unearth this Door," the man continued, still looking over the pit. "And that is not to mention the lengths we went to so that you could be here with us tonight. How ironic: that a Door was to be found in the same pitiful world as the bearer of a Shard! The lock and the key placed next to one another!" He turned swiftly and grabbed Alex by the collar, pulling out the chain hanging around his neck. On the end was the crystal shard, engraved with its miniscule symbol. He yanked it down, ripping the chain.

Blinking away the tears of searing pain, Alex saw, to his horror, the man dangling it in front of his face.

"Just out of interest, how did you come into possession of this?"

Alex didn't answer. He tried frantically to twist his arms out of the invisible lock. He still could not move them and was left wriggling helplessly in mid-air like a wounded animal.

The man laughed coldly. "I wouldn't bother. You'll only tire yourself out." And he flung the pendant over the pit.

It spun meticulously three times, the pointed end

glimmering brightly on each revolution. As it reached the center, it froze, as if caught magnetically. It hung perfectly still for a single, inextricably long second directly over the slot in the stone. Then it plunged, daggerlike, down.

With a high-pitched shriek, silver light rocketed upwards, shooting a column of energy into the darkened sky. It struck clouds and penetrated through them, lost, like a bright searchlight, in the deep purple shadows. The low growl of swift wind swept over the hilltop. Clouds, whipped up by a sudden gale, swept over the bald peak, swirling together to consume the stars and moon. The windstorm descended, blasting over the barren hilltop in a freezing frenzy, crunching the trees in a cacophony of searing whistling. Thunder rumbled from above, and over the surrounding hilltops talons of bright white lightning clawed at the landscape, pulverizing their points of impact in superheated oblivion.

A deep grinding sounded, and Alex looked back down at the pit. The layers of stone were rotating slowly in alternate directions, as if pulled into a predetermined position. They halted with a heavy

The Ritual

crunching noise, and with a crack the topmost level sunk into the second, the second into the third, and so on, seven times until they became level. The dull glow around the now connected pipes intensified, and the same vaporous light surged from the external chute through the newly aligned ones. It completed its circuit and fizzled, grinding to a halt. The silver light flickered and faded. The thunder, wind, and lightning remained.

Now, twenty feet below them, a single circular slab lay, a shimmering, complex rune highlighted in indigo across its even surface.

The man turned back to Alex, smirking coolly. "Lastly . . ." The man strode over to one of the black cloaks, who was holding an antiquated Latin-style scroll. He inspected the miniscule engravings for a moment, evidently translating word by word. "We need . . . blood . . ." He reached into his robe and pulled out a curved dagger. Still reading the inscription, he raised his arm and plunged it into the neck of another nearby black cloak.

The figure gave a low gurgle as scarlet blood spurted around the silver insertion. The corpse

the white fox

sagged to the wet ground.

Lucy screamed, and Jack gagged and vomited a little into the grass. Even the other black cloaks looked apprehensive at their leader's impulsive murder.

". . . blood . . . of an innocent," the man finished. "Ah, well." He kicked the body, and it rolled over the edge into the pit. "He can be the appetizer."

There was a dull clunk as the corpse hit the bottom. Thin ribbons of corrosive steam, putrid blackness, snaked upwards from the chasm, accompanied by the sound of sizzling meat.

He rounded on Jack and Lucy, marching over to where they were held. He leered at them both—held as they were above the ground they were the same height as him. "I'm a generous sort of chap, so I'm going to leave it up to your would-be protector to decide. Who gets sacrificed?" He looked at Alex.

Alex tried again to wriggle out of his confine but to no avail. "If you dare touch *either* of them—"

"You'll what? Wriggle at me? It's either one dies, or they both die. You can choose to save a life or choose not to. It's up to you. I may be wrong, but you're one of those people who *doesn't* want to see others die, yes?"

Alex snarled at him.

"So who's it going to be? Netball player, complete with authentic scream action, or the gaunt teenager, malnourishment-related accessories not included?"

Alex didn't answer.

The man drew his dagger out again and began swinging it between Jack and Lucy like a pendulum, getting closer each time. Both tried to move, but all they managed was to lean their heads back slightly.

Jack looked from Lucy to the dagger. She was past the point of screaming; now she was stunned into silence at the mesmerizing veer of the blade. He tried to speak. "Pick me—" He felt something invisible clamp over his mouth, muffling his voice.

"Hush," the man whispered, raising a finger to where his mouth would be, "it's not your turn. You get your question next round . . . providing you still have a tongue. Or a head."

There was silence. Jack looked at Alex. He was staring at the dagger, his face a mask of indecision.

The dagger swung before Jack, so close that he felt the air ripple around his collar, then by Lucy and grazed her neck. It came back a second time, aimed deep at Jack's jugular—

"No," Alex shouted.

"We have a winner," whooped the man. He lowered the dagger. "Girl, how many people have you murdered, tortured, stabbed, shot, psychologically damaged, or otherwise maimed?"

"None," Lucy whimpered.

"How good of you." He grabbed her by the throat and lifted her into the air. He raised the dagger in his right arm and switched his grip so the blade was pointing downwards.

Jack tried to cry out, but he couldn't even whisper.

The man swung the blade in an arc, ready to strike—

"Wait," Alex yelled.

The man paused and turned his head to look at him, the dagger halted in midswing.

Alex looked from Lucy's terrified expression to the darkness of the hood. Jack could tell he was thinking fast. "Show us your face."

The figure smiled again. "I suppose you're thinking by looking me in the eye and appealing to my better nature you can stop this madness and bring

The Ritual

me over to the side of goodness and justice, and then all evil in the world will vanish forever, and we'll all go and have a tea party in a flowery forest grove with talking animals with names like Bertrand and Alice. Well, it won't. The world's cruel, Mr. Steele, and the sooner you understand that fact, the sooner you'll see true reason. But then, why not try? Why not try and prove me wrong?"

The man reached down with his dagger hand and pulled the hood off his face. Sleek, shoulder-length hair framed a darkly handsome face with fierce blue eyes and a sadistically curved jawline. He looked only about forty, but in his eyes there burnt a light Jack immediately associated with madness—simultaneously old so as to have seen all the evils of the world in their worst form, but at the same time young, daring, and vicious.

"No?" the man said. He leaned closer to Alex. "Has it sunk in yet that you're on your own? No grown-ups here to make it all better. This isn't smoke and mirrors, boy. You aren't about to wake up safe and sound. This is real. Nowhere is sacred, not even your hometown. Does it hurt, knowing what kind of place this world really is?"

Alex stared at him for a moment. He thought he had seen something in that face before, though he could not recall where or even if it was on this man. "What's your name?"

"Icarus. And before you say anything, I appreciate the poetic significance. I chose it, after all—the second great overreacher after Prometheus in classical mythology, the one who aspired to the sun, the symbol of light and life in the ancient world, but ended tumbling down, scorched by the sublime nature of his own ambition, down into bottomless perdition, there to dwell in chains wrought by his daring grasp at the glory of immorality. Now, if we're done with theatricality . . ."

He raised the dagger above his head, its vicious, entwined blade glinting in the red light of the eye above, its shimmering surface mirrored in his own pupils.

Lucy screamed again, louder this time. The thunder and wind still blasted over the hilltop. The cloaks of all the figures around rippled, wraithlike. The crescent moon now shone with purple light: from one angle, a hungry grin.

Alex writhed against the force that kept him bound, but again nothing happened. There was the sound of movement in the background, but Jack did not hear it. He was frozen with fear.

Then a bolt of blue light burst out of the darkness like an enraged beast. It struck one of the black cloaks squarely in the chest, sending him tumbling into the shadows.

Chapter VIII
counterattack

Icarus lowered the dagger and dropped Lucy, whirling around. All the black cloaks turned, searching for the source of the blast.

A moment later, a second shot exploded out of the gloom, narrowly missing another figure. The shock wave blasted her hood off—a dark-haired woman with sagging skin. Then another, which knocked the legs out from under a man to her right. The group abandoned their positions at the pit and drew closer around their leader. The purple light had faded from the moon.

Jack twisted his head and squinted into the dark. Out of the shadows, more figures appeared to be advancing up the hill from all sides. With no moonlight, they were semi-spectral, but a momentary flash of

lightning silhouetted several against the obsidian sky. They were not swathed in ethereal cloaks, but one had some kind of rifle or heavy gun hoisted over its shoulder. In that moment, another threw out their arm, and a flash of crimson light burst out of it, spinning through the air like a throwing dagger and striking a heavily built black cloak in the shoulder. He shrieked and reeled off sideways.

Another burst of light, this time green, shot from the outstretched arm of one of the newcomers, swiftly dodged by one of the cloaks. A newcomer flicked her arms outwards and let loose the orb of golden fire that had been hovering between her palms.

However, Icarus was ready. He raised his arm in a lightning quick motion, and the air rippled around him as the fire was deflected to smoulder in the grass to his left.

Now, the black cloaks began to counterattack. The unhooded woman raised her hand and contorted it. Shiny black tendrils leapt from her fingertips to coil around the nearest figure like writhing serpents. A man, his face still hidden, made a motion like a karate chop through the air, and a wave of indigo energy panned out across the ground, tripping up two approaching newcomers. The hilltop dissolved into chaos—bursts of light being fired, absorbed, and deflected everywhere, augmented by the furious crackling of bullets.

The force suspending Jack released, and he collapsed to the grass, face-first. He moved his arm experimentally, and it worked. He searched around for his captor and saw him flinging crackling black bolts at one of the newcomers—a blonde girl in what looked like a Special Forces uniform of dark Kevlar and body armor. Icarus was nowhere to be seen, but Lucy was a few feet away, spluttering and choking.

He tried to stand, but a blast of red light shot directly over his head. Half-crouching, half-crawling, he made his way over to Lucy. "You okay?" he panted.

"No," she gasped, grasping her throat. She had pink marks around her neck and cheeks where Icarus had held her up.

"What the hell's going on? Who are these people?"

"I don't know." She looked more scared than he had ever seen her, but he saw in her face the same thing that was keeping him from denouncing this all

the white fox

as a hallucination: the impulse to stay alive.

If they survived this, Jack knew he would question whether what he was seeing here was actually real, but this was not the immediate issue. These lights, whatever they were, seemed to be hitting and hurting, and that was good enough for his adrenaline-induced brain.

"If they're half as bad as this lot, we shouldn't be sticking around. Let's get out of here. Where's Alex?" Jack looked around. After a moment's searching, he saw him. He had jumped onto the crescent moon stone and was sparring with a tall and skeletally thin black cloak. He seemed to have abandoned the gun; it took Jack a second to register that what was rotating in his palms were shruriken-like discs of silver energy, which he was hurling at his opponent.

The black cloak deflected three in succession, but one caught him in the stomach, and he doubled over sharply, crumpling to the ground and rasping for breath.

Alex scanned the chaos and caught sight of Jack and Lucy. He smiled.

He's actually enjoying himself, Jack thought, ducking

a whistling wheel of violet flames. It was at that moment that he knew for certain that Alex hadn't been anywhere near a mental hospital. He couldn't help smiling himself. The last eighteen months melted away, and there they were again, the three of them in the orchard, sharing pizza and drinks that Alex had bought from the off-license down the road. Lucy had just said something funny, and they were all laughing. And there was Icarus, laughing along with them, cackling behind Alex, raising his knife . . .

Smoothly, almost artistically, Icarus slid his dagger into Alex's back. The vision melted away as time turned to sludge, everything seemingly slowed to half rhythm. Jack saw Alex's eyes widen, his mouth sag as he fell forward onto the hard stone.

Jack didn't know what was going on. He did not see the blasts of energy shoot past him nor the duelling figures staggering in his wake. He did not feel himself running or the pain in his thighs as he dropped into the pit. He only knew that he wanted to cause Icarus as much pain as possible, and he didn't care how he did it.

Then he stumbled and fell, and time returned

the white fox

to normal. Looking up, he ignored the searing pain in his knees, for what he saw filled him with dread. A column of impenetrable ebony smoke was forming behind Icarus, and, as if from all around, the black cloaks were diving into the pit towards it. They formed a circle—facing outwards around it—standing erect, but the bolts of bright energy shooting towards them from their attackers were fizzling out before they reached their targets. One by one, they replaced their hoods and held up their right hands, palm outwards. Purple thorn patterns traced over the veins, forming into twisting roses, wrapping themselves over the entire bodies and intertwining with the dark smoke. The black cloaks vanished, ghostlike, into the wall of darkness.

Icarus caught Jack's eye. The blue there burned with satisfaction and malicious pleasure. Then he was gone into the blackness and Alex with him.

Jack's gaze switched to the only remaining cloak, just in time to see one of those bolts of lightning arch down onto him. A burst of blinding light, agony, then darkness himself.

Jack came to very slowly, becoming firstly aware of the slight rumbling motion of what he was resting on and then the noise of the engine around him. He finally had the energy to open his eyes. He was staring through a pane of glass, looking at the passing scene of trees and countryside, barely visible by the illumination of amber road lights. He turned his head and flinched as pain exploded into his neck—it was blinding white; he couldn't see; he could only feel again the surge of lightning that had coursed down his spine, setting every nerve alight.

As the pain receded, he became aware of where he was. He was sitting in the backseat of a small, grubby-looking car. Someone was watching him. In the front passenger seat was the girl in the Kevlar he had seen fighting earlier, now with a very out-of-place tan jacket over her body armor. She had short blonde hair and very blue eyes. She could have been only a few years older than Alex, if that.

"Are you okay?" she said. Her voice seemed strangely familiar.

the white fox

"I'm alright," Jack replied, massaging his neck.

"What did they hit you with?"

"What? Oh, this sort of black lightning bolt."

The girl frowned. "You should be okay, I think . . ."

Jack thought about it. His memory was a bit fuzzy. There had been a crescent moon and a hyena-wolf creature and lots of brightly colored lights. And Alex. Then the full magnitude of what had just happened cascaded down to hit him like an avalanche.

"What's going on?" he cried in a voice that was much higher than his usual one. He strained against the seat belt. "Who are you people? Where's Lucy? What was that? Where are we? What happened to Alex?" He faltered. More memories crashed down. The knife. Alex falling. The purple patterns, then black smoke disappearing into the night. Icarus smiling at him. He punched the seat in front of him hard.

"Hey," said a man's heavily accented voice, "don't do that." For the first time, Jack became aware of the driver.

The girl looked at Jack sympathetically. "Calm down. It's okay. We'll tell you."

"Gaby, we can't—"

"Look what just happened to him. I think he deserves to know what's going on."

"Sardâr wouldn't—"

"Well, Sardâr isn't here, is he?" When the man didn't answer, she continued more kindly. "My name's Gaby, and this is Malik."

The Indian-looking man driving nodded at them in the rearview mirror.

"We're part of an organization called the Apollonians. I . . . we . . . help people, in a manner of speaking."

"So you're not with the Cult of Dionysus?"

"Us? No! Definitely not. Actually, the reason the Apollonians was founded was to—"

"Gaby . . . ," Malik grunted warningly, turning left at a roundabout.

"He needs to know—"

"Not *that* much."

"Sorry about him," Gaby said, regarding Malik coldly.

"What happened to Alex? Where's Lucy?"

"Your friend—Lucy?—is safe. Don't worry. You'll be seeing her in just a few minutes. As for Alex, we're not sure. He was obviously taken by the Cult, but we don't know why yet. More to the point, what were *you* doing there?"

Jack quickly recounted the story from when he'd left school to their arrival at the orchard. He left out the part with the fox, although he wasn't really sure why. Maybe they'd think he was mad, or maybe they'd take the crystal that the strange creature had given him. Alex had told him to keep it secret. As subtly as he could, he felt the string around his neck and tucked it lower under his now filthy school shirt.

"Right . . . ," Gaby said, exchanging a look with Malik.

It was clear that they didn't believe him. Through the haze of the headache, he felt a prick of annoyance that he was not being believed by two people who claimed to represent a secret organization that fought off demon-summoning sorcerers. "So, where are we going?"

"We surprised the Cult when we attacked," explained Malik. "They got sloppy and didn't keep their surveillance up. But they'll return with reinforcements within hours. We need to get the two of you out of here. All our agents have taken different routes

Counterattack

back to headquarters to throw off any trackers."

They spent the remainder of the journey in silence. Jack wasn't sure what to think. He could pass this whole experience off as a horrific nightmare and wake up in his bed tomorrow morning with everything unchanged, but it all seemed so real. And there was the matter of the fox. Just afterwards, he had thought that had been a hallucination or some trick. But then there was the hellhound, the crescent moon machine that changed the weather, and these two organizations that appeared to be able to create and throw energy at each other. What little he had paid attention to about waves and particles in physics seemed to completely contradict this. It was like something out of a surreal sci-fi film.

And then he had the crystal, and so did Alex. Where did that fit into all this? The fact that he was being driven somewhere by two complete strangers in the middle of the night barely registered on the scale of events. If they weren't with the Cult of Dionysus—why should they be, having fought them off?—then he was content with them for now. And they said they were taking him to where Lucy was . . .

About half an hour later, the scenery changed. They had exited the motorway onto a rough dirt track that led off between two grassy slopes. Wooden fences with barbed wire suggested sheep or cows, though after a few minutes they passed under the cover of trees. These were not the apple trees of the Birchwood orchard but tall, widely spread oaks. The track continued to the left, showered with autumnal leaves. Straight ahead, a smaller track led up a hill.

The car slowed. They had reached an ornately decorated gateway, the stained and crumbling cherub statues on either column oddly silhouetted in the light of lamps on each side. Jack looked out his window. The manor above them was a block of darkness against the night sky. A few disparate trees were scattered about the hillside like lost children. They began to climb the rough path to the house.

They reached a courtyard-type area, and the car crunched to a halt in the gravel. Malik turned off the engine, and Gaby got out. Jack got out too, and as he stood up he winced. It felt like needles had been ap-

Counterattack

plied to his ankles by a vengeful spinster. Apparently that bolt of energy had done something.

Closer up, it could be seen that the manor was of reddish brick. Tall windows were set at regular intervals on four levels, and Jack spotted three separate chimneys pointing squarely out of the top. The main entrance was flanked by wild, untended wisteria, which almost blocked the front door. There was only a single light, coming from somewhere over a wall to the left of the entrance.

Gaby led the way, and Jack followed. They reached a wooden door that filled the gap between the manor and high brick wall. Gaby pushed it, and it creaked open. The two of them entered. Malik made a brief sweep of the area and followed.

Inside was an enclosed garden. Red, blue, and yellow flowers had probably once formed a heraldic crest shape on the beds, but now the colors had all merged into one another, ruining the pattern. The noise of a fountain, half-blocked, spluttered somewhere behind the shapeless bushes, and a couple of trees crept over the wall and out to freedom in the corners.

the white fox

The three of them took the path hugging the manor. The light up ahead came from an old-fashioned metal lantern overhanging another door, this one going into the building. Gaby reached it and stopped. The others piled up behind her. She glanced at Jack, then pressed her hand against the door. A small symbol, composed of faint turquoise light, traced itself above her palm. She removed her hand and, with her finger, drew a second symbol, this one in blue. The two hung on the wood for a moment, then moved over one another and sunk into the door. It creaked open.

Gaby stepped in and stood aside. Within was very gloomy. Jack glanced apprehensively into the darkness and joined Gaby. Malik entered last and pulled the door shut behind him.

Outside, the wind blew through the oaks, scattering their leaves. The gates rattled, and the chains holding them shut creaked. A sign was framed on the redbrick wall next to it. Though faded with age and with much of it peeled off completely, two words were still distinguishable.

the white fox

Chapter IX
accepting the truth

As Jack's eyes adjusted to the dark, he began to see his surroundings. They were in a wide corridor. A moth-bitten old red carpet stretched down the hall, past some ancient-looking wooden stairs carved with eagles on the banisters. The wallpaper was faded regal blue with chipped gold fleur-de-lis in lines and columns. Ashes and soot had been discharged all around a derelict fireplace, blackening the worn speckled marble. The ceiling and ornamental chandelier were knotted with cobwebs. Used candles and fallen pieces of wood and leaves were scattered across the floor. The only light emanated from an open door farther down.

Malik led the way down the hall. Jack caught his reflection in a stained mirror over the mantelpiece. He

looked a state; his face was shot red with the cold, and his hair and clothes were clotted with mud and leaves.

They reached the door, and Malik motioned for them to stop. He slid inside, and indistinct voices could be heard from within. He poked his head around the door and beckoned them in. The other two entered.

This room was in a little better condition than the hallway. It was quite a large drawing room, with cabinets and bookcases set against the walls, all also knotted with cobwebs. The only light issued from a crackling fire, throwing flickering shadows onto the walls. Two armchairs and a sofa were clustered around a rug in front of the fire. Only three other people appeared to be there—one in an armchair, one slouched on the sofa, and one at a desk on the other side of the fire. The one at the desk was on a laptop. The two next to the fire both seemed to be waiting for something.

Jack heard a scream, and something hurtled at him from his left, almost knocking him off his feet. It took him a moment to realize the bundle of hair, mud, and limbs was Lucy. She was hugging on to him like a small child, her body jerking with badly contained sobs.

Jack was taken aback. He awkwardly curled his arms around her, letting her cry into his neck. He found himself whispering things that didn't seem to register in his brain first—the kind of things, he thought, people must say to comfort others without thinking. He knew, in reality, he couldn't guarantee that it would all be alright, that he couldn't possibly say for certain that it would all be okay, but he supposed that was what she needed to hear. He held her close and hugged her. Now, at the most uncertain moment, he recognized why Lucy was his friend. Underneath the stereotypical teenage persona she inhabited every day of her life, she was just a scared little girl, just as insecure as he was.

Gaby nor Malik nor anyone else in the room rushed them. They stood respectfully by the side, remaining silent, as Jack comforted Lucy.

After several minutes, Lucy took a deep breath and straightened up. Her face was stained red under the dirt, and her eyes were bloated with glassy tears. She wiped them away and attempted a smile. She hadn't let go of Jack's hand. Her palm was squeezed in his, a reassuring lifeline.

"You *finally* made it," said the person on the sofa, acting as if nothing had just happened. He looked slightly older than Gaby and was well built, with a strong jawline and short brown hair. "What took you so long?"

"We got the motorway route," Malik replied. "Where are Linda and Thiago?"

"Still not back," the second person responded. He was sitting in an armchair across from them, wearing an old-fashioned smoking jacket and holding a pipe. African by his looks but Deep South American by his accent, his face was wrinkled but his eyes were bright and alert. "You must be Jack. My name is Charles King." He offered his hand to Jack, and Jack took it firmly, shaking it twice. "I would get up, but as you can see that's not really an option."

Jack looked at Charles again and realized that only one leg reached the carpeted floor.

"Alex should have waited for backup to come and rescue you, but we're obviously lucky he didn't. A few more minutes and well . . ." Charles smiled at them.

"This is Vincent."

The first man nodded. "Call me Vince."

Jack and Lucy smiled back as best they could. In that moment, Jack realized how ridiculous they must look—two mud-drenched, blotchy teenagers in full school uniform, standing in the middle of a derelict mansion. He could barely suppress a hysterical laugh.

Lucy gulped loudly and began to speak, her voice a breathy gibber. "What's going on here? Please, can you tell us now? I've got parents at home. They'll be wondering where I am. They'll be okay, won't they? Please . . ." She faltered, and, as if in compensation, squeezed Jack's hand even more tightly.

"Those are all good questions," Charles replied, "and you deserve answers. We represent an organization called the Apollonians, and, as you may have gathered, we act in opposition to the Cult of Dionysus. And with good reason. You cannot imagine what would have happened if we had not intervened on that hilltop."

Gaby looked pointedly in an I-told-you-so sort of way at Malik.

He ignored her.

"Done," interrupted the man at the desk. "How

143

does this sound?" He pressed a last key and bent closer to read.

Last night in Birchford a freak lightning storm caused mass power cuts across the entire town. Scientists have attributed these events to an unusual movement of atmospheric pressure brought on by the heat of this year's autumn, coupled with rising carbon dioxide levels in the atmosphere. The actual lightning strikes centered on and around the Sirona Beacon, reputedly a sacred worshipping place for Celtic druids in pre-Roman Britain. Meteorologists and geographers have performed initial examinations of the hilltop, and it will be closed to the public until further notice.

"That should do fine," Charles said. "Send it to the press."

"What? You're not going to tell people what actually happened?" Lucy exclaimed. "They tried to kill us! People need to be warned!"

Gaby, Malik, Vince, and Charles exchanged dark looks.

"How many people do you think will believe what actually happened?" Malik responded. "Would you believe it yourself if you hadn't been there?"

Lucy looked down.

"The number one rule of PR: blame it on falling house prices, youth criminalization, or global warming," the one at the desk remarked as he pressed a key. "Have you never read the *Daily Mail*?"

The drawing room fell into silence: the only noise was the whistling wind from outside. Jack watched the flames dancing in the grate. He had so many questions, and he knew Lucy did as well, but he could not think where to begin. What had happened in the last hours of his life had distorted every certainty he had held about the world. He was still half-expecting to wake up at any moment. The demon, Alex returning after so long, a satanic ritual on an ancient holy site, a battle— it was the stuff of a clichéd comic book. The fact that he had lived to see it was something; the fact that he had lived *through* it to realize how inconceivable it had been was even more of an improbable occurrence.

At that moment, he couldn't see how anything could go back to normal ever again. This new world—for that was the only way he could think of it—was terrifying. Part of him wondered how he had allowed himself to be brought here, in the company of people who toted guns and could apparently fire energy from their bare hands. But, he felt—and he knew Lucy thought the same—that these people did not seem bad. And in any event, he had enough of his beliefs to challenge already without questioning their apparent protectors.

So he asked the only question he and Lucy could stomach the answer to at that point. "What now?"

Gaby and Malik looked towards Charles.

Charles took his time blowing out his pipe smoke, appraising them with raven's eyes. "You're not safe here," he said finally. "Not just in this house, not in this country, not in this world. You need to get out, whilst you still can. You've entered a whole new stage of your lives. There is no way of going back. I'm sorry. You need to go—now."

"Go where?" Lucy cried. "My parents have no idea

where I am! How do we know they weren't caught up in all that stuff on the hilltop?"

"We'll send people to check on your parents and fill them in, but by the time we get there, you'll need to have already left."

"You don't know my parents." Lucy sniffed, with just a hint of pride. "My dad works in accountancy. He's *never* going to believe this."

"We've convinced people like him before. We'll show him Sirona Beacon ourselves if we need to. They'll have to believe us—you'll be gone. But don't worry. We'll keep an eye on them."

"No, I need to go back! I need to warn them!"

Charles let out a long sigh. "Right now, you're more of a danger to them the closer you are. Both of you. You've seen too much. So have we, but to the Cult we're established enemies. You have no idea how much damage you could do with the knowledge you now hold. The Cult won't go after your family if they know you've gone, but if you go back, they might be tempted to. I'm sorry. I know it's painful, but you're going to have to let go."

Lucy sighed and let the point rest. Jack put his

arm around her in a comforting gesture. He couldn't relate, obviously, but he knew how close Lucy was to her family. The closest thing he had was the feeling of losing Alex, which, now, he was feeling all over again.

"We'll explain everything to you in due course. But you'll agree to leave with us tonight, then?" Charles prompted.

"I guess we have no choice." Jack glanced at Lucy, who managed a stiff nod. The glassiness had returned to her eyes, and he redoubled his protective arm. "One thing before we go, though. Alex . . . he was with you, wasn't he?"

Gaby looked from Malik to Vince to Charles to the man at the desk. After a moment, Charles nodded at her.

"Yeah, he was," Gaby said finally, breathing out slowly. "He was one of us. An Apollonian. That's yet another thing you deserve an explanation for. He should be here, telling you what happened, but . . ." She trailed off, looking uncomfortable.

Jack nodded. If these people were telling the truth and Alex had been with them, he knew he and Lucy could trust them. What he was nowhere nearer to understanding was why Alex had disappeared, where he had gone, and why he had returned tonight. He wanted some justification, some easy-fix explanation for Alex's disappearance—something that would solve all the problems that had been rotating at the back of his mind for the last eighteen months and had intensified tonight. But, he believed, they would come to understand everything soon enough.

The two of them now had to do something they'd never before done in their carefully managed lives—take a leap of blind faith and hope they ended up on solid ground.

Chapter X
the space machine

"If those people can fly in smoke," Lucy gasped, as they pelted down the stairs, "where on *Earth* is safe?"

Jack, Lucy, Gaby, Vince, and Malik had taken a side door of the hallway that must have once been servants' quarters. Diving down a tightly entwined spiral staircase, they passed a derelict laundry room, a dormitory, and a cavernous kitchen. Vince was leading the way with a relic of a gas lamp, its bobbing orb of light chasing away shadows on the flaked plaster walls.

"Right," Vince began, his voice emanating from somewhere below them, "your crash course starts here. Lesson number one: this one isn't the only world. There are many out there, many different races, many different people. This planet is tiny on the grand scale of things."

"So are you three from another world, then?" Jack exclaimed, slipping slightly on a piece of loose plaster.

Malik laid a steadying hand on his shoulder.

"No," Gaby answered from behind him, laughing slightly, "no, we're definitely earthlings. Human ones, anyway. The Apollonians work in many different worlds, but we try to use people on their own planets. Where you're going, though, you'll need some . . . reeducating."

"Which brings us to lesson number two," continued Vince. "Humans aren't the only sentient life. There're lots of different races in other worlds you won't have come across before, so prepare for some surprises. Elves, dwarves, fairies, goblins . . ."

"Sounds like a fairy tale," Lucy remarked, half to herself.

"Where did you think our stories came from?" Gaby replied. "All stories have a shred of truth. Sleeping Beauty, Isis and Osiris, most Norse mythology . . . they're all accounts of when humans have come into contact with different races. Exaggerated and embellished obviously, but the point's the same. It's not

The Space Machine

a coincidence that people all over the planet recognize dragons. The ancient Scandinavians and Aboriginals had the same understanding of flying reptiles."

"Yeah," Vince added, "embellished or just plain racist. It takes a particular kind of ethnocentrism to confuse elves with fairies . . ."

The three of them all snorted with laughter. Jack and Lucy exchanged bewildered glances.

"So," Jack said, struggling to digest this next big step onwards into regions as yet unknown, "other creatures—elves, dragons, goblins—are real, and our myths and legends are actually real-life stories about them visiting Earth?"

"Pretty much," Vince replied. "And finally, lesson number three. We've found two ways to travel between worlds without having to make a real-time journey through space. The first one is through the Darkness, the way the Cult travel."

"It's much quicker, but it's not a good idea," Gaby put in. "It never ends well."

"The *other* way," Vince elaborated, "is by a machine." The light had stopped bobbing, and as they rounded a corner, they saw him standing in front of an ancient-looking wooden door. He shoved a rusty old key into the lock, yanked it sideways, and shunted the door inwards. It creaked open, and they moved into the space beyond.

There was the sound of a light switch flicking, and strobes spluttered into life above their heads, throwing the chamber into harsh, industrial light.

Jack blinked and looked around. They were standing in what he could only describe as cata-combs—Gothic buttresses of grey stone formed a vaulting bubble around them, framing arch-shaped walls of stone in an octagon. Opposite them, one of the arch shapes was empty, leading to another cham-ber and so on in a long hallway stretching for a few hundred meters in an underground tunnel. This structure, Jack thought, must run under the entire mansion and grounds, some kind of medieval prison or tomb.

It was what was in the center of this chamber, however, that caught his attention. There, set on a makeshift wooden pedestal and illuminated by the

The Space Machine

anachronistic electric lighting, was the most bizarre object Jack had ever seen. Having studied Venice in geography, he thought it looked a bit like a gondola. This gondola, though, was not something you'd expect to find in Renaissance Italy. It was bright turquoise and had a curved underside, like a small aircraft. The helm was carved in the shape of some ornamental bird and the tail end as a kind of jet. Protruding from each side was a pair of flat, eight-foot-long glassy panels, not unlike a dragonfly's wings. He edged closer to see what it was made of. It seemed like wood but had the smoothness of blown glass. On closer inspection, the surface was not a solid coat at all but made up of thousands of tiny interlocking symbols.

"What does it do?" Jack asked.

"It's a dimension ship," Vince replied. "Can you do science?"

"No."

"Well, I won't go into details. Just imagine it like *Star Trek*. Or *Doctor Who*. Teleporting." He turned and vaulted over the side, positioning himself behind the helm like a latter-day pirate—function-driven body armor at complete odds with the carefully crafted swan's neck, embossed with mirrorlike eyes, which formed the helm of the ship.

Gaby giggled.

"Excuse me. I built this thing—"

"And look what happened last time you tried to fly it," Gaby replied superiorly. She ushered Jack and Lucy to the edge and motioned them to climb in.

Jack tentatively stepped over the side, unsure of how fragile it was. Inside were three wooden benches, just like a rowboat. Gaby and Malik settled themselves on the back one, and Jack moved over to make room for Lucy. She looked apprehensive at anything that vaguely resembled a roller coaster cart, but when everyone else was in and staring at her, she seemed to realize she had no choice. Jack steadied her as she clambered in, and she sat close to him on the second row back. They both instinctively looked around for seat belts.

"What are you looking for?" Gaby asked them.

"This thing moves?"

"Oh, don't worry about the seat belts," Vince said

jovially, then caught Gaby's expression.

She pointed at her own socket.

Jack and Lucy found theirs and pulled. As it turned out, Vince had used the term *seat belts* very loosely. They were comprised of a piece of rope that looped over the legs of both people on the bench and clipped together. Very loosely. Jack glanced at Lucy. She appeared equally anxious. He couldn't shake the impression that they were sitting in an oversized holiday souvenir.

"Okay, everyone ready?" asked Vince, glancing back.

"Vince, put your rope on," Gaby said exasperatedly.

"Come on. I've flown this thing hundreds of times. I can deal with anything it can dish out."

Gaby rolled her eyes.

Vince began shifting things on the front panel. It looked like a cross between the controls of a supercomputer and a brightly colored child's toy, with dials, keys, and several other indefinable implements. Vince placed his palm on a crystalline orb on the control board at the front. Immediately, the same symbol-filled light the manor door had opened with spread over the board, changing from red to green to blue.

The wings began to vibrate up and down noisily, sending shudders through the whole ship. As they beat faster and faster, it started to rise off the ground, the pressure building below it.

It was at that moment when Jack noticed something horribly wrong. The opposite end of the tunnel was a flat stone wall—a stone wall, which, even more worryingly, looked as if it had recently been patched up. Panicked, he tried shouting, but the noise of the wings completely drowned out his voice. Worse, no one else, not even Lucy, seemed to have noticed.

Vince brought his other hand down in a fist on the control panel. The ship rocketed forward, the wings pulsating into a hazy blur as they hurtled down the tunnel.

Jack cried out, the air resistance beating his exposed skin. Beside him, he could see Lucy screaming, but the frantic wing beats drowned out all sound. They gathered speed. Vince was bent forward, frenziedly adjusting dials and buttons on the panel, Gaby and Malik, he could only assume, still seated behind them and not ejected backwards out of the ship to be beaten bloody on the underground floor.

The opposite wall blasted towards them, a solid mass of skull-shattering stone—but stone that now seemed to be contorting into a spherical portal of impossibly bright white light. Jack only just had time to fruitlessly shield his face before they smashed into it.

He waited for the impact, but it never came. The noise of the wings and what he now thought must be the roar of jet engines still resonated around him, but they had definitely not hit anything. He dared to open his eyes a fraction. As he comprehended what was around him, he could not help but widen them.

They *were* soaring through a tunnel but not one of stone. This tunnel was of spinning light and energy, lightning-rent storm clouds of rainbow hues, light and dark mingling into every color imaginable. Another noise, something like a sonic boom or roar of portentous thunder, echoed around them, sound and matter churning into a pathway of spatial majesty. A bolt of umber-bronze lightning arched out of the mass some way in front of them, crackling towards their ship, but it ricocheted off. In that second of impact, an electrical buzz of energy sounded, as a dim but durable orb of protective barrier surged around them.

In a heartbeat—or perhaps after several hours—a flash of sparkling white burst before them: the end of the tunnel. Jack was dimly aware of Vince adjusting more controls somewhere in front of him (for distance seemed to have altered the way it worked), before they were hurling towards the core of light. The colors, clouds, eternal hues of bright energy drained away as tangential, all-consuming brightness engulfed them.

Jack's breath caught in his throat. This time, he did not cover his eyes, but he could see nothing; Lucy, Vince, the entire ship, his own body had vanished into the portal of all-reflecting power. Then they hit the ground and skidded, normal light restored in an instant. The noise of rocks and sand showering out behind them, the lurch of being flung forward in their seats, the twinge of the belts cutting painfully into their laps. The ship rumbled to a halt, and Jack and Lucy fell backwards off the benches.

Jack sat up, feeling nauseous. The lights he had just experienced were flashing in front of his eyes, dancing in a dizzying kaleidoscope across the steel-grey sky that he was *actually* seeing. Lucy remained on the floor of the ship, grimacing. Jack had seen that expression before. It was the internal struggle to prevent vomiting at all costs.

Gaby and Malik had already undone their seat belts and got out. Vince was buried in sand a few feet in front of the ship, his head completely submerged.

Gaby went to stand next to Vince. Her momentary attempt to look disapproving collapsed into a fit of laughter. "I think that might be the *ultimate* I told you so."

Vince pulled his head out of the sand, brushing pebbles from his hair, his face burgundy with hilarity.

Satisfied that Vince was alright, Jack looked around for the first time. As the lights in his peripheral vision faded, he could see their surroundings. They were on a rocky beach, surrounded by obscuring walls of white fog. Grey water lapped a few feet down to the right from where the ship was entrenched. Something that sounded a bit like a seagull croaked overhead, swathed in the fog above them. There was no sign of the basement, the mansion, or the forest. He glanced behind him. No wall or bright light, only a low cliff face clustered with sparse yellowed grass and a few boulders.

Jack untangled the rope from around his stomach and clambered out of the ship. He wasn't very steady on his feet. "What just happened? Where are we?" he asked Malik, who was stretching out next to him. Gaby was still occupied with excavating Vince.

"Rauthr. Small Magellanic Cloud. About two hundred thousand light-years away from Earth."

Even the previous day, Jack reflected, he wouldn't have considered looking for signs that Malik wasn't joking. Now, however, he felt he needed to verify anything that might just be true. "And we managed this . . . how?"

"Spatial jump. Don't worry, though. It's only hours after we left. It should be about 3 a.m. on Earth."

Jack took a deep breath. Even with his extremely patchy grounding in physics, he was pretty sure that wasn't meant to be possible. But then, he realized, that was pretty low down on the register of new possibilities he had been assailed with in the last few hours. Demons, secret organizations, and stolen friends came higher on that list. He was glad Lucy was in earshot, and he wouldn't have to face the unenviable task of explaining this to her.

"So if we're on a different planet," Lucy piped up in a high-pitched voice, her grasp of science considerably better than Jack's, "how come we can breathe? And the gravity's the same. Isn't that a bit of a coincidence?"

"It's a lot less complicated than it sounds. Generally, oxygen is a universal requirement for intelligent life. They talk about natural selection and the variety it brings, but really all living creatures are in the same mold. Earth is perfect for life's requirements. Other planets that harbor life are much the same. I think you'll be surprised how familiar the people here are."

Jack and Lucy spent the next few minutes looking

around in awe, studying every detail of the sand, the different rocks, the sea. It was largely the same as any British seaside on Earth. The air tasted cleaner, less polluted, and the larger rocks littered around had a distinct bluish tint. There was no living thing visible, though occasionally one of the seagull-like creatures' cries could be heard. If they hadn't experienced what they just had, neither of them would have noticed anything out of the ordinary.

After they had exhausted all the possibilities for examination on this distinctly boring bit of coastline, they went back to sit in the ship. Neither of them attempted to start a conversation. Both seemed to recognize that the other was trying to come to terms with what had happened to them.

Lucy, in particular, was very nervous, even though, she admitted to herself, nothing seemed to be out of place. She wondered whether it could be a trick. But then after the day she'd had so far, it was just as possible that they were on an alien planet. She shivered at the very thought. Had the Apollonians managed to find her parents yet? How would they take the news? It was bad enough having news about your daughter's drunken antics reported to your door by a disapproving neighbor, but being told that she'd gone to another world . . . Come to that, when was she next going to see them?

Jack, meanwhile, had given up trying to fit this into any frame of reference he had established in his first sixteen years. He knew that the fact they had just moved to another world would not hit him for some time. He would have to see something that could not possibly happen on Earth to convince him fully. Where they were going and from whom and how soon they were going to get all this explained concerned him more.

No one seemed to know exactly what was going on. Gaby and Vince had moved from the place of Vince's landing to the coastline, peering out into the fog. Malik stood nearby, equally silent, checking his watch every few minutes. It dimly occurred to Jack (amongst the many other logical inconsistencies jostling for foremost position in his head) that an alien world couldn't possibly work on the same timescale as Earth.

Then, after about half an hour, something happened. The lapping of disturbed water reached out to them from the shallows, intensified by something beyond their vision. A low bubbling, the frothing of displaced grey water, sounded from behind the white veil. An immense, dome-like shadow, though too faint to make out any details, appeared to be rising out of the water.

None of the other three needed Gaby's and Vince's frantic cries to get up and move closer to it.

Malik took off his watch and tucked it inside his jacket pocket. "Finally."

Chapter XI
the golden turtle

"It's about time," Malik said, striding over to the edge of the beach. The bubbling was receding, replaced by metallic clangs and clunks. Moments later, a wide wooden plank was shunted out of the fog from the direction of the shadow, sinking into the sodden sand, forming a bridge over the shallows. Without hesitation, Malik placed a foot on it, tested its sturdiness, and clambered up it into the mist.

"Go on, then," Gaby said when neither Jack nor Lucy moved.

Cautiously, they approached the edge of the plank. Despite Malik's ease in crossing, it didn't look particularly stable. With an almost cartoonlike gulp, Lucy placed one mud-encrusted trainer on it and entered the

wall of white. Once the wood had stopped bobbing with her weight, Jack followed.

Crossing was unnerving. Immediately as he left dry land and moved over the waters, the fog descended like a white veil, enveloping him entirely in a bubble of sight only ten feet in front of him. The beach soon receded completely in the ivory mass, so that he was standing, entirely isolated, surrounded on all sides by impenetrable fog. He had no idea how deep the water was, how far he was along this makeshift pier, or how long he would have to walk. Gritting his teeth, he moved onwards, completely unaware of what was in front of him.

After a few more feet, he could see the beginnings of something vast emerging from the fog. It looked like he was walking onto a dome of dull gold—a metallic bubble, like that of the Eden Project buildings, but completely opaque. He tested his footing, and it felt solid enough. Scrambling up, half-walking, half-crawling, he soon saw the faint figures of Lucy, Malik, and two others, becoming more distinct as he drew closer. They were standing by a kind of hatch in the top of this dome, the beginnings of a metal ladder visible, descending downwards. Lucy was shivering behind Malik, evidently slightly wary of the two figures Jack could not yet see. He moved up to join her.

Malik finished talking and turned to them. His correspondent came closer out of the mist, the form becoming clearer as she moved towards them. She was a stunningly beautiful black girl, with a round, friendly face and deep brown eyes. Her jet-black hair was slightly wavy and cascaded down to her shoulder blades. She wore a white shirt, a red waistcoat, baggy trousers, and boots. A tattoo in the shape of a stylized lion wove around the upper forearm, and a crimson bandana decorated with a golden turtle was wrapped around her forehead.

"So who are these?" she said.

Her voice brought Jack back to reality. He found he was staring and looked at his feet awkwardly. He suddenly didn't know what to do with his hands. At Malik's beckoning, he and Lucy came closer to the hatch.

"Jack Lawson," Malik said, "and Lucy Goodman."

"Alright, then. How much do they know already?"

"Well, a few hours ago they were nearly murdered by the Cult, so they've seen their fair share. But remember," he replied, looking at her sternly, "Charles slipped up on this one. Sardâr left *very* specific instructions. He wants to fill them in personally. Actually, his instructions were far *too* specific, if you ask me. He always seems to plan for the most unlikely occurrences, and those are the ones that always end up happening. It makes me uncomfortable."

The girl rolled her eyes and looked half-exasperatedly, half-jokingly at Jack.

He suddenly felt very hot around the ears.

"But where would we be without him? He's our next best to Isaac, and he's led us right so far. The sooner he gets back, the better."

Malik shrugged. He turned to Jack and was joined by Gaby, issuing out of the fog like a Kevlar-clad spectre. "I'm afraid this is where we leave you," Malik said, addressing Jack and Lucy.

"Don't worry," Gaby said, laughing at Lucy's scandalized expression. "You're in good hands. Captain

Ruth"—she gestured at the girl—"will take you to a safe location. We've got people on hand there to take care of you. Like Malik said, all eventualities were planned for."

"What about my parents?" Lucy protested.

"We'll handle that. We'll make sure they know what's going on and that you're safe. We need to get back and start sorting out this mess—cover stories, fake scientific explanations, burying the temple . . . It's going to take a while."

"But when can we go home?"

Malik and Gaby glanced at each other.

"We don't know," Gaby replied after a moment, looking sympathetic. "I'm really sorry, but your guess is as good as ours. We're not sure how much damage the Cult managed to do and whether they're planning to come back anytime soon. The idea was to stake out in that mansion until they attacked, then catch them unawares. As you can see, that didn't all go to plan."

"What about Alex? What are you doing about that?"

"We're on the case," Gaby replied, smiling. Jack

couldn't help thinking it was more of a rebuttal than a response. As much as Gaby and Malik had been helpful, now that he was recovering from the shock of the night's events and his sense of skepticism was returning to him, he could not help but feel a little annoyed at the lack of explanation for any of the events that had twisted their world upside down in such a short time.

"Sardâr will explain everything," Malik said tersely, pulling out his watch again and waving it in front of Gaby's face.

As they smiled at both of them (in what Jack thought was a reassuring way), considering what had gone on, he couldn't shake a slight sense of abandonment. Both nodded at Ruth and vanished into the all-obscuring white mass, an exit as ethereal as the entrance the two had made into their lives the night before.

"Who the hell is Sardâr?" Lucy whispered to him.

Jack shook his head, as nonplussed as she was. Both of them stared into the fog for a moment. He felt like a package bundled from one keeper to the next. He heard the clunking of the plank being withdrawn,

The Golden Turtle

along with his hopes of getting back to Earth on the dimension ship. Jack glanced at Lucy. The panic on her face suggested she was feeling the same way and that she was preparing to jump off the side of the ship and demand to be taken home. Half of him got ready to stop her, the other half wanting to do exactly the same thing.

"Well," Ruth said after a minute or two, "I think we should get you into something more fitting. Quentin?"

The other new figure, a man in a poorly fitting Regency wig and ultramarine jacket, stepped up to her side.

"Take these two below deck and give them some new clothes."

"Aye, aye, captain," replied the man in a badly disguised aristocratic drawl.

"Jack, Lucy," Ruth continued, "can you come down to the command deck afterwards? There's someone I want you to meet."

"This way, please," said Quentin. He hoisted himself over the side of the hatch and began clanking his way down the metal ladder.

Jack and Lucy looked apprehensively at one another. Then, one after the other, they clambered onto the ladder and descended into the dome.

Ruth did a quick visual sweep of the area (an action rendered virtually useless by the fog) and shouted into the mist, "All hands below deck." Waiting for the clanging of other hatches to recede, she pulled herself onto the ladder and slammed the hatch shut above her head. Instantaneously, with the sensation of a sinking elevator, the ship started to descend into the water.

Twenty minutes later, Jack and Lucy found themselves standing outside the command deck. Their latest journey had been a blur of bustling men and women, all in a seeming hotchpotch of clothing. Impelled by their guide through a network of tunnels and stairways, all corridors with identical dark wood panelling and lit with soft gaslights, they had been shown the way to their rooms several floors below.

They had torn off their filthy school uniform and netball kit and thrown on a collection of seemingly miscellaneous and mismatched items of clothing and accessories.

Jack was now dressed in a flamboyant waistcoat over a woollen white shirt, with two layers of cotton trousers and absurd cowboy boots. Lucy looked like a fortune-teller in a couple of shawls, trousers straight out of a stage version of *Arabian Nights*, an extra large man's shirt, and several bangles. She had opted to keep her torn-up trainers after offers of clogs, Wellington boots, and leather bags as alternative footwear. Both of them had looked at each other and acknowledged the silent consensus that it was good that their rooms didn't have mirrors.

Jack knocked, the door emblazoned with a stylized golden turtle symbol, and a moment later the answer came.

"Come in."

They opened the door and entered. Whatever Jack had been expecting, this was not it. The walls and ceilings of the room were a single curved dome of glass, entirely transparent, save for the metal framing. Beyond the dome, barely illuminated by the jets of gold projected from the lights below them, was the blue black of deep ocean. They appeared to be surging above the ocean floor at considerable speed. Looking up, only a glimmer hinted at the surface of the water.

"We're under the sea?" Lucy murmured, quite unnecessarily given their surroundings.

"Yes, you are," came a cold reply from somewhere in front of them.

The contents of the room were computer panels and screens set around the edges facing inwards, a dozen crew members keying things in or following readings on numerous radars and relays. In the center, set into an indentation in the carpeted floor, was a large oak table, apparently anachronistic with the high-tech electronics around it. Pinned to it were several faded maps decrying strangely shaped islets and illustrations of fantastical sea beasts around the edges. Ruth and another woman were standing by it, examining something.

Ruth was stunning, but Jack's attention couldn't help but be attracted by the other woman, the one who had spoken. She was like no one he had ever seen. She was taller than both him and Lucy by several inches and extremely slim. She looked vaguely Middle Eastern. Her jet-black hair was plaited down her back, and she was wearing a serene blue tunic with silver trimming. Her clothes would have seemed strangely medieval were they not set next to Ruth's, Jack's, and Lucy's own fashion chimeras. Her eyes were even darker than Ruth's yet surprisingly cool, and her face had an oddly pinched look.

As they came closer, she stood up straight, regarding them imperiously. "So this is Jack Lawson?" she said, her voice calm and genteel.

"Yes," Ruth said, then seeing Lucy's expression, "and this is Lucy Goodman."

The strange woman stepped around the table and offered her hand to Jack. He took it cautiously and shook it. As he did so, he noticed something else. Her ears were pointed upwards ridiculously far, past the level of her eyes, almost to points.

the white fox

"Jack, Lucy, this is Adâ Sharif. She's our escort to the mainland." Then Ruth saw Jack looking at Adâ's ears. "And this might come as a bit of a shock to you, but she's an elf."

Jack was about to challenge this, but then he remembered what Vince had said about becoming reeducated in this new world.

Adâ's hand tightened momentarily, and she looked into Jack's eyes, as if daring him to challenge it. Jack stared back defiantly, and she let go.

Adâ turned, taking no more notice of Lucy than if she had been a balsa-wood hat stand. "I would have greeted you earlier with the others, but I cannot stand that girl Gaby."

Neither Jack nor Lucy said anything. Both knew what the other was thinking.

Over the rest of the day, Jack and Lucy were given a flurried tour around the ship by Quentin. Along increasingly claustrophobic tunnels of panelled wood, they were taken to the kitchen, the dining room, and below to the mechanical workings of the ship—reactors, turbines, and generators that neither Jack nor Lucy thought could ever work, looking as they did like the inventions of a cartoon evil scientist. It took Jack a while to realize that *The Golden Turtle* was not just a name. The entire ship was literally built in the shape of a gigantic metallic turtle, with the command deck as the head.

Though the tour was quite dull (not helped along by Quentin's increasingly monotonous attempts to sound piratey through an Etonian accent), they came across many of the crew who were going about their day's work. From the bits of conversation they had with them, most of them seemed very amiable and friendly. For once, Jack threw himself much more into conversations with strangers than Lucy, who remained stoic and visibly uneasy throughout.

Eventually, the jet lag began to kick in, with the realization that they had been awake for almost twenty hours. After the tour, they were shown back to their own small cabins. Both tried to sleep but found it impossible. Somehow, they had come out on this planet midmorning, despite leaving at midnight. But then, Jack thought, that probably happened when you jumped two hundred thousand light-years through space.

In the end, Lucy managed to doze off, but Jack gave up and took to wandering around, talking to the crew and taking in the atmosphere.

Whilst exploring, Jack discovered an observatory dome on the top deck—one panel of the turtle's shell made of transparent glass rather than metal, through which he could sit and watch. They had risen over the course of the day, so that now they were much closer to the surface. The echo of silver moonlight glittered above, dancing on the surface of the water. Evidently, the fog had cleared.

"So how are you enjoying your first voyage aboard *The Golden Turtle*?" said a voice behind him.

Jack whipped around to see Ruth leaning casually on the railing, her arms folded. "I was just getting some fresh air," he said awkwardly. He felt very like a small child, sitting cross-legged on the floor.

Her expression broke into a grin. "Don't worry. You're not part of the crew," she said reassuringly, coming to stand next to him. "But that doesn't mean I won't give you jobs to do. Everybody's got to pull their own weight here."

"Yeah, Quentin made that very clear."

Ruth laughed. "He's harmless really. The crew joke about him, but he's the one who keeps everyone organized. God knows we need it, with so many different worlds, each with their own missions."

"Missions?"

"We help out the Apollonians wherever they're working—usually ferrying goods and people around various worlds. Mostly humanitarian aid for worlds devastated by the Cult, though we do occasionally get involved with direct conflicts."

Jack nodded, looking upwards. He made out hints of starlight. "There are so many stars. You don't get them like this on Earth."

"Not as many as there used to be."

Jack turned to her, but she offered no explanation.

"What did you think of Adâ?"

"She's . . . nice," Jack said slowly.

Ruth laughed. "She likes being intimidating, and the elf thing doesn't help. We have passengers on board all the time but none—no offence—as completely clueless as you and Lucy. You handled it fine, though."

"Thank you." Jack laughed, a little more at ease.

"So, how are you?" she asked. "Missing home?"

"Not as much as I thought I would," he replied. "I don't have a lot to go back to anyway. I'm an orphan."

"I'm so sorry. Did you know your parents?"

"Never did." He paused for a moment. "Where do you come from? Have you got any family there?" Jack glanced at her. She was staring resolutely at the undersky, watching the crystal clear ripples of light on the waves.

"I don't remember. I don't remember much at all. The Cult . . . they got me about five years ago. My earliest memory is being locked up in Nexus—that's their base world. I don't remember my home, my family . . . anything." She rolled up the sleeve of her right arm and held it out to him. The lion tattoo he had glimpsed earlier was imprinted in black across her veins. "This is all I've got from before I lost my memory. This and a dream I keep having . . ." She faltered. Finally, she spoke again, rolling her sleeve back down. "How did you get through?"

Jack had never been asked that before. When he told people he was an orphan, they were sympathetic for a moment, then avoided the issue for fear of awkwardness or upsetting him. "Friends," he said. "Friends got me through it."

"Yeah," Ruth continued, "I suppose, in the end, that's all that counts. I was lucky. I escaped and got picked up by *The Golden Turtle*. The captain here . . . his name was Ishmael. He took me under his wing. He was like a dad, I guess. But then he died. A blood disease. And the crew elected me captain . . . and here I am." She turned to look at him fully.

He met her eyes. They were slightly red.

They stood in silence for a minute.

"I'm sorry," Jack said.

"It's alright." Ruth smiled. "I can deal with it."

"So, where are we going?" And the conversation

continued from there.

There they stood, two adventurers, lost from homes they never knew, staring upon the underside of the starry dome of darkness and light. In twenty-four hours, Jack's life had changed forever. He had been sent from his home to another world and was now moving, unseen, under the waves towards an unknown destination. On the brink of this brave new world, he at least knew he had someone he could rely on.

And, though it surprised her to think it, so did Ruth.

Part II

"Turning and turning in the widening gyre
The falcon cannot hear the falconer"
"The Second Coming"
W. B. Yeats

Chapter I
lake, mountains, and goblins

After three days of subterranean sailing, they reached their destination.

Jack had finally managed to get to sleep in the early hours of the first night, only to be woken again by a loud bell at seven. True to what Ruth had said about the ship traversing different worlds, every main room aboard the ship had at least nine clocks next to one another on the wall, each with a different series and amount of numbers or symbols. Jack had looked at the others with interest but had quickly given up trying to understand them. Eleven o'clock was equivalent to a squiggle, a blue triangle, a broken circle. Five o'clock, a lightning bolt, a flagon of ale, a spear, a sofa with wings, and a green moose. He could only guess which one their new

destination adhered to.

True to Malik's words on the beach, the crew were remarkably non-alien. Whilst most of them looked human enough, some of them had pointed ears that hinted at being the same race as Adâ. Jack felt he should find out exactly what an elf was, but there were more burning questions he needed to ask. He tried once or twice with different sailors, but they had evidently been told not to say anything about his and Lucy's circumstances, so he gave up.

As it turned out, Quentin was a laughingstock amongst the rest of the crew, who kept joking that he was out to kill anyone who didn't fit into the minutiae of his clockwork planning. They all seemed to view Ruth half as their captain and half as their collective little sister. Many of them made allusions to Ishmael and how Ruth could never have had a better father figure.

They answered Jack's questions about the ship and made constant attempts to get Lucy involved when she was sitting in lonely silence. Jack's suspicions that *The Golden Turtle* was far more technologically advanced than anything on Earth were confirmed. For one thing, you could easily not notice changes in depth or diving and surfacing actions. As his grasp of earth science was patchy at best, he decided not to pursue the subject.

When he asked about what the crew actually did (implying that they were pirates), the two he was talking to, Aonair and São, burst into laughter.

"It's a righ' loose term," Aonair had said in his thick Irish brogue.

"It is indeed," São had continued with a Spanish roll. "Think of all the worlds we go through and all the different countries in those worlds, each with their own laws. We cannot possibly keep track of them all. Anyway, there are some fairly disrespectable regimes in place."

"We make our own and keep to those." Aonair nodded. "And if occasionally we get in trouble with the law, then so be it. They're a righ' side worse than us, but 'cause they're doing it on behalf of a country, then apparently that's all fine."

Exactly as Ruth had said, they had been worked very hard on board. Even though there were no female members amongst the crew, having a woman as the captain meant there was no traditional sexism.

the white fox

This meant that both Jack *and* Lucy, devoid of any sailing or navigational-computer skills, were drafted into the kitchen, peeling white-tinged parsnips and grey potatoes, and running seawater through an ultrafast distillation machine. Lucy had come to expect deferring behavior and selective equality rolled into one. Neither was present aboard *The Golden Turtle.* Jack found her many times during breaks sitting in her room, tinged green with claustrophobia and kitchen odors. It didn't help that Ruth seemed to find this quite amusing every time she walked past.

To his surprise, Jack had been fine with seasickness. He'd been on a ferry only once, on a school day trip to Calais, and had thrown up three times. This was different; he was restrained below deck, and there was no smog being pumped back in his face. He did, however, begin to feel the impact of the enclosed space during the second day. He had never gone so long without sunlight, and though the cabins and hallways were lit softy, he was beginning to feel the pressure for fresh air and openness.

Ruth, meanwhile, was no hypocrite. She mucked in with the rest of the crew, working just as hard, if not

Lake, Mountains, and Goblins

harder, than any of them. The huge disparity between the work ethic of her and Lucy was hard to ignore.

Jack was below deck on day three, catching several well-earned hours of sleep, when he was unusually awakened not by the bell but by Quentin's own rendition of a wake-up call. This comprised of a long poetic monologue about rising from the night into the morning, interspersed with bursts of pirate dialect. In the end, Jack got out of bed just to shut him up.

On the command deck, the crew were frantically preparing to surface. Ruth, Lucy, and Adâ were already there, watching as the voluminous blackness receded into lighter and lighter shades of blue green.

With his bearings completely gone, Jack had no idea where they might be surfacing. As the water pressure thinned, rocky outcrops—pillars of stacked stone reaching up from the deep like giant fingers—became visible around them. A moment later, the briny water around the glass began to bubble frantically, and the water sloshed off it, as if drained away. For the first time in three days, natural light broke through the dripping screen, refracting off the glass in rainbow cylinders. They appeared to be in some sort of lake, surrounded by rocks.

"Come on up to the hatch," Ruth said, leading the way.

Jack and Lucy followed her, Adâ bringing up the rear, through the network of tunnels to the bottom of the ladder.

Ruth climbed up, unscrewed the hatch, and pushed it open. As soon as she was clear of the ladder, the others followed.

The mist was still clinging to the air, though not as thick as before. They were indeed in the middle of a mountain lake, with no apparent connection to any other body of water. Jack could only assume they had come out of some subterranean passage. The lake seemed to be in a valley basin—on all sides, iron-grey rocks loomed, forming into peaks high above them. The only way out of the valley was a rocky path, snaking in between two large boulders and around a cliff face up towards one of the mountains. A small tree, its leaves a dead grey color, sagged on its side on the water's edge, looking as if it were about to keel over into the lake. He breathed in, and the air tasted tangy, as if cooking spices had been evaporated into it.

Lake, Mountains, and Goblins

"Do we have to walk from here, then?" Lucy asked sullenly.

"Yes," replied Ruth. "Yes, you do."

Lucy glared at her.

The tensions between the two had been running high over the last few days, a combination of sleepless nights, a great deal of work, and Lucy's constant complaining. Ruth seemed to be the first girl of Lucy's age who didn't look up to her like some divine sending. It made a nice change, Jack thought privately, though letting it on to Lucy would be tantamount to a signed suicide note.

"Aren't you coming?" Jack asked her.

"Sorry," Ruth said, smiling. "Business calls. This one's another Apollonian mission. No doubt the Cult have stuck their *oar* in somewhere . . ." She did a little drumroll on the side of the rail.

Everyone ignored her.

"The rings?" Adâ prompted her.

"Oh yeah. I won't be a minute." Ruth disappeared down the hatch.

Jack, Lucy, and Adâ stood in awkward silence on top of the turtle, waiting. Jack had barely spoken to

Lucy since they'd arrived on the ship. They'd both been either sleeping or working, or Jack had been engaged with the crew members or Ruth. He now felt quite guilty that he'd left her to flounder for three days. And neither of them was particularly keen to strike up a conversation with Adâ, whose icy temperament didn't seem to have melted at all since they'd met her.

A few minutes later Ruth returned carrying a small box. She opened it and handed Jack and Lucy a burnished metal ring each.

"Thanks, but I have enough jewelry," Lucy said, staring at the offensively unfashionable accessory in disgust.

Ruth laughed. "They're translator rings. They convert the vibrations of someone speaking into ones you'll be able to understand and vice versa."

Jack and Lucy slid them on to their fingers. The metal glowed green for a second, then shrank to fit comfortably.

"How does that work?" Lucy asked skeptically.

Adâ and Ruth exchanged looks.

"You don't want to know."

"Say something in another language," Jack said.

"We'd best be on our way," Adâ said coolly, picking up the bag she'd pulled out of the hatch. She strode off down the plank that had slid out again from the turtle's side, forming a bridge between the ship and the land.

Lucy couldn't quite manage a smile but gave Ruth a stiff nod and followed Adâ.

Jack stood for a moment, almost unwilling to leave. Ruth had been much more fun than Lucy on the ship and had actually made an effort to talk to him. Lucy had been moody and sick all the way, and now he was stranded alone with her and a woman who seemed to have a nihilistic attitude towards life in general, let alone two teenagers she had been dumped with.

Ruth grinned at him. "I'm sure we'll be seeing you soon. You have to come home somehow." She gave him a quick hug. "You definitely need a shower, by the way . . ."

Jack laughed nervously. He stood there a moment longer, then turned to follow the others. He only looked back once he was on dry land and had heard the hatch clang shut.

"Come on, then," Adâ called in a bored tone to him.

the white fox

He jogged to catch up, and they set off.

The pass between the rocks became increasingly narrow, a sleek path driven deep into a mountainside. It sloped steadily upwards, and in some places they had to scramble up near vertical ridges caused by rock falls. Eventually, the incline became so bad that they had to climb in places, something both Jack and Lucy found distinctly gut-wrenching. The path snaked around the side of the mountain, changing direction unpredictably and sometimes disappearing altogether. As they progressed, small breaches in the rock became more and more prevalent, out of which hot gas issued intermittently. They didn't need Adâ's warning to stay well clear of them.

Finally, they rounded a corner, and the path dropped into oblivion. Before them was a massive ravine, a shadowy pit, surrounded by towering cliff faces. Far, far below them, a sleek band of glittering light revealed the existence of a serpentine river. Mountains, all white tipped and some wreathed in clouds, extended up and behind the gorge. A thin, dangerous-looking path slithered around one edge, and on the other jagged rocks jutted out. Something like a falcon swooped high overhead, cawing to the sky.

Lucy made a step towards the path, but Adâ put out her hand to stop her. She paused, listening intently. Then she shoved Jack and Lucy back behind a rock so they were hidden.

Jack listened. Voices could now be heard coming from somewhere behind them. They were rough, high, and scratchy, yet strangely he could understand what was being said quite clearly. Remembering the language ring, he held it up to the light. The single symbol carved in it was glowing faintly green.

"The boss wants us back by dusk," one of the voices said.

"No, he don't," another replied. "He said tomorrow mornin'. You obviously weren't listenin'. He said take as long as you like to find the entrance but don't let anyone see you."

"He didn't. You're just sayin' that 'cause you don't want to go back. You're scared of him, you are. Scared of some fancy alchemy tricks."

"I ain't scared. You're the one who's scared. You're the one who 'fused to go into his tent to tell him about the rock slide!"

the white fox

"Shut your gizzard!"

Jack peered around the rock. Three figures were hopping down the jagged platforms on the left side. Their legs were extremely bowed, and they moved almost like monkeys, using their hands as much as their feet. All of them had scaly, greyish-green skin and huge ears. Their nails were filthy and yellowed, and their teeth were even worse. They looked as if they had been dressed by Quentin; boots, cloaks, chain mail, helmets, gauntlets, tunics, and belts all made an appearance somewhere but not always in the right place. The two in front gripped their blood-dried scimitars close, but the one behind was swinging it round casually like a police baton. Strangely, that seemed much more threatening.

The two in front argued loudly, their raised voices echoing around the ravine. What was worse, they were heading straight for their hiding place.

Adâ bent down slowly and picked up a pebble from the dusty ground. With superhuman speed, she darted around the rock and hurled it as hard as she could. There was a pause, then a cracking sound echoing around the ravine.

The creatures' heads whipped around in unison, searching for the source of the noise.

"You two," said the third, speaking for the first time, "head back that way. I'll go round the side."

The two creatures nodded and scuttled back up the rocks, out of sight. As soon as they were gone, the third glanced around, checking that he was out of sight. Then he leapt into the air. Two bat-like wings unfurled from the creature's back. They began to flap, carrying it up and over the pointed cliff.

Letting out their tautened breath, the three hiders stepped out of concealment.

"What were those things?" Lucy exclaimed breathlessly.

"Goblins," replied Adâ after a moment. "But there's a problem."

"Monsters that look like giant lizards don't count as being a problem on their own, then?" Jack asked.

"They're no more monsters than you or I," she reprimanded him coldly, "but goblins can't fly. That last one at least was something else."

By the time Jack had realized that goblins could now be added to the demon, sorcerer, and elf list, she was already ten feet along the path. He caught up quickly, not wanting to be left as a straggler.

"Will they come back?" Lucy asked.

"Unlikely."

Jack was already starting to find this annoying. Of all the people who could have accompanied them from *The Golden Turtle*, he would have rather it be anyone but Adâ. Plus, he could tell that it wouldn't be long before Lucy shared a piece of her mind with her. Somehow, though, he thought that Adâ's reaction would be more like a pit bull terrier's than a human's.

It took them another few minutes before they reached the top of the path. There, Adâ stopped abruptly, making the others stagger sideways so as to not crash into her. Jack immediately saw why. A large chunk of the path leading to the top of the cliff had crumbled away, leaving a hundred-foot drop directly below them.

"Where do we go now, then?" he asked Adâ.

She ignored him. She seemed to be working something out in her head, looking back at the trail

Lake, Mountains, and Goblins

they had just come up and counting.

After a few seconds' calculations, she took three steps to the left and placed her hand on the rock, just as Gaby had done on the door back in the manor. She muttered a few syllables under her breath. Faint white light began to trace in swirling patterns out from her hand, inlaying the rock with complex illuminations. About a foot either side, the light stopped and surged upwards and over into a tall, thin doorway. There was a low rumbling, and the two halves of the door cracked apart, folding inwards. The gap in between had been infinitesimal and completely unnoticeable just a moment before. What now lay before them was a dark tunnel that seemed to lead directly into the mountainside.

There was a pause.

"Well, it's not very subtle, is it?" Lucy remarked.

Adâ didn't answer. She crossed the threshold and began striding off into the dark.

Jack and Lucy had both given up any pretence that they might have a say in this. Still not speaking to one another, they followed.

Ruth stood in the observatory, looking upwards at the mountainside through the colossal brass telescope that extended from the ceiling. Between two outcrops high above, she saw the trio disappear into the dark arch etched out of the cliff side. As she watched, the double doors rumbled closed, and there was nothing remaining to suggest the presence of a hidden doorway. Still, it didn't feel quite right. Everything was a little too quiet.

Something moved on the upper edge of the telescopic bubble, and she adjusted her positioning. Too big for a bird, it was flapping its way through the ghostly cold air to the east. She unclipped her own telescope from her belt and found it through the lens. It was a reptilian goblin but one like she had never seen. Instead of arms, it had clawed, bat-like wings. She clicked a button on the side of the scope, and the lens changed to red. Through this view, the creature looked very different—a winged wolf, horned like a goat, and buzzing with a cloud of purple energy, like a swarm of dark locusts.

"What is it?" asked Quentin, who had just joined her.

"Demon. Doppelganger, by the looks of it," Ruth replied grimly. She knew this particular form of demon all too well. Doppelgangers were particularly tricky. By devouring a living creature, they could replicate its physical form, in this case a goblin. No one knew exactly what their true form was like, though rumors had arisen about it being a sort of carnivorous plantlike bear with fins. As goblins tended to categorize leadership qualities by brute force, this "goblin" was probably pretty high ranking by now.

"What course of action should we take, Captain?"

Ruth thought for a moment, still following the creature as it disappeared farther into the distance. "Keep to our original plans. But make sure we're ready to return at any time. If there are demons *here* too, then who knows what Sardâr's got himself into."

Chapter II
thorin salr

The tunnel had been carved into the side of the mountain, a path delving steadily downwards into the subterranean depths of the peaks. Though it was straight and clearly purposefully crafted, stalactites still clung to the ceiling, limp claws dripping with moisture. Torches were held in brackets at regular intervals along the cave walls, shedding dim light and sending scattering orange sprites to dance in the stagnant puddles all around. The tunnel was so tall that the ceiling could not be seen—lost as it was in the shadows that seemed to cling like thick cobwebs in the corners and nooks. Shapes formed in the gloom, and in the puddles the reflections of the flames were magnified into strange silhouettes.

Jack got the impression that they were walking through some kind of sewer conduit. Noises from outside were completely muffled, the tunnel instead magnifying every one of their footsteps into rock slides. He could feel Lucy moving slightly closer to him in the dark, whilst Adâ marched ahead.

They must have walked for at least twenty minutes before a small disc of sunlight became visible at the other end. The exit of the tunnel was under an overhanging rock, which they had to stoop under. The moment they were past it, sunlight flooded their vision.

The land before them was another rocky valley, surrounded by a plateau of cliffs that formed the lower steppes of the mountains. The amber sunlight of the onset of dusk cast itself across the plane in angular waves, catching the cliffs to their left and dyeing them a brilliant, rusty red. The light also caught on a multitude of old-fashioned cranes, pulleys, ladders, and counterbalances below them. They were clustered around several smaller ravines, the shadows emanating from them numbing the sunset glow. Figures, tiny from this height, scuttled around or operated the machinery, lifting bundles of rock onto the edges to be hacked away at by more figures. Metal crates and large boxes were stacked beside each pit, and it was into these that the smaller rocks were being placed to be moved by smaller cranes onto separate piles.

The area was far from even. Along the left side a gap in the cliffs, probably from some ancient lava flow, formed a twisting path. It stretched steeply upwards and wrapped around the side of one of the mountains—a starkly pointed edifice of rock, down which the tangerine sun appeared to be rolling, like a massive, shining boulder.

Directly opposite the outcrop on which they were standing nestled under another grey giant was a very unusual structure. It appeared as though the rock had grown out of the cliff face into a sort of colony, an immense extrusion with many different layers and levels. It was, however, clearly inhabited. Gangways and small buildings clung precariously to its sides, connected to or leading into wide openings in the rock. Dozens of rusted chimneys spiked up out of

the white fox

holes in the rock like industrial limpets, thin trails of ashy smoke sweeping upwards above the cliff. A rectangular reddish stone gate was set into it at its foot under a balcony of overhanging rock. It was carved with a stylized axe surrounded by seven stars and a crown. It looked as if there could be an entire city housed inside.

It took Jack a moment to realize that Adâ and Lucy were nowhere to be seen. He scanned the valley for them and spotted them passing between two of the mining pits. Wondering why neither of them had stopped to marvel at the view, he sprinted down the incline after them.

A few minutes later he caught up, panting heavily. Typically, Adâ didn't give him a second's acknowledgment.

Lucy turned back to keep pace with him. "Where do you think this is?" she whispered. She sounded scared, though definitely not on the same level that she had been in the mansion. This place didn't look overtly dangerous, but they could be wandering into anything.

"No idea," Jack replied.

As they continued walking, he looked around. The cliffs, the mountains, and the tower of rock seemed even taller from down here. Now he could just about see the figures working around the mines. They *were* several hundred feet away on either side, but still they all seemed short, only about five feet high. Their faces had a healthy glow and were quite tanned from working in the sun. They were wearing assorted tunics, gloves, and boots, mostly russets and mahoganies. They, like Adâ, were dressed highly anachronistically; Jack was reminded of pictures in textbooks of peasants on medieval farms. Moreover, they were not operating shining futuristic equipment like that on *The Golden Turtle*. There seemed to be only wooden pulleys with rocks and rope, with no electricity at all. And, he now realized, he had not seen anything like a telecom pylon to suggest any electricity since they'd arrived.

The trio of elongated shadows flickered over the uneven rock as they neared the gigantic stone doorway. It was flanked by several more short people, wearing fern-green tunics with bronze shoulder pads and gauntlets, looking even more like medieval militia. They were all holding double-bladed axes with exceptionally sharp edges.

"Yes?" the guard challenged. He spoke in what on Earth would have been something like a Scandinavian accent, but, of course, the language rings translated.

"Adâ Sharif," Adâ proclaimed, stopping a foot clear of the door, "here to see the king."

Jack saw the guards exchanging dark looks.

"And who are these two?" grunted one of the guards after a moment, passing Adâ and staring at Lucy in a menacing way. The ten-inch deficiency in height didn't seem to inhibit him.

"My nephew and niece," Adâ answered shortly.

Jack and Lucy both turned to her, alarmed, but she gave them a look that made them hold what they had been about to say. Jack was sure that Lucy was thinking exactly the same thing that he was.

"Do they have an invitation from the king?" the guard asked, eyeing them suspiciously.

"As a matter of fact, they do." And with a (rather unnecessary) flourish she pulled a thick piece of parchment from her tunic and handed it to the guard.

He examined the writing and wax seal. "Very well," he said, giving it back to her. "They can go."

Adâ removed her gaze from him and stepped towards the door.

Another guard raised his axe and thrust the butt onto a raised panel in the ground. Out of the gigantic gate creaked open a small door, just over five feet high and at least that much thick.

Adâ rolled her eyes and bent over to shuffle through it. Lucy followed her, and as Jack did so he thought he heard the guard muttering something about the impertinence of elves. Jack couldn't help silently agreeing.

The inside of the rock was not at all like the tunnel they had just come through. They emerged into an enormous chamber, though a cave was probably a more accurate description. The walls were the rock that this city was carved out of, and the floor was paced with smooth flagons. Brackets in the walls housed more flickering torches, and huge carved pillars supported the cavernous ceiling.

the white fox

Patterns, symbols, scenes of battles and glorious victories were engraved into the columns, the ceiling, the floor. In the center of the chamber, a raised octagonal roundel encircled by runes depicted a feast, where figures crowded around a gargantuan roasted ram set upon a table. This was illuminated by light issuing from a gaping hole in the ceiling. This sight only added to the impression that they had wandered into a kind of alternative Middle Ages European community, the chamber a monument to the achievements of craftsmen, warriors, and kings.

Adâ led them past numerous hallways. Despite the lack of windows, crevasses in the rock let in jets of evening sunlight, forming jagged patterns on the flagons. The area surged with many more of these strangely short people, most in simple cotton tunics, carrying baskets of food and grain, piles of parchment or crates. Many were clustered in the hallways, looking more like refugees than miners, with their thickly layered worn clothes, carts laden with possessions, and small children playing and chasing each other.

More guards were posted resolutely at various entranceways or else attempting to marshal some order amongst those waiting around.

Through the throng of people, the three of them head and shoulders above the crowd, Adâ led them towards a door at the opposite end of the chamber.

This was a smaller, more refined corridor, devoid of the crowds. Meticulously woven vermillion carpet ran to the very end, flanked by more pillars. At the other end of the chamber were double doors made of more grey stone and carved with the same axe and star pattern. In between each pillar was a plinth, on which rested a bust of a solemn-looking male, staring, pupil-less, into the distance.

They reached the end and stopped. Two guards in green tunics stood before them, their axes lolling lazily in their grasp. One looked ancient, with a white beard reaching down to his boots. The other was younger, his hair bright ginger, but no less intimidating.

"Adâ Sharif here to see the king," Adâ repeated.

The ancient-looking guard nodded slowly and

held out a gloved hand.

Adâ passed over the letter, and he glanced over it.

"Very well," he croaked shakily, indicating the closed stone door behind him.

All three stepped forward, but as Jack was about to pass the other guard, an axe shot out at lightning speed, narrowly missing his chest. He could have sworn it sheared threads off his shirt.

"What are you doing?" the ginger guard said angrily. His voice was much higher than they had expected, so much so that all three stared for a moment before answering.

"We're going to see the king," Jack volunteered hopefully.

"The king is in council with his advisers. No *youths*"—the guard put a lot of negative emphasis on the word—"may pass here without his permission."

"Oh, shut up," the old guard said dismissively. "They're with Lady Sharif." He beamed toothlessly at Adâ, who returned it with an incline of her head.

The ginger guard looked scandalized but removed his axe.

Jack and Lucy passed. As Adâ opened the double doors, Lucy whispered so the guards couldn't hear, "I think he has a thing for you."

Adâ ignored her and walked in.

This room was much smaller but also well lit; another crack above them threw a twisted amber shape downwards. A tall throne of dyed oak, engraved with a multitude of symbols, rose near the back of the chamber. Sitting on it was the king. An undecorated circlet of bronze was his crown. He looked fairly young, although there were flecks of grey in his blond beard and his face held the hint of wrinkles to come. His eyes were dark and his brow strong—they seemed to emanate not only his penetrating sight but that of all his royal ancestors in busts in the corridor outside.

Despite the fact that they seemed to be looking at a member of a historical re-creation society, Jack, and he knew Lucy felt the same, was overcome with an impulse to bow, but Adâ wasn't bothering with such traditions, so they just stood awkwardly behind her. Their glance confirmed that they were both feeling just as ridiculous in their strange mixture of clothing.

Others sat around an octagonal stone table on hide-coated chairs. These people were also clothed in medieval garb but each in a different kind—one in thick overalls holding huge gloves, several with more ruddy complexions and finer woollen cloaks, and one in a more decorated version of the guards' armor. There were also three empty seats. One person, with an extremely long beard in a green and red tunic, was standing up, and a scribe in the corner scribbled on a roll of parchment.

The table was completely covered in what appeared to be an archaic bird's-eye view map on parchment, filled with mountains, dotted and dashed pathways, several twisting rivers. Small wooden figurines, dyed alternately in crimson and grey, were grouped around the landscape. The person in the red and green tunic was indicating areas on the map with a short cane. He seemed to be presenting a report.

The king glanced at them and motioned them to wait.

Adâ hung back, Jack and Lucy at her elbows like

naughty children.

". . . therefore, given the predictions of our scouts, an attack is most likely to be launched from the north."

"Thank you, Ràth," the king said solemnly in a Scandinavian accent as thick as his guards'. "We will hold another progress report tomorrow. Until then."

One by one, the advisers stood up, bowed, and left.

The king's brow furrowed. "Most worrying." He appeared to consider the matter a moment longer, then shook his head and got down off his throne. "Nevertheless, we shouldn't concern ourselves with that now." He exchanged a cordial nod with Adâ. Closer up, he looked exhausted, his eyes sunken and a pallid complexion that suggested he'd lost his natural glow to weeks of sleepless nights. "So these are the ones we're looking after for the time being, then."

"Yes." Adâ pursed her lips and glanced at Jack and Lucy.

"That's no great hardship," the king said, giving them a smile in strong contrast to Adâ's coolness. "As you may have surmised, I am King Thengel Thorin.

221

the white fox

This is the land of my forefathers. I would give you a proper welcome tour to Thorin Salr, though I am afraid your timing isn't the best. You will have seen we're not in an entirely secure position at the moment."

Lucy looked like she was about to elaborate loudly and sarcastically about being very sorry they couldn't have chosen a better time to get involved in an occult ritual and that they'd come back at a more convenient date. Jack put his hand on her arm warningly. She shrugged it off but said nothing.

"What *is* all this?" Adâ asked, gesturing backwards at the way they had come. "I was gone for only one week."

Through the open door, the thick crowd was still visible in the next chamber.

"The next set of precautions, I'm afraid. Things have got considerably worse since you left. We have scouting parties out all over the mountains, and regiments of soldiers have been dispatched to evacuate the villages. We're having enough problems as it is housing *our* people without having to bring the entire kingdom into one valley. Still, war is war." He sighed. "Did you have any problems with greenskins on your way up?"

Adâ quickly related their encounter with the reptilian creatures, though she left out the part about one sprouting wings. Jack would have pointed this out, but a few painstaking hours in Adâ's company had already taught him that keeping his mouth shut was good for him in most situations.

"That *is* worrying," Thorin said, stroking his beard absentmindedly.

"Any word from Sardâr?" Adâ ventured after a moment.

"None, I'm afraid," the king replied. He looked genuinely worried but checked his expression almost immediately. "But let us concern ourselves with that tomorrow. It grows late. I shall get someone to show you to your rooms." He snapped his fingers. Out of nowhere came a woman in a green tunic, clothed far more brightly than most of the people in the hall outside.

"Please escort our guests to their chambers."

The woman nodded, smiling, and beckoned the

the white fox

three of them to the door.

"So why are we here again?" Lucy asked indignantly. "Have we really just been moved into a war zone?"

There was a pause, in which the king glanced from Adâ to Lucy awkwardly. "Um . . . well . . . that is to say . . . the situation was not *fully* anticipated . . . The plan was originally . . ." He stared at Adâ pleadingly.

Jack couldn't quite suppress a smile that this evidently powerful monarch was being ordered around by a teenage girl who currently looked slightly like a kissogram.

"It's alright, Thengel," Adâ said darkly. "I'll deal with them."

Lucy glared at the king as they were led out of the room.

Jack followed, not feeling entirely confident that they would live to hear an explanation tomorrow.

Chapter III
inari

Within a few minutes, they were in Lucy's room. The medieval theme of this place had clearly been hammered down to perfection; a series of old-fashioned candles had been placed around the chamber, sending flickering, angular patterns across the concave ceiling. The floor, like outside, was set with large, cold flagons, covered in thick rugs and furs. A chair, also covered in some kind of animal skin, sat between the wooden bed and a delicately engraved clothes chest, and an alcove led to a small bathroom. One wall was entirely occupied by a tall window, set into the surrounding rock. The view across the valley was deep grey, the mountains only just visible against a slightly brighter shade of indigo. The whole room and its three occupants were reflected in a

tall mirror next to the chair, looking like the set of a period drama.

They had been here for ten minutes, during which time Lucy, seated on the bed, had endured a lecture from Adâ about how to properly address a monarch. There was so far no evidence that any of it had been absorbed.

"Right then," Adâ finished, adjusting how she was sitting, "there are a few things you should know before you really screw things up. It won't have escaped your notice that you haven't only come across humans in the last few days. I myself"—she scratched one of her pointed ears surreptitiously—"am an example of this. It probably hasn't escaped your notice, either, that the people here are a little . . . *different* than what you're used to."

"Different how?" Lucy asked, being deliberately difficult.

Adâ made a "short" gesture.

Lucy raised her eyebrows.

Adâ sighed. "Shorter," she said quietly.

"Sorry?" Lucy replied loudly.

Adâ clipped her around the head. "These people are dwarves. Ruth said Vincent explained this to you already!"

Jack muttered something about the patchiness of the explanation.

Adâ fixed him with a look that would have frozen open flames. "They are *dwarves*—an entirely different race to you. And, quite obviously, this is *not* your home world, and there are no humans here. It would not be wise to draw attention to any differences between them and yourselves. If you do, the king may be brought under pressure to answer some difficult questions about where you're from, and we will be out of here more quickly than an egg poacher from a cockatrice nest, which," she said as Jack opened his mouth, "is *extremely* fast."

"What about you, then?" Jack asked.

Adâ sniffed. "I am an elf," she said curtly but offered no further comment.

"So we're *not* back in time?" Jack asked after a moment.

Adâ looked at him as if he had just asked whether

the Pope was a Christian. "No, we're not *back in time.*
That's impossible."

"So this really *is* a different world," Lucy murmured to no one in particular.

"Yes, and that's something else. Up until now,
you have only had the company of more *knowledge-
able* people. The vast majority of this world's people
are as ignorant as you were only days ago about lands
beyond their own boundaries. King Thorin is an
Apollonian, as are, obviously, the crew of *The Golden
Turtle.* There are precious few others who are aware
of worlds beyond their own. It is of *paramount* importance that you keep what you know secret."

"Why?"

"Has anyone mentioned Isaac to you?"

Both shook their heads.

"He was originally from your world. He founded
the Apollonians about a quarter of a century ago;
he was the first of us to travel between worlds.
Incidentally, he was also the brother of Ruth's adop-
tive father, Ishmael. He built an almanac of laws,
observations he made about the nature of interworld

travel. One major point is that each world is self-contained within its own time frame. This world is at a different stage of development to yours, and many more will be different still. This one happens to be in the equivalent of your past. Isaac placed it at roughly the ninth or tenth century. A crossover of time periods could have cataclysmic consequences beyond our understanding. For example, if we allowed guns from your time into this world, things would escalate out of our control. This means you must guard your origins vigilantly. For now, you will be Jack and Lucy Sharif, my nephew and niece."

"But we look nothing like you," Lucy exclaimed, half-indignant, half-relieved.

Jack looked again at Adâ. She *was* human shaped, remarkably so, he supposed, considering life could have evolved completely differently on her world. She was, however, at least six inches taller than Lucy, very slender—almost pinched looking—with pointed ears, darker skin, and a different shape to her face and features. It was quite a big difference.

"That's why we need this," Adâ said, producing

from her cloak something that looked like a metal egg. It was dusty brown, held in the same bronzy clasps as their rings. She held it out to Jack and Lucy, who leaned back instinctively, unsure of what it was going to do.

Adâ whispered a single syllable, which neither Jack nor Lucy could make any sense of. The egg glowed bright luminous green and floated out of her hand. It hung in the air for a second, then spun around the room like a high-tech toy, humming slightly. When it had made two full circuits of both Lucy and Jack, it dropped into Adâ's hand and dulled again.

Jack looked at Lucy and got a slight shock. The girl in front of him was still recognizably Lucy: she was still hazel eyed and reddish-brown haired, but she was different. Her ears were elongated and pointed at the end, just like Adâ's. She was taller and slightly slimmer, and her face seemed to have become thinner. Her skin was a lot darker, and her head was more circularly shaped. She now definitely resembled an elf, if not a blood relative of Adâ's.

He stood up and studied himself in the mirror.

Exactly the same change had happened to him, but whereas Lucy's slightly curvier figure looked squashed, he thought the look rather suited him. He stepped in front of the mirror, blocking Lucy's view to it. Her shock, he reasoned, wouldn't do any of them any good.

"How the fu—"

"Bedtime," Adâ said loudly over him. "There are new clothes in your rooms. Good night." She left the room, leaving the door open behind her.

"Night," Jack called as she turned the corner. He waited for the slam of her door and then began talking. "So what do you think of this place?"

"I'm not sure," she said, standing up to lean on the windowsill. "It's just all so . . . alien. We're on a different *planet* . . . Does that mean these are aliens? It's not how I imagined them at all . . ." She stared out at the darkened sky.

Jack waited for her to say something more. This was the first chance that they'd had to talk since *The Golden Turtle.* Realistically, the first time they would have talked since before all this started, and now she didn't seem to want to. "And the king?"

"Bastard. He's just the same as Adâ. We're nothing more than packages to them."

"I thought he seemed nice. He did say we'd talk about it tomorrow . . ."

"Are you siding with them?" She looked at him sharply.

"No, of course not. It's just . . . it could have been a lot worse, couldn't it? The Cult could have got you . . ." Immediately he regretted saying it.

Lucy stared blankly out the window, not replying.

With a sudden, internal jolt, the full magnitude of what had happened to Alex hit him again. He could be being tortured. He could be dead, for all they knew, standing here in relative comfort in a warm, dry room . . . He felt slightly sick at the thought.

"I'm sure Alex is okay," he said, though it didn't sound convincing, even to him.

She didn't reply but continued to stare out the window.

Jack decided to give her some space. On his way out he thought he heard a muffled sob, but he didn't

Inari

go back in. He got the impression he would be co-opted as the nearest and easiest target for blame.

Jack went to his room. It was exactly the same as Lucy's but flipped so that the bathroom was on the right side. On the bed were a pile of sandy gold and blue tunics; wide, Arabian-like trousers; a pair of rough leather boots; and a belt. Looking down at his pirate gear, he realized that he hadn't changed his clothes in four days. Shocked and slightly disgusted, he stripped off his top layer and headed into the bathroom.

The room was just as rocky as the previous one, but the entire floor was a basin-like bath full of steaming water. A pummelled crack in the center of the bath spurted the water upwards like a Jacuzzi or a hot spring, and chutes around the edge filtered some out again when it got too full.

Jack removed the last of his clothes and sunk into the water. It was luxuriously warm and a strong contrast to freezing seawater. Salt and dirt dislodged from his skin and hair and were sucked away down the chutes. He didn't feel any taller, but he definitely was, and his new body, however it had come about,

the white fox

was quite a bit more muscular than his last.

He stepped out of the bathroom, scratching his wet hair, and froze.

There were several people Jack could think of whom he would gladly be discovered half-naked by, particularly with this body, but a glowing, vocally enabled fox wasn't one of them. It took a minute for his brain to kick into gear.

"Don't move," he said through gritted teeth, holding his towel up whilst bending down to grab his new clothes. "You've got a lot of questions to answer."

The fox said nothing, just inclined his head.

A moment later, Jack reemerged from the bathroom to find the creature still on his bed. Keeping his distance, he sat on the chair slowly. The new clothes were far more comfortable than Quentin's nautical amalgamation had been.

So what do you want to know? The creature sounded strangely like a well-spoken Englishman, with an impeccable BBC accent.

"Everything! What are you? Are you even a fox? How can you talk? Why is the Cult of Dionysus after us? Where's Alex?" After the minimalist explanations from Vince and Adâ, he was keeping his expectations low for any answer to these.

"I'll try my best." The fox stretched out, and Jack thought he saw him smile slightly. *"Firstly, I am—"* He sounded as if he wanted to carry on but looked as if he were choking on something. *"Damn this restricting form. As much as I would like to tell you who I am, I can't say. I can tell you what I am, though. I think so, anyway."*

"That wasn't a good start. So *what* are you?"

"Loosely speaking, an ancient elemental force, bound in corporeal form."

Jack raised his eyebrows in annoyance, but then, he thought, talking to a glowing animal that could understand and talk back, he really wasn't in a position to be making judgements about what was real or not.

"It's not as grand as it sounds. I'm not like other spirits. You have to walk around looking like a miniature snowstorm, and the hair balls are horrendous."

"I thought only cats got hair balls."

"I thought so too, but something obviously went wrong

in the transfer. It's really not pleasant. Be thankful you mortals invented baths."

"Right . . . Who put you in that body? Did you choose to be a fox?"

"Ah, now that would be telling," replied the fox slyly.

Jack got the distinct impression that the fox was enjoying himself.

"I believe your next question was why the Cult is after you. Actually, they weren't. They tracked down what they were looking for—a Door to Darkness—and it just so happened that it was in your town. They needed Alex's Shard, and so they targeted your friend Lucy on the expectation that he'd come running. They were right. Unfortunately, you saw too much, and you needed silencing. And your escape the first time has only made that a more urgent priority for them. Then there's the matter of your Shard, though I doubt they know about that . . . yet."

Somehow, Jack thought, this wasn't much better. Being in the wrong place at the wrong time was just as bad as being actively searched out. He pulled out the Shard from under his tunic and let it hang in the lamplight. He'd almost forgotten about it on the journey.

"It's not really mine, though, is it?" he asked, pondering its gleaming surface. "I mean, you gave it to me. I don't own it."

"Of course you do," the fox replied, hopping off the bed and coming to sit in front of him. *"Trust me. It would be a grave mistake to part with. Keep it on you at all times."*

Jack shrugged and replaced it under his top. It hadn't proven itself to be of any particular significance yet, other than that it was a gift from a glowing animal spirit and that Alex had one just like it. "What about Alex? Did you give him his too?"

"No, I didn't, but I believe it was an allied agent who did. I'm afraid I don't know what happened to Mr. Steele," the fox said, and for the first time he sounded worried. *"I'm sorry,"* he added in response to the morose look on Jack's face.

"I'd—*we'd* waited for him for over a year . . . and he'd only just come back . . ."

There was silence, in which the fox didn't move but just stared at him.

"I'm tired," Jack said finally. He took off his top

and got into bed, pulling the covers up over him. It was extremely comfortable—some kind of stuffed mattress with about five sheets piled on top. He closed his eyes and left himself open for sleep to take him. The candles, flickering in the slight brush from the disturbed sheets, were still lit.

"Do you think you could turn those off?" he said to the fox, yawning. Before he had even realized that he had just asked an animal to put out the lights, the flames were extinguished. The weaving patterns of smoke faded away into the now dark room.

Well, it would have been dark, except that the fox was still glowing with the brightness of a firefly on ecstasy.

"Can't you put your light out?"

"That's one thing I can do." A moment later the light faded into complete darkness. *"You know, Jack, I like you. I was worried you'd be more pompous, just like everyone else involved in this mess of a war, but you're not."* The irony that this was said in what amounted to an upper-middle-class southern English accent did not escape Jack.

"You really think it's going to come to war?"

"I know historians don't like the word inevitable, *but this pretty much is. And it doesn't look like we're well prepared. I've seen many wars, and this one looks like it's going to be particularly nasty. And yet, statesmen who should be protecting their lands just sit in council rooms splitting grungles over the minutiae of fiscal policy, whilst their worlds fall apart around them."*

"The Apollonians have been around for hundreds of years?" Jack asked sleepily, the dates not adding up even in his state of sliding consciousness.

"Not as such, no. But there have always been some *people who opposed the Cult. The Cult's been around for a good few hundred years now, but the imperialist escapades are relatively new. In fact, even before the deluge of Ndiuno—"* The fox spluttered again, his words apparently cut off against his will once more.

"What's a grungle?"

"Troll hair. Trust me, you don't want to know."

"Oh. Right. And what's a cockatrice?"

"Did you ever see Sesame Street?*"*

"Yeah, I think so."

"*Think Big Bird but with fangs, talons, and a poisonous tail.*"

"Oh." In the shadows, Jack smiled. He was beginning to like the fox, not least because he was giving him some straight answers that seemed so rare around here, even if they were being rooted out by some invisible force. "How the hell did you get here? From Earth? We had to fly this dragonfly machine thing, then spend three days in a turtle submarine."

"*Oh, I managed it much quicker than that. But sorry. That's on the blacklist too.*"

Jack thought for a minute. "Do you have a name? Or does that come under who you are?"

"*That, my friend, is called a loophole. My name is Inari.*"

Inari

Chapter IV
resolutions and preparations

Jack rolled over in bed. Light filtered through his window in a broken block, highlighting the spiralling sheets
of dust sifting through the air. From outside, the drifting noises of bustling crowds and the protestant grunts
of machinery signalled the start of a new day.

Someone screamed.

Jack sat up straight in his bed and listened. There
was another scream. He hoisted himself out of bed,
threw on a tunic and a belt, and rushed out of the room.

Lucy's door was open. She stood, looking horror-
stricken, staring at her own reflection in the mirror.

Adâ joined Jack in the doorway. She didn't look
very pleased.

"What the *hell* did you do?" Lucy shouted at her,

indicating her altered body.

"It's necessary for your disguise," Adâ said, sounding a little wary for the first time.

"Put them back!" screamed Lucy. She looked as if she had been about to point to her breasts, but realizing Jack was there, had thought better of it.

Both Jack and Adâ stared in silence. Then, when Lucy didn't speak, each slowly backed out of the doorway in opposite directions.

"Be quick. We're having breakfast with the king."

Jack returned to his room and put on the pair of boots. They were extremely thick and at first hard to walk in but quite comfortable. He shuffled out of his bedroom, trying not to trip over himself. The other two were waiting outside, Adâ impatient, Lucy seemingly quite a bit happier. Looking at her now, Jack thought, she must have dropped at least a size. There was obviously some compensation.

A female dwarf was waiting at the end of the corridor, ready to descend with them into the administrative chaos of the colony-city-fortress. Just as the previous day, the hallways were throttled with

Resolutions and Preparations

people, and it looked as if the refugees had spent the night there. Only a narrow stream in the center allowed for the free movement of guards and miners. Weaving down the path of least resistance to the floor below, their guide led them finally to another pair of large double doors. She conversed with the guard for a moment.

He nodded and pounded his axe upon the floor as the one outside had done. In the same way, a five-foot-high door sprung open out of the larger one.

The dwarf headed through it, followed by Adâ, Jack, and Lucy.

This next chamber was roughly the size of the entrance chamber—another cavern that seemed to be hollowed out of the innards of the cliff. Rows and rows of hefty wooden tables filled its floor space, surrounded by dwarves in lines, eating, drinking, and talking. Magnified a hundred times by the cave-like ceiling, the cacophony was astronomical; the roar of voices, clinking of goblets and cutlery, creaking of benches and noises from the other hallways and chambers echoed all around them.

the white fox

The dwarf guided them down the aisle between the two central tables, passing a multitude of dwarves. Jack noticed a definite segregation here—separate tables for fine-tunic officers, other guards, male and female miners, others in overalls, and several more who appeared to be scribes or civil servants. The chamber was full to the breaking point. Through another pair of wide doors to their left, he spotted a thick queue of refugees packing in towards a kitchen, apparently receiving their own rations to take back to those waiting in the hallways.

At the end of the chamber, a few stone steps led to another door. On it were carved several runes, but after a moment's examination Jack realized he could read them. He glanced at his ring, but it was not glowing.

WEST DINING ROOM—ANNEX

The dwarf paused outside the door, then motioned them to go inside.

Adâ turned, one foot on the step, looking the

Resolutions and Preparations

other two up and down. "Lucy, do something with your hair. Jack, your tunic's back to front."

They made their adjustments (Adâ replanting her sapphire hair clip on her scalp) and straightened up.

The elf opened the door, and they headed inside.

This room was far smaller, only a little bigger than Jack's bedroom. An octagonal stone table, like the one in the throne room, dominated the space, though this one was littered with the remnants of crispy-looking meat and thin slices of something like bread. A few crusty cheese rinds were scattered on the plates, and a large lump of what seemed to be a golden-brown roast, its original animal indistinguishable, sat in the middle of the table like a strangely overcooked Christmas turkey. It was already partially eaten with the dull white of bone visible, and a knife was planted vertically in it like a sword.

Several people sat around the table, with several more attendants standing behind them in between now empty trays. The king was seated directly opposite the doorway, with a similar-looking but younger dwarf next to him. On one side of them was another dwarf, dressed in the same curious grey overalls as his fellows outside, his face black with soot and goggle marks etched around his eyes. A pair of scaly, elbow-length gloves was tucked through his wide belt. On the other side sat a tall figure—recognizable as an elf by his pointed ears and Arabic look. Reading glasses rested on the bridge of his nose, and he wore a deep crimson tunic and a gold-laced robe.

"Sorry we're late," Adâ remarked, taking a seat. "There was some confusion over cleavage."

Jack snorted but managed to turn it into a cough.

Lucy did not look amused at all.

"No matter, we saved some for you," the king said, gesturing to one of the attendants.

He sprung up between them with three plates of crispy meat, a few slices of bread, and a slightly green-tinted cheese.

"And feel free to help yourselves to the roast. I apologize; your first meal here should have been somewhat more extravagant, but I have vowed in these troubled times to eat only as the most meagre of my subjects. How can we hope for others to act for

Resolutions and Preparations

the common good if we do not ourselves?" Thorin looked at the three newcomers. Adâ nodded, but Jack and Lucy glanced at each other, unsure of whether this was a rhetorical question.

"So, what's the plan, Thengel?" the burnt-looking dwarf asked of the king after Jack and Lucy had been given the chance to begin their surprisingly famil- iar-tasting meals.

Thorin nodded at the attendants, and they bowed and left the room by the same single door. "Well—"

"I think these two need to be filled in first," the male elf said, interrupting the king.

"Yes, yes, of course." He turned to Jack and Lucy. "I know from yesterday's experiences that you are already aware of the presence of greenskins in the mountains. These are uncivilized, brutish creatures; they are naturally nomadic, with no fixed abode, and so usually take to pillaging our outlying villages in tribal raids. Over the last several weeks, however, changes have become more and more evident in their organization and actions. Raids have been coming thick and fast from the east, with forces numbering

the white fox

far greater than before. Of those villages that have been attacked, there have been few survivors. I have recently decided to evacuate all villages. We have several greater colonies arranged over these mountains into which refugees have been pouring for days now. As you will have seen, we are struggling with the increased demands on space and rations."

Jack was trying to listen, but Lucy didn't help things by rocking back on her chair repeatedly in a bored sort of way.

"And there are the additional rationing problems caused by the loss of most of our arable farming land due to a bad harvest season—"

"Alright, Thengel, I think they have the general idea," the male elf asserted, as the king looked as if he was beginning to list all his current grievances. "What matters to *them* is Sardâr's current predicament."

"Indeed, yes," Thorin continued, acknowledging the change of subject. "You probably know by now that Sardâr Râhnamâ is the leader of the Apollonians. A week ago, he disappeared. He was in this colony, and we have reason to believe he has gone to investigate the causes of our problems. It appears he left on a dangerous mission in secret to prevent endangering anyone"—he looked at Adâ—"who might have insisted on accompanying him. We are debating as to whether to send a search party out . . ."

There was an exchange of looks around the five senior members of the table. Adâ glared at the younger dwarf next to Thorin, whilst the other dwarf and elf seemed to share a reserved understanding.

"So . . . what's the plan, then?" Lucy ventured, nonplussed by the series of silent exchanges.

"Well, Adâ has wanted to send a search party since Sardâr disappeared. Meanwhile, Bál"—he glanced at the younger dwarf to his right—"argues that we cannot spare the resources for the time being."

"Especially not for one who isn't even a countryman of ours," Bál put in. "We're virtually in a state of national crisis, and we have to care for those within our walls."

Adâ renewed her glare with increased vigor. "This is *so* much bigger than you can possibly imagine, *dwarf*—"

"Adâ, that is *enough*," the other elf said sharply. "At any rate, Smith and I agree that Sardâr is more than capable of handling himself. He is our most experienced agent, and I, for one, have complete faith in his judgement. He would not have allowed himself to become embroiled in anything he cannot handle."

The grubby dwarf, evidently Smith, nodded in agreement.

For once, Adâ kept her silence.

"And so," Thorin continued wearily, "we return to square one. But with your arrival, I believe we can come to a solution. Before Sardâr left he said that in the event of anything *untoward* occurring in relation to the Earth operation, nothing substantial was to be said or done without his presence. Another example of his seeming omniscience. So, the choice is yours. Do we leave him to his mission and trust that he is well or send out a search party?"

Jack and Lucy looked at each other, taken aback by the surprise choice before them. Having been so close for so long, they could tell what the other was thinking without speaking. Both seemed to

Resolutions and Preparations

view this as a choice between unknown quantities. But Jack recognized in Lucy's face the same propelling yearning to get some concrete answers about their extraordinary predicament. And if finding this Sardâr was the only way that could happen, then the choice suddenly seemed very simple.

"Yes," replied Jack, "send a search party."

Lucy nodded.

"But on the condition that we get to go." Jack could tell with this secondary request that he had lost her support. Unsurprisingly, he supposed, she felt she had been shifted around enough for now and would want to wait in this colony-city in relative comfort for some answers. But he could not square that with his impulses. He needed answers, and he needed them now. More, a voice said in the back of his mind, for Alex's sake than for his own. But then, Lucy didn't have a glowing fox spirit harassing her with enigmatic hints at awkward moments.

The five around the table were silent, evidently surprised. Entirely different expressions moved between them, from Thorin's shock to the male elf's wry smile.

"I say let them go. They deserve answers as quickly as possible. And if Bál's complaint is about not being able to set aside resources, then they should adequately fill two places on the search party." The male elf took out a wooden pipe and lit it with an ornate leaf-shaped lighter.

Bál looked mutinous at his own argument being used against his cause. Adâ appraised them coolly, her gaze flicking between the two. Thorin and Smith exchanged a shrug.

"That's decided, then. Mount Fafnir. You leave this afternoon." The king stood up, as did everyone else around the table. Nodding at them solemnly, he left the room.

"I'm sorry, but we weren't properly introduced," the burnt-looking dwarf said to Jack and Lucy. "Smith Brassmelter, Forgemaster," he said, smiling toothily from under his skullcap-like helmet and offering his hand to Jack.

He took it and shook it vigorously.

"Hakim Morabbi, Chancellor of the National

Resolutions and Preparations

Academy of Khǎlese in Tâbesh, at your service," the elf said, shaking Jack's hand perfectly normally. "And this," he continued, when the remaining dwarf failed to introduce himself, "is Bál Thorin, His Majesty's nephew."

Bál grunted at them, doing an excellent impression of Lucy on Monday mornings. Jack got the feeling that he resented missing his chance to leave the room with the king.

A moment later, Bál and Hakim made their excuses and hurried off, though a considerable distance apart.

"Come on," Smith said. "We've got to get you sorted out for this afternoon."

Jack followed Adâ and Lucy out of the chamber, leaving his empty plate behind.

Outside, the dining room was still as busy as before, except that the overflow of refugees seemed to have spilled into here as well, with some chewing meat next to their bags and carts in corners and others having commandeered a table. Smith marched away with surprisingly long strides towards the opposite door.

Just as they were about to follow, Adâ faced them. "Thank you," she said quietly before bustling off behind the forgemaster.

Jack turned to Lucy in mock shock, but she was clearly not in the mood for jokes, having just been volunteered against her will for a mountain expedition. As Jack followed, he reflected on his mixed feelings about Adâ. He could not suppress the notion that they had been manipulated by her into getting her own way. But, he acknowledged with some surprise, he pitied her. *He* knew what it felt like for someone close to disappear suddenly without a trace, and, he supposed, being put on babysitting duty for two thankless teenagers must have been very frustrating when she was so worried about Sardâr's well-being.

A few minutes later, having climbed through the innards of the cliff via more flights of stone stairs, they emerged into the light. They were standing on an open air metal platform that seemed to fill a gap in the cliff face, affording them a phenomenal view over the valley. The mining machinery they had seen

Resolutions and Preparations

the day before was working just as it had been, beneath the magnificent grey peaks that brushed the lower cloud banks. Directly below them, another mass of refugees thronged towards the main gate, escorted by a group of the green-tunic guards.

Smith led them along the gangway, which clung to the side of the cliff. Both Jack and Lucy kept well back from the edge. They couldn't see what was supporting the metal bridge, and neither really wanted to find out that it was nothing at all. A large doorframe was set into the rock at the end of the gangway, and it was to this that Smith moved.

Inside was extremely hot. Jack looked down and jumped backwards in shock. The gangway continued into this chamber, but now it suspended them over a lake of deep crimson liquid. Patches of black rock formed on the surface here and there, and every so often a bubble popped loudly on the surface.

Dwarves, clad in scaly-looking aprons and gloves, were hunched over on high platforms raised above the lake by thick, charred columns of rock. Some funnelled the liquid up in metal chutes, others fed it into what must have been miniature furnaces, whilst still more beat weapons into shape on the anvils above. Rails were suspended by poles from the ceiling, a series of hooks hanging from them. More dwarves added the completed weapons to the hooks and gave them a hefty push, sending them rattling down to the opposite end of the chamber.

"Is this . . . molten lava?"

"It's from the mountain," explained Smith as they crossed the gangway over the pit. "Magma is channelled into this chamber and cools, so we can use it as a natural forge."

"*This* is cool?" Lucy said incredulously.

Smith chuckled, showing his wide teeth again.

They reached the end of the gangway and passed under another doorframe. As they walked, Jack noticed that there were two massive holes in the rock on either side of the gangway through which the rails swerved together and continued. In the next chamber on the other side of a rock partition, the rails curled around and lined up to form a sort of bizarre department store. He had to look at it more closely to realize that the room was an incredibly huge chamber; where they were standing was only a platform overlooking a massive cavern full of the rails, all with metallic objects hanging off them. Some dwarves stood near the entrance, sorting the arriving goods onto rails. More were standing in the aisles on the lower levels or crossing the further matrix of gangways to reach items on higher rails.

Smith beckoned one over and gave him a series of instructions. The dwarf nodded and scuttled away to look amongst the racks.

"This fortress was the first of the seven that are the strongholds of our kingdom. Our ancestors built this one around the use of weapons . . . We were a more warlike people then . . ." Smith glanced over a few documents on textured parchment. "This forge has been here for hundreds of years, and our mechanisms haven't changed very much. All the major doors are operated by axes. Even the emblem of the royal family is an axe."

"Well," said Jack offhandedly, watching several swords appear through the hole in the wall and swirl down to the store, "you're always ready for a fight."

"Don't mention fighting," Smith replied darkly, still scanning his documents. "Ever since Sardâr disappeared the king has been extremely jumpy. He's convinced that we're about to be attacked at any moment. It is understandable, given that he has direct responsibility for so many refugees within this city."

The dwarf returned, his platform now laden with a multitude of different plates of armor and weapons.

Smith straightened and looked Jack and Lucy up and down. Instinctively, Lucy covered her chest.

"Both of you are too tall for dwarf armor," he remarked. "Luckily for you we have some spares for other races, usually commissioned and then never picked up by visitors. We don't get many of those, though." He siphoned through a few unidentifiable pieces of armor. "Try these on."

A few minutes later, Jack and Lucy were clad head to foot in dwarf-made armor. It mostly consisted of a thick, scaly hide, backed with leather, which Smith explained was troll skin (this didn't encourage either of them, particularly after what Jack had heard about

Resolutions and Preparations

grungles the night before). There was a chest plate, gauntlets, a metal-topped helmet, and another pair of protective boots. In addition, they had each been given a rather cumbersome large sword and a round, dull silver shield. The entire thing was absolutely stifling in the intense heat.

"Of course, depending on how long you stay here, we might have to invest in a custom-made suit for each of you," Smith said, stroking his beard.

As Jack tried to loosen his tunic slightly under the armor, he had the painful inkling that this might be necessary.

After thanking Smith excessively, they followed Adâ out of the forge and into the open air. The fifty-foot drop to the rocks below did nothing to ease their light-headedness.

the white fox

Chapter V
mount fafnir

The journey was extremely strenuous.

To the south of the colony-city of Thorin Salr, an ancient flow of lava had cleaved a gap between the high rocks. There, a trail of volcanic rock, dulled in color over the aeons, rose. It wove steeply up from the valley, cutting into the edge of the mountain as it climbed. The sparse vegetation found in Thorin Salr became less and less prevalent and eventually ceased altogether.

Each time they reached a bend in the trail, they were afforded a view of the surroundings. The mountainous valley was directly below, falling farther and farther with every glimpse. To the north, the mountains gave way to hills and then rocky, grassy plains that looked like they could have recently been used as arable land.

To the east and south, the massive effigies of rock disappeared into the mist, with the dull grey mass of the sea in the distance.

The search party had, in accordance with Jack's request, featured himself and Lucy. Accompanying them were Hakim and Adâ, three dwarf soldiers, and, much to the surprise of them all, Bál. They could only assume that the king had commanded him to go. His attitude was one of sullen resentment from the moment they had left.

Jack, for one, was extremely uncomfortable. Apparently, the armor he wore hadn't been designed for elves. It was particularly height restricting, so that the bottom edge of the breastplate cut into his diaphragm, and the boots reached only halfway up to his knees. The helmet did not well accommodate pointed ears, and he had removed it several times to feel deep, sore grooves in them. On top of all this, the temperature was tangibly increasing as they climbed higher.

Lucy wasn't particularly happy, either. Her parents "not believing in exercise" (although she had considerable natural talent at netball), she was having serious difficulty keeping up with the rest of them. Every so often, Jack had to wait two minutes for her to struggle up the slope to join them, by which time the rest of the group were two minutes ahead. In addition, she seemed to have decided that being concussed by a falling boulder was preferable to helmet hair.

In the first stages of the journey, Hakim had hung back to talk to Jack. Jack quickly gathered that he was feeling a little guilty about Sardâr's instructions.

"This mountain," he had said, "is supposed to be a relic of an ancient epoch. According to legend, a malevolent dragon was slain here by the patriarchal dwarf hero Rofhæle. The beast's body fell into the heart of the volcano, and its spirit was fused with the mountain itself. It's an old dwarfish superstition that when the mountain erupts it is the ancient dragon taking revenge on the descendants of its murderer."

Jack nodded, genuinely interested. He had always enjoyed myths and legends at school, and a small part of him—the seven-year-old part—was revelling in this opportunity to almost live one. But for now, what concerned him were the matters immediately at hand. "What's up with Adâ?"

Hakim smiled slightly and lowered his voice. Adâ's long dark plait was swaying down the back of her travelling cloak some twenty feet ahead. "She's going through a tough time. Sardâr left without telling anyone, not even her. She's normally perfectly amiable, but I must admit, I don't envy you two being escorted around by her in her current state . . ."

After at least an hour of trekking, they reached the end of the trail and halted. A doorframe, like the ones leading into the forge, had been set into the rock here, carved with numerous runes and symbols. In stark contrast to the cool mountainous air, the gap in the rock exuded heat like the breath of a sleeping beast; the hint of extreme incandescence far below was augmented by the fiery glow.

Hakim felt the scorching air with his outstretched hand, then turned to talk to Adâ. He whispered something in her ear. She appeared to consider for a moment before nodding.

"Right, let's go," Hakim said finally. He headed

Mount Fafnir

into the cavern with the four dwarves and Adâ. With a growing sense of foreboding, Jack followed.

The heat became steadily stronger as they descended. Jack was becoming increasingly uncomfortable. It was claustrophobic in the dark narrow tunnel, with people clustered closely together and only a menacing orange light to show the way. Even Lucy's attitude of bad-natured rebellion was gone, replaced by a lurking fear that was hard to identify.

Finally, after what seemed like days, the tunnel widened, and the red glow became more pronounced. Hakim rounded a corner and disappeared, and Jack followed.

The heat hit him like a blast of boiling water. He'd felt nothing like it before. It was like all the sunburnt weeks of August rolled into one, with midday at the equator thrown in for good measure. His eyes were forced shut by the wall of inferno heat, so it took him a moment to gauge their new surroundings. They were standing on a small crag of rock, suspended about halfway up the volcano. Before them, expanding outwards for what could be miles, was a pit of crimson liquid. There was no scraggly skin on top of this; instead it bubbled and frothed like a stormy river. Thick walls of steam rose and coiled into the air like snakes, disappearing into the distant, gold-tinged blue, which was the ring of sky above. Indistinct and cloudy, the arms of the rocky cliff face reached around the fiery pit and met in a rough circle on the other side of the crater over a hundred yards away.

Strangely, the wave of heat seemed to have little to no effect on the dwarves. Jack was already sweating profusely, and Lucy's normally straight hair was becoming more and more bushy by the second. Adâ maintained a look of serenity, slightly offset by the flush of scarlet that had flooded her face the moment they had entered the cavern.

Hakim bent down, examining the edge of the rock.

Jack moved over to him, careful not to look down. "What's the matter?"

"Something's not right," he said and looked up at Jack, gesturing to the edge below him.

Down a sloping ridge of rock, there was the beginning of what once must have been a bridge—a pair of basalt grey rams on pedestals, flanking a stone walk-way. Only a few feet protruded over the pit, where it had been broken off unevenly. Jack knelt down to look more closely. It was at least five feet thick under-neath. Whatever had taken a chunk out of this bridge must have been absolutely enormous.

Lucy, having recovered from the heat shock, was now deeply regretting allowing herself to be talked into this. Her feet were throbbing, she was filthy with dust and sweat, and she could tell she looked a mess. She slunk over the rock, her arms folded defiantly, kicking small rocks out of her way. She reached the end of the platform and gave the deep sigh of a spoilt little girl out of her depth. In fact, it *was* the sigh of a spoilt little girl out of her depth. As this thought oc-curred to her, she gave an extra vigorous kick to a pebble positioned just by her foot. It soared through the steaming air and plummeted over the edge, plop-ping unseen into the expanse of magma.

A moment later, she realized that something was wrong. Surely the lava hadn't been rippling like that a second ago? Just as she was deciding that she was imagining it, a small amount was thrown up to sizzle next to Hakim.

The elf stared at it, then grabbed Jack and yanked him backwards. More magma splattered the edges of the platform, and the steam coils changed to erratic zigzags. All the others gathered as far back as they could without disappearing into the tunnel.

The fact was, none of them could see over the edge. If they'd been able to, they would have noticed that the magma was sagging in the middle, as if someone had pulled the plug on the mountain. It sucked downwards like a whirlpool, and something else—something the shade of bone but much, much bigger—became visible within. Then the lava exploded upwards in a wave.

A massive shape spiralled out of the molten rock. The steam instantly dissipated, as if afraid of what it was concealing. As red liquid poured off it and out of its orifices, the thing became visible.

Lucy and one of the dwarves screamed.

Towering over them was the most horrific creature Jack had ever seen, far surpassing the hellhound. It resembled a gigantic lobster, but it was positioned like a hunched humanoid. Armor of charred bone covered its form, and the gaps between seethed with dark energy. Six appendages extruded from its hide, four like spider's legs and two, the top two, ending in pincers the size of small houses. Its flat head stretched horizontally, its mouth a circular gash, and its eyes burned with the same otherworldly phantasmagoria that had occupied the skull of the demon on Earth. It opened its maw and roared, displaying at least ten circles of razor-sharp fangs.

Jack stumbled backwards, his heart pounding in shock. He had not wanted to see what came out of that steam. He breathed in shallowly and gagged. The same stench of darkness penetrated his nose, searing this throat and making him retch. This was far, far worse than the hellhound. Jack just stared upwards, the height of the being before him seeming to exemplify the hopelessness of their situation. He knew for certain this was a demon, but the last one had been a fraction of the size, and Alex had said that a bullet could keep it at bay only temporarily. How were they supposed to defend themselves against this thing, let alone when their choice of weapons was confined to the Dark Ages?

Hakim was the first to act. He flung the others behind him and flourished his staff expertly, but before he could do anything, he was knocked across the platform by the blow of one of those huge pincers. Another swung diagonally down, narrowly missing Lucy.

Jack leapt out of the way of a third blow and landed hard on the rock. He scrambled to his feet.

The rest of the party were spread out, each having drawn their weapons. Adâ had twin curved blades, and all the dwarves had axes of varying sizes. Hakim was nearby Jack, not moving.

Slowly, so as not to attract attention, Jack sidled over to the fallen elf. He bent down and listened for breathing, and to his great relief, he found it. Still trying not to make himself noticeable, he grabbed the elf under the arms and began to drag him towards the mouth of the tunnel. If he could just get him out of the heat . . .

A horrific screech made Jack drop Hakim and cover his ears. He saw Adâ in front of him, holding the two blades in an X above her head, sparks flying everywhere as she blocked the blow of one of the pincers. The demon retracted its appendage and smashed it down again harder, knocking Adâ to the ground. The pincer opened, and tendrils of some pulsating, dark substance snaked out through the air, wrapping around the elf's body like serpents.

Jack gripped his sword handle and pulled. It caught in the scabbard, ripping off his belt instead. The scabbard clattered to the ground a few feet away, and at the same time, Adâ's head was disappearing within the black wraps. Abandoning caution, he sprinted over to her and began tearing at the cords with his bare hands. The repulsive octopus-like tentacles felt rubbery to the touch but were clamped like a vise over her body. He yanked one with all his might, but as soon as it came free another took its place, hiding the strip of cloth he had managed to uncover.

Out of the corner of his eye, he saw one of the dwarves pulling Hakim into the mouth of the tunnel, whilst the other three formed a kind of phalanx at the back of the platform with the hefty metal shields they had been hoisting on their backs up the mountainside. For some indescribable reason, a page from one of his old history textbooks flickered to the front of his mind—the difference between a phased withdrawal and a retreat. For a fraction of a second he envisaged escaping—charging up the passage, leaving all this behind—leaving this crazy world, with its elves, dwarves, and demons, and running back to the lake, back to Earth, back to the way things had been before this madness.

But no. There was Lucy inside the tunnel, watching with pallid horror. There was Hakim, hunched against the rock face, unconscious. There was Bál, strident before the beast, ready to parry any of its blows. And there was Alex, though somewhere in an unknown dark oblivion amongst the stars, who Jack knew needed help. And there was the second pincer swinging out of the roasted air, catching him in the stomach and launching him off his feet, his fingers scraping uselessly at Adâ's glutinous cage as he soared through the air, tumbling downwards into oblivion.

Mount Fafnir

Chapter VI
sərdər

"You really need to start saving yourself, you know."

Jack heard the voice inside his head, somehow distant. Fearing what he might see, he opened his eyes.

He could see the churning lava beneath him, hear the shouts from above, feel the heat, and yet he seemed to be suspended in the air on his stomach. Inari was floating in front of him, resting on his front paws, his glowing fur oddly unremarkable in the crimson light emanating from the magma below.

"What . . . ?" Jack managed groggily. Then he actually cried out as he realized he was lying on a narrow rocky ledge below the original platform about three feet away from fiery oblivion.

The fox inclined his head but said nothing.

"What happened?" Jack said after a few moments, pushing himself as far away from the drop as possible.

"*You fell,*" Inari replied.

"Where are the others?"

"*Up on top still, I assume.*"

"Couldn't you have checked? Couldn't you have helped?" Jack said exasperatedly.

"*I can't directly interfere with mortal affairs. And besides, if I'd gone, you could have fallen.*"

Jack glanced at the bubbling liquid below and decided he was glad Inari hadn't left. "Can we go back up?"

"*Yes. But you won't be seeing me for a while now.*"

Instantly, Jack felt the absence of stomach you get going down a roller coaster, and he began to float upwards. Through the miasma of heat he could make out the hulking form of whatever the grotesque creature was. He saw that the lower part of its form was anchored in some kind of black rock that clung to the surface of the lava like a magnet. Somehow it seemed less terrifying than before. With a slight lift of hope, he realized that they were now dealing with a known quantity. He had seen the worst this thing could do, so now they knew what they were up against. And they could fight back.

He reached the edge of the rock and was roughly deposited on the side, apparently unnoticed by anyone else. He straightened up and surveyed the scene, but, once again, the ivory fox had vanished.

Those black, rubbery tentacles were extruded from the massive pincers; six bundles of dark wire hovered eerily in the air, the steam cascading up and around them. There was only one free person left—even Lucy had been apparently absorbed—and it was Bál. He was in the same position as when Jack had been knocked off but looked much more battle worn and exhausted. The heat finally seemed to be getting to him. Even as Jack watched, another set of tendrils began to weave out of the

the white fox

pincer, snaking their way like eels over to Bál's swiftly failing body. He started to batter them away, but as he knocked one, another coiled in at a different angle, darting closer and closer to scraping his armor and enfolding his skin.

Jack took action immediately. He leapt onto the rocks, grabbing his scabbard as he went. Rolling with surprising grace, he landed, gesticulating on the hard, warm ground. He lurched upwards and drew his blade. The silver caught the fiery light and glinted. Simultaneously, Bál collapsed, and the tendrils began to slide over him like sinisterly solid water. This time Jack wasn't taking any chances. With a gasp of effort, he raised his sword above his head and sliced down through the tentacles.

It was not elegant or particularly efficient, but it worked. With a rumbling crack, the demon's head twisted around to him as the split tendrils writhed in apparent agony. The creature growled (a sound like millions of cars smashing to the lowest point of the Grand Canyon at the same time), and the second pincer swerved out of nowhere at his abdomen.

But Jack was ready. He rolled to the left, dodging the blow, and extended his sword arm.

There was the satisfying squelch of severed sinew, and Adâ collapsed to the ground, covered in reeking black liquid. She clambered to her feet, looking shocked but resolute. "Thank you," she gasped, spitting out more slime. "You cut the others open. Leave this to me."

Jack nodded, and as he moved to break more cocoons he heard the familiar screech of pincer on metal. Soon all of them were free, and the platform was drenched in thick black liquid. Lucy looked dazed, which was a good thing, because she probably hadn't been that filthy before in her life.

Hakim staggered to his feet and raised his staff. "Jack, take the others and get out. Leave this to us."

"No," Jack said, looking him right in the eyes, "I've got to fight." He felt dazed also, but it was mixed with a strong sense of righteous vengeance. He felt anger bubbling under the surface, ready to explode outwards. This was for Alex. Even if the creature had nothing to do with the Cult, to him it was the same

the white fox

entity that had taken his closest friend. He had been powerless last time. Not again.

Hakim's eyes softened. "You've done brilliantly, but we can take it from here." The elf ducked as the pincer, now mobile from lack of victims, arched over him, cutting a ream through the steam. He raised his staff and roared an incantation.

A bolt of bright blue lightning shot over Adâ's head, striking the creature in the chest. It looked perturbed but not beaten, and Hakim joined Adâ, one deflecting blows, the other firing spells.

Jack watched with the others from the mouth of the tunnel, Lucy by his side. The dwarves, even Bál, seemed to have recognized that they could do no more against this foe and were showing no great impulse to leap back into combat. Jack felt a growing sense of panic as the battle became closer and closer cut, not even trying to explain to himself how Hakim seemed to be shooting electricity from wood. Even his poor basic knowledge in chemistry told him that this was physically impossible, just as it had done back on the hilltop on Earth.

Once or twice, Adâ was knocked sideways, momentarily stunned, and Hakim had to swiftly dodge a blow. Finally, the decider came. Adâ raised her sword to block another strike, but at the last moment the pincer opened, the lower half taking out her legs. She collapsed forward hard, one of her swords spinning over the edge to be swallowed up by the fire. Hakim's staff crackled as he cut off the bolt and thrust it into the air. A diamond of crystalline light swirled around him and Adâ, but even as it faded, the second claw came back to strike anew . . .

Jack hardly knew what he was doing. Before the rational side of his brain had had time to react, he was charging forward and jumping under Hakim's outstretched arm. Arching back his arm, he threw his sword upwards with all his might.

Time seemed to slow down. He was dimly aware of something shining bright white at his chest, but his gaze was fixed on the spinning blade. It cycled through the air, turning over and over, and struck the beast directly in the throat.

Time returned to normal in a flash. The creature

screamed (adding an aircraft carrier to the cars) as more white light burst from its throat, scouring a deep gash in the rock above. It writhed and screeched, and the inferno at its center seemed to intensify. The exoskeleton was melting away, sinking back into the lava like disease-ridden treacle. With a final, almighty roar, blackness engulfed it, and it imploded into nothingness. Jack's sword extruded itself from the vanishing darkness and dropped like a falcon to land on the platform, the blade driven impressively deep into the rock.

No one moved.

"Good throw," Adâ said weakly, picking herself up.

Jack just stood and stared at the space where the creature had been. There was no indication that it had ever existed. What was more, the air seemed somehow cleaner, as though purged from an unhealthy spore. He was dimly aware of people moving around him and dragged himself back to reality. "Is it dead?" he said bluntly to Hakim.

"I highly doubt it. We'll just have to . . ." He trailed off, staring at something above him.

Jack followed his gaze and immediately recognized what was strange. Twisting out of the air into existence was a thick, charred chain.

As Hakim had already guessed, the presence of such a powerful demon had caused reality to warp around it, some things appearing and others disappearing. The cage now conjuring itself out of the steam had originally been forged by ancient dwarves to imprison their most heinous criminals, and therefore was not Dark alchemy in and of itself. Of course, modern-day dwarves were much more civilized and did not suspend their victims over lava pits for days on end until their internal organs failed from excessive heat. No dwarf of the contemporary age would dream of performing such a heartless punishment—hanging, drawing, and quartering the condemned and then dropping their remains off a mountain for birds of prey to devour was seen as much more humane.

The chain swirled onwards, and out of the clearing steam something resembling a giant birdcage loomed.

"Can you get it down?" Adâ said, turning to Hakim.

"That shouldn't be a problem." He raised his staff

and intoned a few words under his breath. The symbol on the wood glowed, and the cage began to rattle along the chain towards them, apparently of its own accord. As it drew closer, Jack could see something hunched in the corner. Shocked, he realized it was a body.

The cage creaked to a halt on the edge of the pit, and Hakim and Adâ hurried over, followed by Jack and Lucy. The door had no lock, but ash and blackened, warped metal had welded it to the side. Hakim gestured them to stand back and placed his hand on one of the bars of the door. Searing golden light flashed over the frame, and it whiplashed open with a small explosion.

They all peered inside. In the opposite corner was the huddled figure. His clothes—what could have been a fine cloak and tunic, though Jack couldn't tell—had been scorched and reduced to rags. His dark hair was matted and reached his shoulder blades. As he raised his head, Jack recognized the iconic pointed ears and Middle Eastern complexion of an elf.

The prisoner struggled to stand, gripping the cage door for support. Hakim grabbed his hand, hauling him out of the cage and onto the rocks. The elf swayed, looking dazed, but righted himself and looked around. Grime covered his fine, angular face, though his bright blue eyes were alive and alert.

"Sardâr," Hakim said, awed, and pulled him into a hug. The man's face broke into a grin as they split apart and Adâ immediately took Hakim's place.

"I knew you'd do it," he said, wheezing, easing Adâ off him. "I knew you'd come through. A little earlier would have been nice, though," he added but only half seriously.

The dwarves had made their way over and were standing a respectable distance away, watching him. Slowly, Sardâr's gaze moved around the circle until it came to rest on Jack and Lucy. "So, here you are. You must be Lucy Goodman." He inclined his hand to her, and, a little surprised, she took it. He kissed her softly on the knuckles, and her already scarlet face pinked slightly more. "And you," he said, turning to Jack, "you're Jack Lawson. Alex has told me all about you two." He offered his hand to Jack.

"We'd like some answers, please," Jack said a

little coolly, ignoring his outstretched hand. The raging river of adrenaline pumping around his body had not drained in the slightest, but he was feeling oddly clearheaded considering what he had just done.

"Now, Jack, is that really reasonable?" Hakim reprimanded him. "He's just come from—"

"No," Sardâr interrupted, "he deserves them."

"I do?" Jack said, a little surprised.

"Of course you do," Sardâr replied, almost quizzically. "You've been carted from one world to another, come into contact with the Cult, faced down, I presume, a growing number of adversaries that you could have never contemplated only days ago, and you don't know what's happened to you. Of course you deserve to know!"

Adâ avoided both Jack and Lucy's eyes slightly sheepishly.

Sardâr took a step forward but staggered and was caught by Hakim. For the first time, Jack noticed that his leg was twisted the wrong way under him. "However," he said weakly, "I would appreciate it if we could get back down the mountain first." Jack nodded.

Bál led the dwarves and Lucy out. Hakim followed, beckoning Jack with him. They hoisted Sardâr onto their shoulders, and, with Adâ in tow, returned up the tunnel.

Chapter VII
the risa star

The journey down the mountain was much harder than the way up. The heat of the volcano had faded, but the uncomfortable rubbing of the armor was still there, coupled with a new soreness. Jack's adrenaline seeped away, and he found himself exhausted.

He and Hakim had to support Sardâr all the way down, something made far more arduous by Jack realizing that his helmet had become a permanent addition to Mount Fafnir when he'd fallen off the rock. He flinched every time a few pebbles scattered down, though no one seemed to notice.

Once or twice, Hakim had to change his grip on Sardâr, and on those occasions Jack noticed just how underweight Sardâr was. Out of the crimson light of

the volcano, he looked extremely pale and worn, as though he'd had to keep a permanent level of stress on himself all the time he'd been imprisoned.

They arrived in the valley through the same wrought-iron gateway as they had come. Under the purple-streaked orange sky, the miners were wrapping up their day's work and returning to the fortress for a well-earned dinner. Another crowd of bedraggled refugees was clustered around the open gate. Many of them paused in the midst of their slow influx to gaze, puzzled, at the disaccorded party of charred-looking elves and dwarves pushing past them into the entrance hall.

Bál and the other three left for the barracks soon after—one to report to the king—and Hakim told Jack and Lucy to go and get cleaned up, then meet them in Sardâr's room.

Almost an hour later, after they had showered, changed, and eaten a quick dinner, they knocked on the door.

"Come in," came the tired reply from inside.

Jack pushed on the wood, and it swung inwards.

The interior chamber was slightly larger than Jack's room, with another door leading into a bedroom on the left. The wall to the right was dominated by an oak bookcase, whilst the one opposite held a large window, showing the pitch-black valley below and the slightly lighter sky. No lamps were lit. Instead, to their left, Sardâr, Adâ, and Hakim sat in armchairs next to a flickering grate beneath an ornate fireplace. As Jack and Lucy walked over to them, the latter two elves stood.

"Oh, don't leave because of us," Jack said hurriedly, but to his surprise, Adâ did not look angry or disdainful. Surprise quickly turned to astonishment as she smiled at them and patted Jack on the shoulder.

"You did well today. Sardâr is going to explain things to you. We'll see you tomorrow."

Hakim nodded at them, and the two elves left.

"What happened to her?" Lucy whispered as they continued to Sardâr's chair. Jack shrugged, perplexed.

"Sit down, please," said the elf kindly. He was wrapped in a light robe over a soft snowy tunic, bright against his desert-darkened skin. He looked something like a Zoroastrian prophet, seated next to the sacred fire at the heart of a temple. A flagon of a steaming drink was clasped in his hands. He still appeared gaunt and tired, but most of the volcanic grime had gone, and his shoulder-length dark hair was sleek and clean. "Now, you will understandably be wanting an explanation for everything that's happened."

"Yes, we've been waiting for quite a lot of time," Lucy said. Jack got the impression that she didn't want this opportunity to slip away. He shared her anxiety and leaned forward slightly in his chair.

"Of course, you deserve one." In an opposite motion to Jack's, he settled more comfortably in his armchair. "Well, where to begin? Adâ has already filled me in on what has happened to you in the past few days, and I must say you have held up valiantly. Not many people could cope with the Cult of Dionysus, let alone young Vincent's flying skills." He smiled encouragingly.

Lucy, however, seemed to feel that they were getting nowhere. "Yes, but what does that *mean*? Who *are* the Cult of Dionysus? Why are they still after us? Why did we have to leave Earth?"

Sardâr surveyed her for a moment. "You must understand, I tell you this in the deepest confidence. This information is only known, bar a few scholars and traders, to the Apollonians and the Cult of Dionysus. Before I tell you, you must swear to me that you will not disclose it to anyone."

Jack and Lucy looked at each other and nodded in unison.

"What about Adâ and Hakim?"

"They both belong to the Apollonians. They have known for quite some time, as does Thengel. However, the vast majority of the dwarves in this kingdom have no idea. It would be extremely irresponsible to jeopardize their ignorance." Sardâr paused, apparently aligning his thoughts. Then he picked up an ancient-looking book off the top of the pile next to him, and, flicking through, found a page with a piece of parchment leafed in. "Sorry about the basic translation," he explained before reading off the parchment.

the white fox

You must, my people, understand that we live in an essentially dualistic universe. We are caught between two opposite poles of reality; the Light, the positive, the logical, the ordered: and the Dark, the negative, the primal, the chaotic. Light and Dark exist within all things and are in constant opposition. It is an age-old battle. For in the beginning, the exemplar of Light, Elysia, fought her opposite, the Dragon, and the universe was born from their struggle. My people, you do not know what your ancestors sacrificed for you. The Light fought the Dark again, and the supporters of Elysia were driven back to the ancient kingdom of Tiberisa to make their last stand.

When all hope seemed lost, in their hour of need, salvation arrived. A fallen Star named Risa. It shattered into seven Shards as it landed. Envoys from each of the races under the Light—dwarves, elves, fairies, men, and zöpüta—were sent to find these Shards. They returned, imbued with great power, and partitioned the Light and Darkness,

separating the two. We reside in the Light, and
the Dark Realm is separate. Be thankful, my
people, that fortune and Elysia have smiled
upon us so.

"That," finished Sardâr, "is from the *Testament* of
Arafat, who was a priest active in my home kingdom
eighteen hundred years ago. There are similar tales
from almost every world." He began taking books off
the pile and depositing them on the table. "*The Gospel
of Prorok, Tiên Tri's Reading of Ultimate Truth, The Divine
Message of Yeeonja . . .*"

"But it's all just a myth, isn't it?" Lucy didn't
sound very convinced. "It's etiological, a prescientific
explanation, like the plagues of Egypt."

"We thought so too," Sardâr replied darkly. "We
thought it was all a fairy tale from some ancient religion, long since dead. We *thought* we'd narrowed
our existence down to complete rational understanding through science. But we were wrong. We
never thought that a war—*one* war—could draw in
so many different worlds and peoples. The more

the white fox

we dug, however, the more we came to realize our distant ancestors established links between worlds long before we originally thought—we thought *we* first discovered them. But being able to travel between worlds isn't the worrying part of the legend. The worrying part is the existence of Darkness as a real, substantial force in our world."

The atmosphere in the room darkened distinctly. The shadows seemed to become more pronounced; the lines of Sardâr's face accentuated. He took to gazing into the fire, the flickering serpentine patterns dancing across his tired features.

"We reside in the Light," he continued, "but there is a flip side to our existence, which permeates our universe. Not a physical world like our Light Realm but a Dark Realm. It is a world of the collective, monolithic, formless force of destruction. All things are part of this struggle between Light and Dark. The question is: will the Light irradiate the Dark, or will the Dark consume the Light? You have obviously come into contact with demons now. They are not creatures as we in the Light understand them. They are not individuals but an embodiment of a single collective force, compressed into physical form by the constraints of the Light. They are, to all intents and purposes, anti-mortals. They possess no emotion or sentiment; they are merely tentacle-like extensions of the single Darkness with the sole drive to consume the Light."

Neither Jack nor Lucy said anything, nor did they look at each other. Jack was remembering the ethereal gleam in the eyes of the hellhound and whatever they had just faced. It was the same shared gleam of rapacious hunger.

"What about the Cult of Dionysus?" Jack ventured after a long silence.

"We know very little about them." Sardâr finally broke his gaze from the fire. "Though we are certain that they are all potent sorcerers who have no qualms about using the Darkness to their own ends, despite the horrendous implications such actions have for the mortal form. So powerful that they have found ways to travel between worlds without vessels."

"But what do they want? Why did they come to

301

the white fox

Earth?"

"We believe that what the Cult desires is nothing less than the domination of as many worlds as possible. They believe, not without reason, that unparalleled power can be attained by communion with the Darkness. Foolishly, though, they think they can manipulate the Darkness to their own ends. Our intelligence suggests a plot to create something akin to a superweapon: the Aterosa; some sort of device powered by Darkness itself. That, I believe, is why the Cult came to your world. It appears that one of the few remaining connections to the Darkness—a temporal Door—has been left untapped nearby your home."

"So you're telling us," Lucy said, "that Birchford, the least exciting country town in England, actually houses a gate to another dimension, and the reason we're here is that it was found by a cult of satanic wizards trying to build a magical bomb?"

"Yes. A very insightful judgement on your part."

Lucy looked stunned.

Jack could relate to her disbelief. He had been

pleasantly surprised at his ability to accept a monster hound, a group of sorcerers, a world-traversing turtle ship, and their arrival in a medieval kingdom without too much fuss. The problem was, now that everything was starting to fit together, it was forming an increasingly unassailable mental wall.

"So that thing inside the volcano . . . that was another demon?"

"Yes, and I'd wager a much more powerful one than the last ones you came across. It must have taken a colossal source of energy to summon such a creature. Which reminds me . . ." Sardâr reached around his neck and pulled out a cord. Dangling on the end was a bright Shard of crystal, glimmering in the flames, almost identical to Jack's.

Instinctively, Jack took off his own and held it up to the light.

"I thought as much," Sardâr said quietly, a glint of understanding in his eye. "Hakim and Adâ told me about your impressive exploits earlier today. I mean no offence, but I doubted that a teenager with no training in any sort of combat, let alone with a sword, would have been able to do that."

"So these are the Shards in that story? And Alex has another one?"

"Yes, it appears that these are two Shards of the Risa Star. But we must be certain." He held it up to Jack's.

From the center of Sardâr's, an inferno of crimson light rose. From Jack's, tangential pure white dissected it. The face of each of them was illuminated with the other's light. Lucy's face was oddly bi-chromatic in the twin glows. After a few moments the lights faded, and they both took back their Shards.

"Yes," said Sardâr, "the Seventh Shard, if I'm not mistaken. The one I hold is the First."

Jack braced himself for the inevitable question of where he had gotten it. For some reason, he was unwilling to talk about the glowing fox. It shouldn't seem strange in light of all the things that had happened to him, but he felt there was something about it that was different.

To his surprise, Sardâr moved on. "They originally were used to seal away the Darkness. Whether they will again this time is still in question."

"What do you mean this time?" Lucy asked.

"Well, the Apollonians were formed about thirty years ago to combat the Cult. Since they appeared, the Cult has been attacking a variety of worlds, destroying all their defenses, enslaving the population, spreading despair, making them perfect prey to be absorbed into the Darkness as broken fragments. With each world that disappears, the Darkness encroaches into the Light, bringing them one step closer to the completion of their superweapon. To open a Door to Darkness requires a phenomenal amount of energy: that is why, we think, they too are after the Shards. I've been told that you have witnessed an almost completed ritual to open such a Door using another Shard—it is hard to conceive how close your world came to destruction." Sardâr contemplated the fire.

For a moment, there was absolute silence. No noise came from the floors above or beneath them, no birdcalls from outside the window.

Sardâr blinked and turned back to them.

"What's going to happen to us?" Lucy repeated. "And what about our families?"

the white fox

For the first time Sardâr looked a little uncomfortable. "What happens to you is up to you. We could return you to Earth, but I would strongly advise against it. The Apollonians have headed off a major attack, but as long as there is a Door to Darkness there, they will return and in greater numbers too. You are most welcome to stay here, and we can keep an eye on you that way."

Jack and Lucy looked at each other, weighing the options.

"If we stay," Jack said, "can you teach us how to use magic?"

Sardâr stared at Jack. "I understand the others have tried their best to keep this a secret from you?"

Jack and Lucy nodded.

Sardâr thought for a few moments. "I must apologize for this. We did not want to shock you . . . although in retrospect it seems pointless given what you have now seen and survived. What people from your world call magic, we call alchemy. Just as the Cult draws on the raw power of Darkness, so we in the Light can draw on the natural power of our world.

I will explain it to you in more detail another time, but it does exist and can be very powerful and very dangerous. Its use, like anything else, varies across different worlds. We in my home city, Khălese, use it in everyday life. The dwarves here despise it, which is why I presume Adâ thought it would be so easy to conceal its existence from you while you were here, although without Hakim's considerable skill with defensive spells, you both would have boiled inside Mount Fafnir. The people of your world used it in the past, but it was never approved of by certain authorities. More recently it seems to have been abandoned in favor of technology. When you do learn about it, you will see just what folly that is."

"So you'll teach us, then?"

"Yes, I think that would be a good idea. You will need to be able to protect yourselves."

"And to fight too?"

"I'm sure that can be arranged. Certainly, Adâ and Hakim would be more than happy to help with that, and some of the dwarf militia are very talented in that area. You will need to become acquainted with the weapons of this world, as tiresome as it may seem, though more generally useful self-defense techniques will not go amiss, either." Sardâr finished his drink.

The fire flickered, the shadows shifting across the uneven stone floor. The soft swish of the wind could be heard from outside the window.

"Well," said Lucy resignedly, "I can't leave if Jack's still here. I guess I'll have to postpone going home." She smiled at Jack, and he returned it.

Throughout it all—the shopping, the bullying, the attacks by dark sorcerers—he knew he could count on Lucy.

Chapter VIII
elves and dwarves

Jack woke up the next morning extremely sore. The parts of his body where the armor had gouged marks were still red, and a hot bath the night before had done nothing to ease the pain. Getting dressed was a chore.

He and Lucy came out into the corridor to look for Adâ, but her room was empty of her and all her belongings.

Instead, they saw Hakim ascending the stairway towards them. "Adâ's staying with Sardâr now. Come on. We've got a job to do."

They went down the stairs and across the hallway to the cavernous entrance chamber. Like a massive network of arteries and veins becoming clogged with cholesterol, more and more refugees were crammed against the wall, and even more could be seen issuing group by group

through the entrance gate. The difference now was that the queue for the dining hall seemed to be weaving downstairs and into these corridors. Dwarves in guard uniforms were distributing rations amongst those too old or too young to queue up.

Jack spotted Sardâr, his dark skin and tall figure easily recognizable amongst the dwarves around him. Adâ was nearby, handing out bread to a group of children. Again, Jack found himself wondering about the differences between elves and dwarves in height, figure, and skin tone.

"Oh, good, you're here," Sardâr remarked as they drew closer. "We're stretched really thin today. Grab a basket of bread, and you can help."

They all spent the next hour passing out bread and milk to the refugee dwarves. Jack was struck by how exhausted they all looked. Not only did they seem to be worn down by the long trek on foot, but most were very thin and looked malnourished. The elderly were the feeblest. Some carried stumps of wood to help them walk with, and others too degenerated to make their own way had been laden on the wooden carts along with sacks of possessions.

There were many small children, and though they seemed in much higher spirits than everyone else, they too looked thin and pale. In particular, he noticed the age gap between the children and those of middle to old age. It was as if a generation were missing, and he did not like the thought of these crowds trudging across mountain terrain without any able-bodied young adults.

"So what *is* the difference between elves and dwarves, then?" he asked Sardâr as the two of them gave loaves to a family of eight.

"Very little," the elf replied, smirking slightly at one of the guzzling children, "and a lot less than both sides would like to admit. There are elves in this world, just as there are dwarves in my world, which is why we're able to get away with this. Incidentally," he added, leaning closer, "you're doing a very good job of being one of us."

Jack felt nonplussed for a moment, then looked down at his new body. It had become so natural to him in the last two days that he had almost forgotten what had changed. "So does that mean there are elves—and dwarves—on Earth?"

"Well, there were," Sardâr said, giving a flagon of milk to an old woman. "That's another bit of evidence for our ancestors discovering how to travel between worlds hundreds of years before we could. Where do you think all your folktales came from? Sleeping Beauty? Snow White and the Seven Dwarves? The Elves and the Shoemaker? Mind you, most of those are highly embellished. As you can tell, we're not pocket-sized, and, to my knowledge, none of us have tried our hand at nocturnal tailoring . . ."

Jack laughed.

"And trust me; I could count the fairies I know on *one hand* who would be willing to queue up to give gifts to a human baby."

"So how many different races are there?" asked Jack. He was genuinely interested. Now that he had just about come to grips with the idea of other worlds, he wanted to find out as much as possible, particularly as they would be here for a while.

"We're not really sure. The numbers are poten-

Elves and Dwarves

tially limitless, given how many planets there are, but some are obviously more affluent than others. A few continually crop up in ancient myths—elves, dwarves, humans, fairies, goblins, and zöpüta. Isaac theorized that these six are the only sentient ones—they're higher evolutionarily than say bears or fish—but there are many more. Trolls, merpeople, giants . . ."

"And each world has got its own continents, countries, cities, languages?"

"They're all at least as diverse as your world is."

They were joined by Adâ, who was being encircled and used as some kind of living maypole by the children she had just served. Jack was struck by the transformation that had come over her. She was no longer aloof and cool but could barely conceal her bright smile; she was laughing with the children and grinned at Jack when he caught her eye.

"Having fun?" she asked playfully as the children ran off.

"I've just been explaining to Jack about elves and dwarves."

"Ah yes, that's a fiery relationship there."

the white fox

Hearing that, something occurred to Jack. "You're speaking differently."

"I'm sorry?"

"Your accent is different. It's sort of . . ." He was going to say Persian or Arabic but realized that wouldn't mean much to either of the elves.

"Oh, we're speaking in Khălesen. It's our native language. But that's no problem for you," she said, pointing at his ring. It was glowing again, but now with teal rather than green.

Jack became aware of a guard standing nearby, waiting to speak. They turned towards him.

He looked flustered, and, unlike the others, he was in armor without any rations to distribute. "His Majesty, King Thorin, requests your presence at an urgent war meeting."

Adâ groaned but stopped at a reproachful glance from Sardâr. "Very well. We'll go now."

The guard nodded and left.

"What do you think it's about?" she asked.

"I'm not sure, but it can't be good. Jack, find Lucy. I think you two should hear this."

A few minutes later, Jack, Lucy, Sardâr, Hakim, and Adâ arrived at Thorin's throne room. He was pacing when they came in, his violently ginger beard frayed and unkempt and his eyes ringed red and weary. Jack had seen him only the day before, but he already looked a shadow of his former self, as if he had been pacing around the throne room all night. Another dwarf was seated next to the throne, and he looked even worse for wear; his arm was in a sling, and his face was cut and bruised.

An attendant scuttled over to them and motioned for them to sit.

"Once again, Sardâr, it is a great relief that you are safe," the king said.

"No thanks to you," Adâ retorted, and Jack noticed that she was talking in the more rough Scandinavian accent he now associated with whatever the native language of this kingdom was.

"Quite," Thorin replied, "but we have more pressing matters to deal with. There has been . . . well, the captain can explain it better than I . . ." He motioned to the seated dwarf, who cleared his throat painfully.

"We were on a surveillance expedition to the coast," he began, "and they're bringing in giants."

Jack could tell this meant something to both Sardâr and Adâ, for they sat bolt upright in their chairs.

"Are you sure?"

"Absolutely. Colossal dwarves, the size of large trees. The stories are true."

"So whoever's behind this has gone to the bother of shipping in giants," Sardâr said, rubbing his chin. "That *is* something."

"Exactly," concluded Thorin, "which is why we have no time to waste. We have passed the time when we could have abated this conflict before it started. Now it is unavoidable."

"Excuse me," interjected Jack, "but why is it unavoidable?"

Thorin turned his head to look at him.

"Because," answered Sardâr when Thorin said nothing, "if whoever is behind this is bothering to ship giants in from other countries, possibly even other worlds, then they mean business. They won't answer to a truce."

Elves and Dwarves

"It could just be a threat," Lucy said.

"Possibly," said Sardâr, but he sounded unconvinced. "Thengel, have there been any other sightings?"

"A fair few," replied Thorin, "though nothing like this. Trolls have been seen, though they're nothing unusual around these parts. Plenty of greenskins, of course. Filthy, slimy, reptilian—"

"Thengel," Sardâr interrupted.

"I know. I know," the king snapped back, "but it's in our nature to hate them. Our people have been enemies for as long as anyone can remember."

"As have yours and mine, and yet we manage. Or would you like to take a few of us down to the mines and chain us to the axes?"

The king flushed. "That's not all." He motioned for the captain to continue.

"These goblins and giants were led by elves. Well, I thought they were elves; they were taller than us. All of them in black cloaks. They were sorcerers. They killed my entire regiment and . . . left me alive to carry back the message." He looked down, as if the memory pained him more than his injuries. "The leader . . . he

the white fox

told me to say that Archbishop Iago sends his regards and will be in contact shortly."

Jack saw Sardâr and Adâ exchange looks, mouthing the name to each other, evidently not recognizing it.

"He said," the captain continued, looking as if he was forcing out the last words, "that you may remember him by the name Zâlem Khâyen." Sardâr's normally amiable expression darkened instantly. Hakim and Adâ exchanged shocked looks, laden with understanding.

"Who's Zâlem?" Lucy asked when no one endeavored to explain.

"Zâlem Khâyen is no more than a traitor, a thief, and a murderer."

"A murderer?" said Lucy, intrigued, but Sardâr seemed unwilling to say any more.

After a pause, Hakim took up the story. "Our home country, Khălese, is ruled by a president who is elected every five years. Twenty years ago, a member of the house of Khâyen was elected. His son was Zâlem. He was a brilliant sorcerer and the perfect student: intelligent, ambitious, and engaging. I can tell you that from being his teacher. However, there were people in the academic community who . . . distrusted him."

"There were rumors," carried on Adâ, "nasty ones. A few of his rivals at university picked on him or else achieved better and gloated about their success. They were never right again."

Sardâr seemed to not be able to resist having his say. "I filled in for one of the history teachers whilst he was on sabbatical and I taught Zâlem. I won't deny he was brilliant. He had ideas about politics and history no other student or teacher could imagine. But as Hakim said, he was ambitious. He was a radical politician who believed that Tâbesh and the entire kingdom should be for elves only. Now that kind of talk in a seminar will earn you a bit of attention and debate, but to actually carry out the kind of ideas that he was suggesting would take an enormous amount of resolve."

Hakim continued. "Sardâr uncovered a plot headed by Zâlem to take control of the kingdom . . . a plot which entailed killing the president."

"His own father?"

"Yes. Zâlem had become tired of his father's liberal approach, and he decided to take matters into his own hands. You see, we elves don't have it very easy, particularly around dwarves." Hakim glanced at Thorin, but the king wore a stony expression and was staring straight ahead. "Dwarves in both this world and ours have tended to have a history of colonization. There have been some very expansive dwarf empires in the past, and often these have been at the expense of the native elves. In past years, it has even been known for dwarves to enslave elves . . . and there's often still prejudice about it. Zâlem believed that his people deserved the right to take back their honor at the expense of other races that coexist with us in our kingdom. He gathered the usual crowd for a radical orator—a mixture of enthralled fanatics, ambitious young political cronies, and thugs looking for a break into major business. It was a serious threat to our democracy and security.

"Sardâr rushed off to tell me and the president. Of course, the president wasn't having any of it. And you can't blame him; it was his own son. So we took to guarding him secretly . . . which wasn't easy, given his complete denial of any danger. Then one night, whilst Zâlem's fellows subdued our guards, Zâlem managed to get into the president's bedchamber whilst he was sleeping, but Sardâr arrived just in time to prevent the murder. They fought, and when Zâlem was rendered defenseless, the president woke up. He saw both in his room, Sardâr holding a dagger, and, well . . ."

"It was a choice between an academic and the president's son," said Adâ. "Naturally, the president exiled Sardâr and let his son go free."

"So what happened to Zâlem?" Jack asked, intrigued.

"He disappeared a few years later after completing his education. The president might not have liked it, but Sardâr has quite a following in our community. They believed his side of the story and didn't take kindly to him being exiled by the person he was trying to protect. Zâlem didn't have much choice; once his father was shunted out of office he was on his own."

"So he's back," Sardâr remarked, staring in the distance.

There was silence. Noises from outside seemed numbed. Everyone in the room was focussed on Sardâr, who was in turn apparently focussed on the king's throne.

Finally, after several full minutes, Sardâr spoke again. "Well, I can't say I'm surprised that he's ended up with the Dionysians. Ambitious, fanatical, a firebrand orator and commander—everything they could want in a recruit. And he's risen up the ranks to control an entire operation." He directed his next remarks at the king. "We suspected the Cult was involved with the stirring up of war here, but this is far worse than I thought. We need to discuss matters . . . alone. Hakim, Adâ, if you would please take Jack and Lucy and leave."

Both nodded, their expressions grave.

Jack's last look at the room was to see Sardâr get up and begin pacing in a mirror of the king's movements. He could only pity the surviving captain caught in the middle of this.

Chapter IX
security and defense

The four of them spent the rest of the morning distributing food and drink to the refugees. Very little was said. The tension within the main chamber had risen considerably and not just amongst them. Already, rumors of what had befallen the erring scouting regiment were dispersing through the fortress quicker than the bread and milk. The miners still worked, the refugees still trickled in through the main gate, and the guards still patrolled and handed out rations, but everything seemed more hurried. Jack noticed the increased amount of disconcerted looks being thrown at the wide open main entrance. He could tell that the guards on the gate in particular were eager for the flow of refugees to cease, so they could barricade themselves behind the

thick stone and wood.

After several hours, Sardâr emerged from the throne room corridor, looking raw but resolute.

Jack, Lucy, Adâ, and Hakim virtually dropped their baskets of bread and hurried over to see him.

He assuaged their inquisitive looks with a brush of his hand. "We have been discussing additional security arrangements. The night guard is to be bolstered, and the fortress secured from the bottom up. The gates are not to be opened after nightfall, and no one is to enter or leave the fortress. Additional regiments are to be dispatched daily to escort arriving villagers into the valley. We've reasoned that the only feasible course of action is to lock down our defenses and wait. We don't know what Zâlem and his cohort are planning, and we can't take any serious course of action until we do."

"This would be so much *easier* with technology that wasn't just wood and stone," Adâ muttered. Jack and Lucy both nodded.

But Sardâr shook his head. "You know the consequences of that. We'll just have to make do."

Security and Defense

"Yes," said Hakim, "a weapons crisis, on top of everything else, is the last thing we need. Did you get a chance to ask the king about the tutoring?"

"Yes, I did. He agrees that, given the circumstances, Jack and Lucy need to be as prepared as everyone else here." He turned to the two of them. "Learning how to defend yourselves is no longer a matter of leisure. We will begin classes tomorrow. I will have to share my time between teaching you and dealing with matters here, so if I take the mornings, then Adâ and Hakim can take the afternoons."

The two other elves nodded, as did Jack. Lucy seemed less enthusiastic. Despite her multiple certifications that she would rather be back at home, the prospect of something akin to school did not spark her imagination.

Jack and Lucy spent their first proper evening in Thorin Salr with Hakim and Adâ, as Sardâr was attending to the implementation of the new security measures. They ate some kind of charred meat and smoked cheese that tasted delicious in the East Guest Hall and sat for a while as the sky began to darken around them.

After a few minutes of silence, toastily comfortable in the warm cavern, Lucy spoke. "So what do people do around here for fun? I mean, are there any bars? Rec room? Anything?"

Hakim pondered this for a moment. "We could go downstairs. If I've got my days right, you should be in for a treat."

They followed the two elves out and down a few passages and a flight of stairs. They crossed the entrance hall and went through another larger door Jack hadn't noticed before. This chamber was about the same size as the East Guest Hall, with lines of benches filled with dwarves and a crackling fire in a grate in the center. At the opposite end, a stone plinth rose up with a single stool on it. The walls were hung with animal furs and the same fine cloth as the soldiers' tunics, woven into meshed, swirling patterns.

The four of them took seats at the back of the hall.

Jack recognized several of the soldiers from their expedition, now in ordinary clothes, and the king's nephew. They were all talking loudly, and frothing flagons were passed around, splashing over the stone floor.

"What are we waiting for?" Lucy called over the racket.

"You'll see," Hakim replied, smiling, turning to talk to a dwarf in the row in front.

Several minutes passed uneventfully, during which a few more people arrived. Then from somewhere in the mass before them, a dwarf took the stage, emanating a wave of expectant silence. He was the oldest person Jack had ever seen. His beard was almost pure white, reaching down to his boots and tucked into his belt along the way. His eyes were grey and ridden with cataracts, but he fixed his audience with an encompassing gaze as he took his seat on the stool and began.

Jack had been obliged to take English literature at school, and he had been reasonably good at poetry. He could tell a ballad from a sonnet, a haiku and blank verse, and could give you a B-grade answer on

Tennyson or Wordsworth. But this was poetry as he had never heard it. Perhaps it was the language ring, but he could hear the rhythm and shape of the language in the original *and* understand its meaning.

It was the story of a dwarf who saved his kingdom from a marauding swamp monster and descended into the Wastes to tackle the monster's kin. He became king, enjoying a long and rich reign, only interrupted by the attack of a fire-breathing dragon. He slew the dragon, casting its body into a chasm, but sustained a mortal wound and died soon after. Jack could not tell how long it lasted, maybe five minutes, maybe five hours, but he didn't care. The dwarf's voice cracked when he finished, and there was silence. He nodded and returned to his seat.

Slowly, the noise began stirring up again.

Jack turned to Hakim, lost for words.

The elf smiled. "You enjoyed that, then?"

"Yeah . . . ," he managed, blinking. He looked around to Hakim's other side. Adâ appeared impressed. Lucy was flopped against the wall, eyes closed and mouth open, sound asleep.

East of the fortress on the edge of the Stórr Mountains in the valley of Sitzung, a solitary figure stood on the edge of a cliff. The peaks spiked up behind him and curved around to the left; to the right they dissolved into plains and misty marshland. The blade of the wind followed the curvature of the scene, slicing above through the peaks and down across the open plateau. Here, nothing grew well, only sparse, inedible roots and a few disparate shrubs. This marked the border between Thorin Salr and the Wastes.

Camps spread out under the cover of the mountains. The fiercest gales came from the south, yet they still blasted through the valley like thunder. The edges of taut, tattered tents flapped noisily in the breeze, and the wild boars, tied by the necks to deeply driven posts, grunted and shuffled their feet. More posts all around were lit at the top, the flickering flames barely penetrating the pitch darkness.

Despite the camps, no goblin was taking shelter. All were outside, the valley full of shadowy, bow-legged reptilian figures hunched together in almost complete silence. All pairs of bulbous, snakelike eyes were fixed upon the crest of rock high above, where a cluster of thirteen black tents, subtly styled with silver symbols, was pitched. The corn-yellow moon swam above it, casting its ghostly glow into the oily reflection of those thousands of eyes.

The figure stood on the crest of the rock, gazing down on his assembled forces. Twelve more of his fellows stood behind him, their black cloaks fluttering in the wind. The leader judged the time to be right. He spoke, his voice magnified a hundred times over the gale. "Brothers! Greenskins!"

Every creature in the valley broke into growls and cries of anger. *Greenskin* was a derogatory term that could be used to refer to any creature, though particularly goblins, which was an enemy of the "civilized" species.

"You have come from every corner of the Wastes, rival tribes and clans all gathered here, and for what purpose? You have come to avenge yourselves on those who drove you out of the mountains! Those who would call themselves your enemies yet treat you like animals! Who are they?"

Roars of rage erupted from several groups. The different tribes could be clearly seen—groups of goblins huddled together under tents displaying different totems and banners. But as the screams grew, the tribes took to their feet. The noise rose out of the valley and upwards into the starry night like a billowing sky beast, and the tribal differences were washed away by the cascade of rage and purpose. Thousands of voices blasted out in a barely discernable howl: "The dwarves!"

"Yes, the dwarves," replied the leader, his boom still overcoming the shouts, "and now we know how to enter their kingdom. Go, brothers! March to Thorin Salr!"

The screams rose to a crescendo, the sky beast purring in pleasure as its form was augmented by the waking cries of hulking giants, chained in one edge of the valley.

The leader smiled to himself. This was too easy. He was a populist by nature—he could metamorphose

the white fox

even the most indolent crowd of divided moderates into a revolutionary mob with a few sentences—but this was barely a challenge. He turned to face his twelve fellows. "I think we've incensed them enough."

Several of the figures laughed cruelly.

"We will *all* lead the march."

The surrounding figures nodded and turned to packing up the tents, quenching the fire, readying their own mounts—not pigs, but lizard-like reptiles they had acquired in this world—and dispatching orders to the goblin chieftains.

Before long, the leader was left alone on the crest of rock. Far below, campfires were being dissolved and replaced by flickering torches hoisted in the arms of marching soldiers. There was a general surge away from him, as the mob looked to quit the valley through the narrow gorge opposite the cliff face. He snapped his fingers.

A shadow materialized out of the darkness next to him—this one in hulking armor, hunched over a black horse. Most notably, where its head should have been, there was just a stump of severed cloth.

Security and Defense

"Go and kill a few. That should give them the energy to last the night."

The shadow gave no noticeable sign of recognition but whipped its horse into action, spurring it forward and off the cliff.

The next few weeks were very busy for Jack and Lucy.

Before their first lesson, Sardâr took them aside with a grave look on his face. "You must understand the significance of this. You may have already seen, but Thengel is something of a revolutionary amongst his fellows. As a member of the Apollonians, he understands fully the importance of interworld cooperation against the Cult. Traditionalist dwarves have disagreed with him, calling him weak. Even his own nephew, Bál, is distasteful of his stance. Many dwarves take pride in their racial stereotype—being extremely proud, quick to anger, and particularly hateful of alchemy. It is the highest betrayal of these principles for alchemy to be used in their own fortress. It is extremely inconvenient for Thengel for us to be doing this, so you must show him the utmost respect. Is this understood?"

They both nodded.

"Alchemy," Sardâr began, "is a science and not so mysterious as it may seem. As I said before, the Cult manipulates the yin in existence—the primal Darkness—which is inherent in all things. We—by which I mean those of us who align ourselves with the Light—choose to tap into the yang, which equally permeates our world. Whilst Darkness is destructive and negative, Light is creative and positive."

At this point, he pushed aside a large ceremonial rug in the center of the room, revealing a circle surrounded by symbols etched in charcoal on the flagons. He motioned to each one of the four symbols, each at a compass point, in turn. "Light is made up of four elements: fire, water, air, and earth. These are not the elements of which objects are *physically* constructed—that is the territory of chemistry and physics—but rather the essence that sleeps within them that can be manipulated by sorcerers."

Jack nodded, but Lucy seemed less sure. He wondered what Dr. Orpheus would make of this.

They only briefly touched on Dark alchemy.

"The basis of Dark alchemy," Sardâr said gravely, "is the exploitation of the negative—moral or natural evil—to the ends of the sorcerer involved. Whilst it may initially seem more powerful than Light alchemy, the consequences for the soul are dire. It draws its power from the Darkness, tempered by anger, greed, lust, envy, or hatred from within the person who uses it. There is no such thing as defensive Dark alchemy; it can only cause pain and suffering." That was all that was said on the subject.

"We live in a Realm of Light. Everything in nature is a mixture of the four alchemical elements; a tree is rooted in earth and water, whereas clouds are linked to water and air, and stars with fire and light."

They were both taught how to recognize which elements composed different natural objects, something Sardâr said was vital to effective spell-casting. Jack's curiosity was piqued at this, having been interested in comics at a younger age. Lucy, on the other hand, was

the white fox

becoming increasingly bored. Her interest in trees, beyond their capacity to be seated under at a party with a member of the football team, was nonexistent.

They arrived in the study on the sixth day of their lessons to find the desk, bookcases, and chairs cleared to the side of the room to leave a large open space in the middle.

"Today you will begin to practice alchemy for real."

"Now?" Lucy exclaimed.

"Yes. It will be hard, but I'm confident that you can get through it."

And the lessons did indeed live up to his word. Jack, who had been hoping for an easier ride with the Seventh Shard, was told to take it off. "You need to learn how to use alchemy before its power is magnified a thousand times. The incident with the volcano demon was extremely lucky. I'm surprised something didn't go disastrously wrong."

"Alchemy is not something that can just be pulled out of thin air. It takes great effort to draw it out of the natural world, far more to shape it into a form that isn't lethal to the user. Observe." Sardâr made

Lucy jump as a fireball appeared in his hand. "In an unskilled sorcerer's hands, this fireball could have been an inferno that would burn down the entire fortress. Excess is just as easy as deficiency. Control is the mark of the strongest sorcerers." He then let Jack and Lucy have a go.

They spent most of the following lessons with Sardâr seated in two identical circles to the one he had shown them on the first day. They sat cross-legged in a meditation position, whilst objects were placed in front of them and they were told to bend its power to their will.

Jack had been thinking a lot, and he had come to the conclusion that the only other time he had used alchemy, when fighting a demon, was in a fit of momentary (and uncharacteristic) courage. It was much harder now. He thought it was something like searching for the end of a roll of tape. It was very difficult to find, and once you had it, it was very difficult to hang on to. A couple of times he felt the same surge flow through him, but in his excitement he let it fade away again.

341

the white fox

Lucy was having no such luck. According to her, she had never once felt the slight pull of alchemy when she got near it. By the end of their first lesson, she was red in the face and extremely irritable.

This continued until the sixth day of their lessons. At about ten thirty, at this point with a lit candle placed in between his knees, Jack got hold of it. Determined not to lose his concentration this time, he focussed on it and pulled with his mind. It was as if he'd been plugged into an electric mainframe; he felt an incredible surge of dynamic energy alight every one of his nerve endings and burst through him. "I've got it!"

"Good. That's raw alchemy. Now close your eyes and try to—"

There was a pop, and the desk exploded into flames.

"Sorry," Jack said sheepishly.

Sardâr smiled and flicked his hand at the desk. Invisible wind blasted over it, the flames dissipating, leaving it unharmed.

Later that day, Jack managed it with a bowl of

water, but this time, he waited to let it go. He allowed it to expand, filling up every particle of his body. Focussing on it, keeping the surge from breaking out, he shaped it into the form Sardâr had described to them. He held on to it, and as he felt his head was about to explode with the effort, he let it loose. An orb of water, completely defying gravity, floated upwards out of the bowl and blasted from between his fingers, shooting across the room like a miniature comet. It collided with the bookcase, knocked a whole shelf of books on the floor.

"Excellent," cried Sardâr, waving his arm vaguely so that the books replaced themselves. "That was the first controlled piece of alchemy you've performed. Now let's try something a little different."

Lucy looked distinctly put out at this.

Every day, after a short lunch, Jack and Lucy went down to the training grounds at the back of the fortress. This was a large room, where a smooth wooden platform occupied the majority of the floor and benches and weapons racks lined the walls. When they arrived, a regiment of dwarf guards were in the midst of an exercise drill, some jogging around the room, others doing press-ups, and still more practicing combat with axes and swords.

For the first week of afternoon lessons, Adâ was their tutor. She took them through the basics of weaponless self-defense: punches, kicks, blocks, and counterstrikes. She used Jack as her dummy for every example, through which Lucy nodded interestedly, and he winced every time her fist or foot stopped within an inch of him.

On the sixth day of their training, on the day Jack had first successfully practiced alchemy, Adâ announced the two of them would have their first free-sparring match.

"I won't go easy on you," Jack warned Lucy as they clambered onto the platform. She shrugged.

Adâ clapped two pieces of wood together, the signal for them to begin.

They started circling each other, gazes flicking between the other's face and hands. Several dwarves, having finished training, watched from the sidelines. Jack took a deep breath and moved in to punch.

Five seconds later, he was on his back, coughing heavily, with no idea how he'd got there.

Adâ was applauding, and the guards were roaring with laughter.

Lucy stood over him, grinning. "Did I never tell you I took karate lessons when I was younger?"

"You kept that quiet," he spluttered as she hauled him to his feet.

"I thought I'd get some fun out of it one day. Never this much, though." Lucy giggled. "You were too busy throwing water balls to notice."

After several more days of weaponless combat, Hakim and a friendly dwarf called Captain Umrád equipped them with some protective padding and a wooden sword each.

Lucy's initial reaction was one of disdainful disbelief. "Don't we get guns? Alex had a gun on Earth . . ."

"On *Earth*," Adâ explained, "a gun is completely normal. Too normal, in fact. Here it would have disastrous consequences for the dwarf-goblin weapon escalation."

Jack expected something like fencing, but this was completely different. The movements were not at all showy, part of a "gentlemen's agreement," they were purely practical and often brutal. Lucy, to Jack's great surprise, was a natural at this too. With agility and a quick eye born of her netball training, she darted around the platform, disarming him three times during their first session. He had to admit to her afterwards that, whilst she couldn't climb a mountain as well as he could, he knew which skill would come in more useful in the future.

This culminated when, three weeks after they had begun, Jack was becoming an increasingly competent sorcerer. He could now levitate light objects, manipulate water and air into shields, freeze objects, and conjure fire as Sardâr had done on the first day. Meanwhile, Lucy was increasingly skillful as a fighter both with and without a weapon; she could now fend off many of the dwarf guards who trained with them as well as Adâ and Hakim. And whilst she could easily outmatch Jack in the training room, she was still fruitless in her attempts at manipulating alchemy.

At the exact three-week mark of their training, the two of them sagged into chairs in Lucy's room, exhausted. Lucy's face was flushed—Jack had never seen her so well exercised—and he was aching from their recent bout as well. Despite Lucy's playful denunciations, alchemy took a surprising amount of mental and physical application, and his legs were sore from being crossed for so long. She looked as he had never seen her before; her face had a lot more color in it, and she had taken to tying her hair back in a ponytail rather than constantly messing with her fringe.

"You know," Lucy breathed, unwrapping the bandages they had been using as gloves from her fists, "this place isn't so bad after all. I wish we did this in *real* school."

Jack smiled. He was glad Lucy was finally settling in. She had even stopped talking about her parents at every opportunity, and Jack could tell that whilst she was still concerned, she was allowing them to dominate her waking thoughts less. Though he was happy to accept this—her attitude had improved a lot recently, and they were getting on as they used to—something nagged at the back of his mind. *His* concern for Alex had not diminished at all, and whilst he convinced himself that by learning these skills they were preparing to help him, he was still raked at night by the recurring fear of what had befallen his friend.

Chapter X
the impending storm

Over those three weeks, very little changed in the fortress of Thorin Salr. The new security measures Sardâr and the king had drafted were put into place almost instantly, but this did nothing to stem the influx of refugees. Disused rooms and hallways had been opened up for their use, so that the strain on the main chambers was lessened. Shifts of guards were on full patrol constantly, and, true to his word, Sardâr did not allow either Jack or Lucy outside the fortress. Jack thought it was a good thing that the two of them were so busy, or the atmosphere would have been stifling. After what had befallen the last scout party, no others were dispatched, but even so nothing was heard of the growing goblin army—or the Cult—at all.

Then, just as Hakim and some of the dwarves they spoke to were beginning to hope that the problem had gone away, everything changed.

Jack awoke on the morning that would have been their twenty-second day of teaching to another burst of loud noise. Looking out his doorway, something was different. There were dwarves running at top speed up and down the corridor, carrying a plethora of different objects and looking distinctly flustered. He checked Adâ's room, but it was empty.

He met Lucy in the corridor. "Where's everyone going?"

"I'm not sure." She looked worried.

One of the dwarves clipped them as she ran past, her towering stack of parchment flying everywhere. "Sorry," she said, looking scared.

The three of them clambered around the corridor, picking up all her sheets. The dwarf was about to run off again when Jack asked, "What's going on?"

She looked at him a little strangely. "They're here!"

"Who?"

"The greenskins! They're here! Inside the valley!"

"What?" There was a pause in which he and Lucy glanced at each other in awe.

"Did you see an elf go past?" Lucy asked.

"I don't think so . . . but the king and a few elves are up on the south balcony."

"Which way is it?"

She gave them directions.

"Okay, thanks." Jack and Lucy sprinted off down the corridor, leaving their bedroom doors wide open.

A minute later they were there, pushing open the door, and were hit with blinding sunlight. Blinking, they saw Sardâr, Adâ, and Hakim standing to their right and to the left the king, Bál, and several other dwarves Jack recognized from the council.

"So what's happening?" Jack asked.

"They've got through the Great South Gate." Sardâr pointed out across the valley.

Jack and Lucy stepped closer to the edge to get a better look. Just visible (for the sunlight was blasting in their eyes) was the rocky ledge that led the tunnel out on to the ravine. The entire valley was deserted, the cranes unusually still, but on that ledge there were silhouetted figures amassing. More and more of them were swarming out of the tunnel; some looked human sized, but there were a few that towered over the rest. Of the ones he could make out, Jack could see the strange reptilian creatures that had so nearly caught them on their way in to the valley.

"How did they get through the tunnel?" Jack asked, confused.

"That's what we're just wondering."

One of the dwarves—Jack recognized him as the only survivor of the scouting party—clapped his hands to his forehead and shouted, "The scouts. My regiment. They had axes on them."

"Why is that a problem?" asked Sardâr.

"The Great South Gate can be opened either by the password or a dwarf axe placed in the right position on the wall," explained an aged dwarf. "It dates back to the days of our ancestors. All axes are shaped so that the momentum of it falling activates a pulley system inside. But they couldn't have got in by having only an axe. They must have known where the gate was."

"But how?"

"It doesn't matter," Sardâr said exasperatedly. "What really matters is how we're going to deal with them now that they're here."

"Don't worry about that." Thorin waved a finger at him tauntingly. "I had a solution installed as soon as the giants were sighted. Einhendr, Nyr, if you please."

Two dwarves walked out from behind the door, carrying bows. Notching arrows to them, they held them up to a flickering brand by the king so the rag-wrapped heads lit.

"No, wait!" cried Sardâr, but even as he said it they let loose the arrows. They soared over the edge of the balcony, not anywhere near where the enemies were congregating. For a moment, Jack thought they had fallen short, but they were both veering in the same direction. They flew into the center of the valley, where he saw a large cluster of strange-looking metal objects heaped in a mound in between the mining pits. Then there was a terrific booming, and dust and chunks of rock flew into the air from where the arrows had landed.

the white fox

"What did you do?" Sardâr roared over the rumbling.

"We laid explosives down, so now there's a gorge between us and them." Thorin looked pleased with himself.

"What!" Sardâr erupted at the top of his voice.

The cloud of dust was beginning to clear, and Jack could see the mining pits had been extended to form a single, massive gorge, at least half the distance of the valley, creating an impassable barrier between the two halves. Bits of broken wood and rock were scattered around the edge, the remnants of the dwarves' livelihoods.

"What's the matter?" Thorin sounded confused.

"Explosives! They aren't due to be developed for hundreds more years! Do you realize what you could have done?"

"Calm yourself," said Thorin. "We developed them ourselves. Strictly within the boundaries of our time period."

Most of the council were looking confusedly, even scared at their king, not least because he was speaking as if he could tell the future. Jack couldn't help thinking that Sardâr, for all his talk about keeping their true origins a secret, had just broken his number one rule.

"Come on," Adâ said quietly, for it looked as if Sardâr was about to overflow with rage. She pushed Jack and Lucy ahead of her down the stairs. Somewhere behind them, another kind of explosion was going on.

Jack and Lucy spent the rest of the day training for battle. Adâ watched over them from the sidelines, but there was an oddly subdued nature, even amongst the dwarves. It was as if the explosives had blown the buoyancy out of everyone. Even the weather was overcast, dark clouds hovering ominously overhead, waiting for the chance to break upon the valley. Sardâr had still not returned.

At around five o'clock, by which time Jack and Lucy were thoroughly worn out, a messenger arrived requesting that they come to Sardâr's study at once.

When they entered, Sardâr was sitting in his armchair, looking uncharacteristically weary. For the second time, he showed Jack and Lucy to their seats.

the white fox

"How did the argument go?" Jack asked before Sardâr could say anything.

Sardâr smiled wryly. "Thengel still fails to recognize that he has done anything wrong."

"Has he?" Lucy asked.

"Yes, many things. He introduced anachronistic technology into this world. He has virtually destroyed the economy of his people, not to mention sealing us completely into this valley with no escape. He's been driven to action by extreme stress and pressure from his military advisers to do something about the goblin army."

"Why do we need to escape? And anyway, can't we get out up the mountain?"

"That trail, like this valley, is enclosed on all sides. As to escaping, Thengel seems to think it's safe, but the rest of us don't. We know that the Cult of Dionysus control these goblins, and *they* certainly will not be deterred by a mere boundary of earth or lack of it."

"Can Thorin actually do anything useful as king?" Lucy asked exasperatedly.

Jack smiled, but Sardâr did not.

"True, Thengel has many deficiencies. He was the next in line for the monarchy, but he is not considered highly amongst his fellows. The dwarves of Thorin Salr are stereotypically stubborn and shun the help—or pleas—of other races. Thengel has led them out of this stereotype somewhat, but in some dwarves' opinions he has gone too far. Even in allowing us to use alchemy here his support amongst his people has slipped. I doubt those explosives are going down well, either. Many think Bál would make a model king, as he is the complete traditional dwarf: brave, stubborn, powerful, and disdainful of alchemy, and, as I'm sure you've seen, other races." Sardâr regarded them.

"Are we going to do any alchemy today?" Jack asked, trying to change the subject.

"Given the lateness of the hour, I think we will leave it today." But then, seeing Jack's disappointed expression, he added, "I see no reason why we shouldn't continue with the lessons tomorrow. As grudgingly as I admit it, Thengel's actions make any immediate attack very unlikely indeed." He looked at them a moment longer. "Go on back to your rooms. I have to send a message."

The days were shortening now, and a relatively early darkness had fallen upon the valley. Stars glittered across the sky, embellishing its obsidian sheet with silvery lights. However, whilst the fortress and the majority of its inhabitants slept, and the guards kept their weary watch, the other side of the gorge was very much alive.

The figure looked up, feeling the scent of alchemy on the breeze. It was subtle, possibly just a lamp being lit by a spell inside the fortress, but, of course, dwarves didn't use alchemy. He turned to a second figure on his right.

"Yes, I sense it too." His voice was low and growling and slightly muffled by the black hood.

"What do you think it was?" The first figure's voice was higher and delicate. The lizard-like beast he was sitting on gave a slight grunt in its sleep.

"A weak sorcerer, perhaps?"

"No *dwarf* is an alchemist."

"Then . . . ?"

"An elf. One I know well."

The second figure did not inquire. His commander was very secretive. When he had been inducted, he had brought with him a group of other elves from his homeland. Although many theories had arisen amongst the Cult as to his origins, none of those elves had ever been persuaded to disclose their reasons for joining. Past experience had told him it was better not to ask.

"So do we do it now?"

The leader did not reply, just gazed out over the valley. His expression was fathomless under the hood.

"Archbishop?" he prompted.

"Yes, I think so." The leader turned around.

Their army, too large to fit in the tunnels, had moved to fill the entire valley on the other side of the gorge. Ragged tents of cloth and crude wood had been set up like those in Sitzung. Goblins slept

the white fox

inside, whilst the three giants looked like part of the valley themselves, their hulking forms almost indistinguishable from the extrusions of the rock. The snoring was horrendous.

"Chieftain," the second said, a little louder than usual.

A nearby goblin, one of the few not in a tent, raised his head. He had been slumped against his mount—a massive dirty brown wild boar—his helmet pulled over his head to shield it from the moonlight. "Now?" he grunted, raising his head higher.

"Yes. Awaken the troops." The cloaked figure turned to the front. The leader reached into the depths of his cloak, pulling something from a breast pocket. A jet-black stone, almost perfectly round, carved with the ornate rose symbol of Nexus. Although it was purely black, where the light shone through it, its shadow gave a red gleam, throwing his face into harsh relief. Under the hood, high cheek bones, pointed ears, and prominent scar were now deeply shadowed. He lifted the stone above his head, muttering a few words under his breath.

The stone began to shine with a bloodred light, which intensified with every syllable the leader spoke. The last one was shouted, the harsh sound echoing around the valley like a bark.

There was a pause, then a beam of pure crimson light erupted from the stone, shooting like a meteor diagonally upwards into the sky. At its very tip the storm clouds began to swirl around it like a whirlpool, obscuring the moon and many stars. There was a phantasmal flash, an unearthly wail, and black rent through the sky. There, high above them, hung a disc of the purest darkness, red light radiating from its center like a chained star. The clouds burnt around it, fizzling out as they got too close.

The second figure glanced around. All their monstrous allies were awake now, gazing in awe at the sky. The shine was reflected in their glass-like eyes, and they were swaying as if in a light breeze. "They feel it too?" he asked his superior, surprised.

"Strange," he commented, "I would never have thought so. Perhaps there is some worth in them after all."

the white fox

"You are regretting what we're about to do?"

His face split into an evil grin. "Not in the slightest. It will be most satisfying to be rid of them."

The second man cackled. "How long do you think it will take them to notice?"

"Not long, but by that time it will be too late."

"I meant the dwarves."

"Oh, within the hour. Those sensitive to alchemy will feel it in their sleep.

There was a moment when they both contemplated the fortress. The few windows there were now shining red and black in the dual skylight.

"Now what?" the second asked.

"Now we wait," replied the elf.

The scene below them was apocalyptic. The valley was bathed in a sinister crimson light, the moon and stars completely eclipsed by the black clouds. The opposite end of the valley swarmed with their enemies, the irradiance revealing how massive their force really was. Right at the back, the hulking form of the giants hunched, looking like miniature mountains themselves. There was not a part of the rocky ground they could see under the horde of creatures, except for at the front. There, a small clearing in the swarm marked several figures out. They were too far away to see clearly, but everyone present seemed to have accepted the worst-case scenario.

"But what's the point?" asked Thorin. "There's no force that can form a land bridge strong enough for that army, is there?"

"None that *we* know of," Adâ replied.

Jack looked at Sardâr. He had said nothing since he had been alerted to the danger. Jack wondered why he was holding back.

Jack scratched his neck again in discomfort, trying to ease the pressure on his upper spine. As soon as everyone had been alerted, Adâ had run him and Lucy down to the armory, where Smith, panicked amidst the chaos of arming an entire fortress at such short notice, had handed over their specially commissioned Dvengr-style armor. It looked beautiful—shining silvery gold, encrusted with rubies on the shoulders, chest, helmet, and forearms. It was made up of a sallet, which left only his face exposed, a cuirass, twin pauldrons and vambraces, tassets and greaves. Along with the chain mail underneath, it was extremely heavy and oppressive in the most uncomfortable places, although better and more accommodating for the ears than the ones they had borrowed.

Lucy was next to him in a similarly encumbering suit. Despite the situation, he smirked when he remembered how she had protested about looking like an obese astronaut.

"What *are* they doing?" Thorin fumed.

No one answered.

This seemed to aggravate him even more, because he started pacing up and down behind them.

Still, no one gave him the slightest bit of attention.

There was movement on the rock below. All the creatures began moving outwards, away from the front and center where the thirteen Cultists stood. The one at the very front seemed to be holding something up, as if to the watchers on the balcony. A metallic clang sliced through the air, and whatever he was holding sparked red momentarily. Everyone looked up. The black eye had started to pulsate like a beating heart. A red light had compressed into a tiny point in the center, forming a concentrated beam that struck like an arrow into the depths of the gorge. It illuminated the rock walls, the broken and useless chunks of machinery hanging on the edges, but even it could not fathom the very bottom.

The portal seemed to groan. Its blackness was congealing, extruding something of itself out of the celestial pit. A moment later, it came free. The immense, shadowy rectangular mass sunk slowly downward, tracing the path of the red beam of light. As it sunk, the liquid darkness solidified, its matter shaping, the color lightening to a charred bluish grey. Then, with an almighty crunch, it landed, its ends making a solid rock pathway between the gorge edges.

the white fox

Chapter XI
the ram released

Jack struggled to understand what he was seeing, then everything, like the bridge, clunked into place. The volcano. The pit. The mysteriously missing bridge. The Cult must have taken it from there in anticipation of just this. But that was too much of a coincidence. There must have been some other way . . .

Jack's thoughts were interrupted by the unmistakable unsheathing of a sword. He turned and was shocked to see Sardâr with his blade out, one edge pressed to the throat of the surviving captain of the search party. Everyone else on the balcony, including Adâ and Hakim, looked dismayed. The one with the sword to his throat, however, did not.

"Sardâr, what on earth are you doing?" shrieked

the king.

"This is not one of your captains," he replied, his eyes still locked on his captive. "This dwarf died, along with the rest of his regiment, three weeks ago."

Thorin spluttered loudly but was unable to form any words.

"This creature was sent back to you to pose as the surviving captain and has been a spy in our camp ever since. Has he been aware of the decision to use explosives? The Cult could not have thought to remove and retain that bridge from Mount Fafnir unless they suspected they might have to use it. And, of course, we spoke openly about interworld travel in front of this 'dwarf' when he first returned, and he made no surprised reaction at all. So, tell us, what are you exactly?"

The dwarf smiled, exposing razor-sharp fangs and a forked tongue too large to fit in his mouth. The thing began to contort, its eyes turning inwards in its head. All its limbs stretched straight outwards, and a pair of rubbery, bat-like wings burst out of its spine. Now there was no hint of a dwarf left but instead a five-foot tall, hunched humanoid, its skin greyish-black with talons extending from its fingers and toes.

It lurched towards the king, but before it had got within a foot of him, there was a thunder-crack noise as Sardâr's blade, charged with ivory light, swiped cleanly through it. The top half of its body toppled off, severed from the legs, but even as it hit the floor both parts exploded in smoke and disappeared.

"Doppelganger," Sardâr muttered, retracting his smoking fist.

The king, along with everyone else, looked dumbstruck, staring at the place where the demon had just disappeared.

They were reawakened to the situation by a great wave of primal noise. The mob below had begun to charge across the stone conduit. The few giants there were thundered in their midst, undoubtedly crushing some of their smaller fellows as they rushed towards the fortress. Those on boars—two on each, one riding, one firing flaming arrows upwards at the exposed gangways and windows—reached the front first.

The guards on the parapet along the wall

appeared horrified, and civilian dwarves, watching from the windows and open gangways of the fortress, all seemed to cry out at the same time.

Thorin had recovered himself and was bellowing orders to the three remaining captains. "Umrád, ready the men for battle. Ásjá, the Forge. Tell them to load and position the firespitters and empty the weapons store. I want every male dwarf able to fight— including the refugees—armored as soon as possible. Veita, make sure all the women and children are barricaded in the West Dining Hall, with a single guard unit protecting them. And, one of you, send an urgent message to the thanes of the surrounding lands: Thorin Salr is under attack, and we require immediate fulfilment of their oaths."

The captains hurried off.

Adâ turned to Jack and Lucy. "Get down to the dining hall. Now!"

"No," interjected Sardâr. His face was ashen but set. He lowered his voice. "That hall is fraught with weaknesses. I've tried to tell Thengel, but he's too confident in the handiwork of his ancestors to listen.

There are many safer places than—"

The entire fortress seemed to shudder as the first boulder made impact. It was followed a moment later by several more, threatening to throw them off the balcony. Keeping low, Jack and Sardâr crept over to the side. The horde had almost completely crossed the bridge and were now bunched up about a hundred meters away from the terra-cotta gates. The giants were projecting the scattered debris at the wall of the fortress. Already parts of the stone were cracking and splintering apart. It would not be long before the weight of the broken rock brought the entire front wall down.

Fireballs arched from the upper ramparts of the fortress, showering the enemy with miniature comets. On top of the fortress, cannon-like objects with their metallic barrels in the shape of dragon heads had been wheeled out and were now spitting flaming rocks down on the horde. Several of them struck true, squashing a group of goblins or knocking a giant back into the gorge, but most missed or fell short. Still, whilst the ammunition lasted the horde could be kept

the white fox

at bay. For the time being at least.

There was a shout behind them, and Hakim appeared in the doorway, still in his dressing gown. He ducked and shuffled over to them. "I've just been helping refugees into the safe chambers. What's the plan?"

Before Sardâr could answer, Lucy cried, "Look!"

Sardâr, Jack, and Hakim spun around. Out of the darkness, from the bridge below, dark smoke was lacing through the air straight towards them. It splayed out over the balcony in front of them, coiling upwards. The darkness began to take shape, forming into a tall, black-cloaked figure.

He was not hooded. His robes fitted tightly, just like the coiling darkness. His face, Jack could tell, had been handsome, but now it was anything but. His eyes were so far sunken into his head that, under the dark shroud of the sky, a subtle glint was all the evidence that they were there. Pointed ears were just visible under his wild, beast-like mane of hair, and a scar bisected his face from his left eye socket down to the edge of his curled lip. Though his skin was the typical olive dark of Tâbeshic elves, it had long since lost its healthy complexion, and he looked drawn and austerely pale.

"Well, well," he said quietly. His voice carried a drawling grandeur that Icarus's had lacked. "Look what the dragon dragged in."

"Zâlem," Sardâr said with a forcibly controlled voice.

Jack stared at the figure before him. So this was the elf who had forced Sardâr to flee his own country and become alienated from his people. He was caught off guard by the same almost irrational hate he had felt for Icarus.

"It's Archbishop Iago now, actually. And, Hakim, I haven't seen you in a few years." He looked the second elf up and down. "The school business isn't going too well, is it? Adâ, radiant as always." He smiled lustfully.

Adâ scowled at him.

"I see you haven't changed your ways," he remarked, regarding Jack, Lucy, and the dwarves with distaste, "mixing with humans and dwarves. You insult our sacred bloodline."

"Yet you still choose to serve a non-elf master.

Or are the rumors about your Cult's Emperor inaccurate? You always were good with lies."

Iago's face contorted with anger, and his voice slackened to a growl. "He has promised me kingship of Tâbesh. No more will our kingdom be commanded by pathetic bureaucrats who think of only peace and equality. I will lead our country into a new age. We will retake the world that's rightfully ours, then take the battle to others. An empire, Sardâr. Like the ones of old."

Sardâr considered him for a moment. "At what cost does he make these promises? From what I have heard, the Emperor of Nexus does not grant wishes lightly. Tell me, are you still intact?"

Iago grinned again, even wider this time. "I'll show you," he whispered and clicked his gloved fingers.

Instantly, a pit of darkness formed next to him in the balcony. Out of it rose a macabre figure—a knight, encased in spiked, silver armor, astride a horse of the same attire. Both the knight's and steed's eyes glowed crimson just like the other demons', but the rider carried its helmeted head under its arm.

"You fool," Sardâr said quietly, his gaze fixed on the demon.

"Abaddon, a seventh-level demon. That is the price you pay to join the Cult of Dionysus—be bound to a demonic familiar. It's hardly a price, though. Just look what it can do." Iago clicked his fingers again.

The knight bent low in the saddle, and the steed charged directly at Lucy. She raised her arms to shield her face . . .

Abaddon lurched off Sardâr's alchemical barrier, backing away slowly. Jack noticed that Iago was pained by the knight's impact too, as if it had been he who had collided with it.

The Cultist clicked his fingers, and the knight disappeared in more black energy. "You'd protect these lowlifes with your sorcery?"

"Of course. I have a duty to them. I don't think you're familiar with that concept, are you?" Despite the situation, Jack couldn't help feeling a swell of pride.

"Very well. Protect them from this." Iago clapped, then raised his arms.

There was a cracking sound. Jack looked around

the white fox

to see a rend in the balcony behind him, the part with him and Lucy on it sliding away from the rest. He cried out, trying to run back towards it, but it was no use. The segment came clean off, and a fifty-foot drop loomed underneath them.

Jack suddenly felt a force under his arms. He and Lucy were being hoisted over the gap and back onto the fortress. As soon as they came to rest with Adâ, Hakim, and the dwarves, they turned. Sardâr was drifting away through the air on the floating rock. Jack made to jump back at it, but real arms, this time Adâ's, held him. He could only watch as the two old enemies faced off against each other, suspended over the bottomless pit.

The air sliced around the two of them like knives, ruffling Iago's robes.

"Let's give ourselves a bit more room, shall we?" Upon a wave of his arm, loose rocks from below leapt upwards onto the balcony, extending the platform by at least twenty feet.

Sardâr stepped back to the edge, taking care to note how much room he had. He knew Iago's strategy, and he had the advantage in this arena. However, if he could catch him at the right moment . . .

"I'm going to enjoy this," his enemy said. "Vengeance is sweet."

Sardâr did not reply, merely unsheathed his blade from the scabbard strapped to his back. He had never carried a shield before—using a traditional Tâbeshic blade didn't support it—but he felt a twinge of longing for one now.

"Still using a sword? How archaic." And with a whirl of dark energy from the air before him, Iago drew two vicious-looking, long-shafted lances. With a tug, Iago undid the clasp of his cloak, and it fell backwards to reveal a full suit of silver armor and dark chain mail.

They faced each other. Sardâr was in full golden armor, his dark hair cascading in the wind. Iago was his exact mirror—covered in riveted silver, black cloak now a cape billowing menacingly around him,

the white fox

his black mane making him look even more like a limber beast. The sounds of the siege below—the hurled rocks and roaring fire spitters—were oddly muffled. The crimson light highlighted the uneven rock.

Then Iago leapt forward, his spears raised. However, Sardâr was ready. He sidestepped at the last possible moment, parrying the edge of the lance with his blade. And the two of them were dancing, ducking, dodging, blocking, and counterattacking through the air, a dual whirl of supernatural swordsmanship.

Sardâr reflected Iago's blow with the butt of his sword and kicked him hard in the stomach. Iago staggered backwards, momentarily stunned. Sardâr took the advantage. He launched forward, the tip of his curved blade pointed directly at Iago's heart. But his enemy whirled and struck back—it had been a feint. Sardâr felt the edge of a wicked metal spike collide with his back, and a spark of lightning shot through him. He fell forward.

Iago stepped over him, the edge of his lance brushing Sardâr's neck. His eyes were ablaze with savage pleasure.

Sardâr's gaze slipped to the right. His sword was lying motionless a few feet away. If he could just reach it . . .

"Well, Sardâr, you really have lost your touch," Iago said erratically, not bothering to conceal his glee. "I expected this to last at least a *little* longer. I'll raze this fortress to the ground, and the Emperor will reward me with Tâbesh on a platter. Very soon the throne room in Khălese will be back in use. It might comfort you to know that you died to save your kingdom from decadence. Then again, maybe not. You always were a traitorous fool."

He raised the spear, about to strike, but paused. "Oh, and comfort yourself also that Adâ won't be grieving for too long. I always had a soft spot for her. She shall make a fine queen consort in the new state—"

"No," roared Sardâr. He released a blast of alchemical energy, and his blade flung back into his hand. In the same motion he leapt off the ground, flipping over Iago. He twirled on the spot, slicing with his blade. However, Iago was quick enough. He blocked the strike with his spears crossed in an X, but Sardâr had been expecting this. He brought his gauntleted fist crashing into Iago's stomach, and this time he felt it connect properly and something crack underneath.

His enemy staggered back a second time, clutching his stomach, his face contorted with agony.

Sardâr waited, catching his breath. A trickle of blood ran down his mouth, but he ignored it, his gaze fixed on Iago.

Iago, still breathing heavily, raised his arms and let go of the lances. They hovered in midair, soon joined by five more that spun into reality. The elf turned his hands, and the spears all turned to point directly at Sardâr. Iago lowered his arms, and the spears sped towards him like arrows.

Sardâr immediately threw a barrier around himself and felt the first two arrows strike. But they were too strong. Driven by Dark alchemy, they spun around him in a tornado formation, coming closer to his body with every revolution. The whipping air was too fleeting to breathe, sucking air out of his lungs. Soon he'd either suffocate or be shredded to pieces. He clutched the Shard around his neck. He knew

The Ram Released

what he must do. But did he dare?

Fire exploded outwards from Sardâr's body, breaking the whirlwind of lances and sending them clattering across the rocks. As Iago watched with horror, the inferno expanded, and out of its peak rose Sardâr, eyes ivory with spiritual energy, enthralled in hornlike flames. The ram gave a beautiful, terrifying cry and launched at the dark elf. He was knocked flat, and there was Sardâr above him, his blade raised, incendiary sparks encircling him like a gigantic halo.

"I would give you mercy, Iago," Sardâr said in a deadly whisper, "but you deserve nothing less than to die an extremely painful death. And I have no qualms about giving it to you." He moved the blade from Iago's neck over to his heart.

But in that moment, the elf had drawn something from his robe and was grinning evilly at Sardâr. "That's right. You know what it is. Pure haruspex— extremely brittle. If you kill me, this stone breaks. And you know what happens then, don't you?" The look of shock and comprehension must have been clear on Sardâr's face, for Iago grinned even wider.

the white fox

"Not that this hasn't been fun, but I think this is where I step out. And mark my words, Sardâr Râhnamâ, you will rue the day you crossed me."

Before Sardâr could register what he meant, Iago, laughing manically, was becoming less and less corporeal, and in a second he was gone with a trail of smoke. Sardâr made a grab for the stone, but it was too late. The shiny black surface collided with the stone and exploded in a flash of crimson smoke.

As the balcony sank gently back to ground level, Sardâr despaired in horrified realization. There was an immense cracking above him. High above, the disc was fissuring, thin sinews of darkness weaving like a spider's web over the crimson core. It shattered.

Chunks of the same black and red imbued glassy substance smashed to the ground all over the battlefield. Everywhere they hit, the shadows gathered, forming pits of dark energy. So the myths were true. The Cult had discovered a substance—haruspex—that could channel the Darkness under mortal control. But if that control was broken, then there was a direct and unfettered rift through which Darkness could surge.

Everywhere around him, demons began rising out of every pit. They were all recognizable from the mythological almanacs he had studied—amphibious preta, slithering drekavacs, winged lempos, grinning, hyena-like hellhounds, and even hideous, terrifying furies. In the sky, where the disc had shattered was now a maelstrom of churning darkness, a crack in the fabric of space.

Slowly, Sardâr stood and picked up his fallen sword. He was standing in the middle of the bridge, now devoid of goblins. He was dimly aware of the battle between dwarves and goblins somewhere behind him—a battle of mortals, who had no real quarrel. A meaningless battle, one that would bring only needless suffering to both sides, but one, thanks to Iago, that would soon be over.

Demons were moving towards him in both directions. Raising his weapon, he gave a terrible shout and readied himself for a battle to the death.

the white fox

Chapter XII
a new alliance

The West Dining Hall was lit by lanterns hanging from the walls. There had been an echoing explosion only moments before that had sent the mass of dwarves contained within it—not only refugees but civilian inhabitants of the fortress—into a frenzy of panic. The long wooden benches had been pushed to the edges, ready to barricade the doors if necessary. Guards stood around the room, and many looked just as frightened as those they were charged with protecting.

Jack and Lucy were in a corner. Jack was seated on the hard stone floor against the wall, whilst Lucy was pacing relentlessly up and down. Evidently, she had learnt *something* from Sardâr. Jack and Lucy knew what the other one was thinking. They had just spent three

weeks of intense training learning how to defend themselves, and now they were stuck in this room, unable to help with the battle.

"We've got to help," Lucy said finally, halting her pacing for a moment. "What's the point of all *this*"—she gestured at the rather unnecessarily embellished armor she was clad in from neck to foot—"if we can't use it?" Her hands were clenched into fists.

Over their time here, something had awoken in her: Jack saw in her a new force he could not have imagined only a month ago. No, that was unfair. He had known it was there all along, that underneath the shallow obsession with being a normal teenage girl there had been a steel—an urge to take life by the horns—in Lucy, ready to break out. He had sensed it back in the orchard after their trip to London, but it had taken an entirely different world to set it loose. Now it was here to stay. And he was not going to let himself pass up the opportunity to match it with his own awakened vigor.

Jack stood suddenly and strode over to the door, which was flanked by two guards in green tunics.

Lucy grinned and jogged over to join him in sizing up the guards. They both appeared distinctly nervous from the crashing noises coming from outside.

"I'm sorry, but we've been ordered by the king to not let anyone in or out of this hall. It's for your own safety."

"But—"

"No. Please make your way back inside."

Lucy looked like she was ready to punch the guard who had spoken, but Jack placed a warning hand on her arm. He hoped this could be settled without the lasting damage that Lucy's fists were now able to inflict.

There was a small flash of white light, and both guards lulled forward onto their knees and fell to the floor.

Jack glanced around, but no one seemed to have noticed. "Let's go."

"Will they be okay?" Lucy asked, only slightly concerned, as they passed them.

". . . I hope so . . ."

Jogging, they reached the Entrance Hall only a few minutes later via the West Hall. An eerie silence had descended over the place and not just because it was completely deserted. Shouts could still be heard from somewhere above, but there seemed to be no more rubble being hurled at the fortress or mechanical fire spitters firing flaming ammunition. Did this mean the battle was over? The churning Jack was feeling in the pit of his stomach told him that wasn't the case.

They turned to the right towards the main entrance. At the sight of the sealed inner door, Jack suddenly realized they had no way of getting out. There were, of course, no axes just lying around to open the gate with.

But before he could voice the problem to Lucy, there was a shout from behind them. "What are you doing here?"

They turned to see the king's nephew, Bál, and a regiment of guards behind the wooden roundel in the center of the chamber making their way towards them.

"Civilians are meant to stay in the guarded areas."

Jack glanced at Lucy. She had that look in her eye—the same look she'd had in the training room and when demanding answers from Sardâr. She was ready to make her stand, and so was he. Just as he could see her hands curling into fists, so he began reaching for the end of the alchemical mental tape.

"We're going to help Sardâr and the others," she said defiantly, staring down at Bál. *That*, Jack could see, was something she had learnt from Adâ.

"We don't want to fight you," Jack added, trying to lower himself to the dwarves' eye level without labouring the point about the difference in height. He looked Bál straight in the face. In those normally disdainful eyes, he thought he could see the same sense of duty that he was now feeling to those trapped outside. The dwarf stared back at him, not coldly, as so often he had done before, but with a new sense of shared goal. He said nothing for a moment, and Jack did not look away.

"So do we," Bál said finally, facing his regiment. "I do not expect everyone to follow us. It may well be a suicide mission. But we have a warrior's duty to those outside. If any dwarf wants to leave, let him leave now."

the white fox

None of the dwarves moved. On the contrary, many of them unsheathed their weapons and nodded at him.

He turned to Jack and Lucy, who also nodded at him. He smiled a little awkwardly. This was really the first time they had found themselves speaking, let alone on the same side. "This is very brave for elves," he remarked, though not unkindly.

"We're not elves," Lucy blurted out. Bál looked confused.

"We'll explain everything if we survive this," Jack replied, smirking slightly at his own optimism. Bál shook his head, evidently deciding that now was not the time to open up a discussion about race relations.

One of the dwarves placed his axe into the slot in the stone, and the door sprung open. Jack looked to his right at Lucy and to his left at Bál. They both nodded in solidarity. Then they all turned and proceeded out into the darkness.

The valley was completely devastated.

Rocks hurled by the attackers and parts that had crumbled off the fortress were scattered everywhere, interspersed with fallen metal gangways and pipes. Corpses of goblins were visible, some crushed by piles of rubble, but most bearing gaping wounds. The giants were landmarks in their own right, the wild crimson light gleaming off their bald heads and huge stomachs. Bile-inducing creatures—they could only be demons—crawled over them, devouring their flesh like a swarm of carnivorous insects. The entire scene reminded Jack of photos he'd seen of bomb attacks in Afghanistan or Iraq. He could only think that the Cult had summoned the demons and fled the carnage—he could see no black cloaks anywhere.

Bál signalled for Jack, Lucy, and the troops to come closer. He was some way off to the left in front of a high, sloping rise of rubble.

Checking to see that their presence was as yet unnoticed, Jack and Lucy made their way over to him, keeping low. Closer in, they too could hear scuffling on the other side of the rubble, the noises of people trying not to be seen or heard.

Bál held up his arm for silence, then, as quietly as he could, clambered upwards to look over the edge. As he glimpsed what was on the other side, he shouted out in shock and anger. There were cries from whatever was on the other side, though they didn't sound like dwarves or demons.

The others drew their weapons, and Jack leapt up the rise ahead of Lucy. There, cowering below a large chunk of the fortress wall, was a small group of reptilian goblins. Bál raised his axe to bring it down upon them, but Jack caught his arm and pushed it aside.

"What are you doing?" the dwarf hissed at him furiously.

"They're not going to hurt you," Jack reprimanded him. It was true; the goblins hadn't even drawn their weapons. Moreover, they looked in a seriously shaken state themselves. They were covered in debris and dust, and one of them was putting pressure on a blood-soaked shoulder wound. Glancing around the immediate area, Jack could make out the half-buried corpses of their fellows. He felt a surge of sympathy for this band of survivors.

"We don't want any trouble," said one in a Slavic accent, possibly Russian, her bulbous eyes still firmly fixed on Bál's axe.

"We promise we'll just go," another put in. He looked like he was in medical shock. "We didn't really want to come in the first place, but the man in black came along and killed our chief, and . . ." He trailed off, blinking, as if trying to erase an image perpetually burnt in front of his eyes.

Jack found himself feeling slightly surprised at just how normal these goblins were. Having spent three weeks enclosed in an environment highly hostile to them, he had taken the dwarves' word for it without questioning it himself. But then, he supposed, that was racial stereotyping—just the same here as it was on Earth.

"What happened?" Lucy asked the group at large.

"We were attackin' the fortress," a third said, this one seemingly the leader, "giants and all, and then the black sun shattered everywhere . . . and demons started comin' out of the ground."

In unison, Jack, Lucy, and all the dwarves looked upwards. There was no longer the obsidian black orb with its red core hanging amongst the clouds like a gigantic celestial sphere. In its place, there was some-thing that could only be described as a tear in the fabric of the sky. It was a pit of the deepest black imaginable—everything around seemingly drawn into it. Staring at it made the bile rise in Jack's throat, just like it did when he saw the hellhound and the lobster demon.

"Look," he said, tearing his gaze away from the whirlpool above them, "we're going to search for our friends who were fighting here. There might be more of yours still alive too. We could use all the help we could get."

The leading goblin turned to his group. Slowly, with wide eyes, they all nodded, even the one with the bleeding shoulder. He got to his feet, followed by the others. "I'm Vodnik." He offered his fist to Jack, evidently surprised when he shook it. It took him a few moments to explain that it was customary in his tribe to press knuckles together as a sign of greeting.

All the others were introduced in the same way. When it came to Bál's turn, there was a moment of hesitation. If he had only just managed to stomach

A New Alliance

cooperating with elves, Jack didn't want to know what he must have been thinking about engaging in friendly relations with his age-old racial enemy. But after a few seconds, he exchanged knuckles and afterwards stared at his own fist suspiciously, as if surprised nothing had rubbed off on it.

So, as an unlikely group of humans, elves, dwarves, and goblins, they made their stealthy way through the valley. It felt like a graveyard, the crimson light and oppressive silence giving a deadening sense to the place. No sign of goblin or dwarf life stirred on any side. Farther on, the fallen body of one of the giants barred their path. They stopped, all intensely aware that they could not stay in one spot for too long.

Something shifted in the shadows above, and a shape leapt from the top of a corpse to land in front of them. It was a hellhound, its skull-like head twisted into a horrific grin.

Jack felt the taste of bile rising in his throat again, and the image of Alex being stabbed rose in his mind once more.

More demons were weaving in and out of the rubble around them, congealing from shadows as if little more than dark liquid.

"Up there," Vodnik shouted, gesturing to a pile of low rocks to the right of the giant corpse.

They hurried over to it, and as they scrambled over the top, Bál swung his axe, colliding hard with the snapping hellhound's skull. It was knocked sideways, but almost instantaneously it got back to its feet, shook its head, and began stalking towards them. Apparently stunned by the ineffectiveness of his prized weapon, the dwarf scampered over the top and joined the others in the huddle on the other side.

More demons were oozing out of the shadows here, and the ones that had just apparently escaped were climbing over the corpse to cut off their path to the fortress. Faced on all sides by enemies, the group formed an outward ring—the dwarves hoisting their axes, the goblins drawing thin scimitars from sheaths on their belts, and Jack and Lucy lifting their brand-new broadswords from the scabbards clipped to the back of their armor. Both of them almost instantaneously dropped them; they were much heavier than the wooden swords, and it only then occurred to Jack that they hadn't actually used any real weapons yet.

Meanwhile, the demons were drawing closer—some resembling wolves, others more serpents or lizards, and still more that could not be compared to anything in the natural world. Jack could feel his heart pounding against the metal plating of the armor. Glancing around, he noticed the goblins and dwarves looked equally scared. For all their combat training and drilling, they had never faced foes like these.

Then, through the haze of fear, an idea occurred to Jack. "Everyone, link arms."

Bál looked incensed. "A love-in with greenskins is one thing, but there is no way—"

"Just do it!"

This time, he obeyed.

Jack hooked his arms through Lucy's and Bál's and steadied his breathing. These were creatures of pure Darkness, as Sardâr had said. So, the only thing that could harm them was pure Light. He now understood what Alex must have done to the bullets in his hand-gun, what Sardâr must have done on the balcony only hours ago—and, he supposed, what he must have done to his sword fighting the lobster demon.

It didn't take much effort. He could feel the power flowing through the Seventh Shard around his neck, waiting to be challenged. He let it rush outwards, tapping into the essence of the elements around him—the rubble for earth, the humid moisture for water, the billowing clouds for air, and the burning debris scattered around for fire. Combined, they formed bright white Light, and it was this that every scimitar, axe, and sword in their circle now shone with incandescently.

"That is *so* cool," Lucy breathed beside him.

The others looked equally impressed with their newly empowered weapons, even Bál, who Jack knew shunned any kind of alchemy on principle.

The demons looked momentarily perturbed, but with their numbers swelled, renewed their assault. Another hellhound leapt at Bál, but this time he was ready. Rolling forward to meet it under the highest point of its arc, he plunged his shining axe upwards. The hellhound gave an unearthly shriek as the weapon sliced through it like gas, the creature evaporating into black smoke and disappearing.

The remaining demons froze, snarling, coming no closer. They could not be described as a single conscious being, but the primal Darkness that made up their instincts recognized the power of the Light they now faced.

The group of elves, dwarves, and goblins began backing away from them, all waving their weapons like flaming torches in front of them as deterrents.

Jack heard a shout from somewhere behind. He turned his head and saw that their path to the bridge was now clear. Moreover, there were people in the middle of it, though these were not demons—he could make out the tall figure of Sardâr amongst others. "This way," he yelled.

With a last wave of their weapons, they all turned and sprinted towards the bridge.

Jack did not look back to see whether the demons were following them or not. But he could see that the others were some distance in front of him. He stumbled and fell, breathing heavily, his skull feeling more and more as if there was some great pressure on it from the inside. He heard a call from Bál to the others up ahead and became dimly aware of the dwarf running back to him.

"Come on, elf . . . whatever you are. We're not leaving you here."

And Jack was slung over Bál's shoulder and carried at a run towards the bridge. A moment later, he was thrown down on the rubble-dusted bridge flagons, Bál breathing heavily next to him.

Jack's head was still pounding. "I . . . I can't sustain it," he gasped, and with a rush he felt the pressure lift from his skull. He leapt to his feet, suddenly wide awake.

"Of course, *now* you're fine . . ."

But Jack ignored him, staring at Bál's weapon. The gleam around it was fading and dying, returning to its normal state, losing its ability to destroy demons. Bál noticed what he was looking at, and, glancing back the way they had come, he saw that the demons had noticed it too and were now charging, slithering, or in some cases flying towards them at extreme speed.

"Come on," Jack called to him, and they both sprinted the length of the bridge side by side towards the group Lucy and the others had joined.

They ground to a halt as soon as they got there and drew their weapons once more. The warriors they were now amongst were a mixture of dwarves and goblins, all looking distinctly battle weary, though none seriously wounded. Bál's regiment and the goblins they had met previously had joined their fellows in slumping against the sides of the bridge and exchanging information about the battle.

Sardâr stood in the center with Lucy, Adâ, and Hakim. And behind them—Jack had to blink to make sure this was what he was really seeing—Ruth and what seemed to be most of the crew of *The Golden Turtle*. They turned as the two stragglers reached them.

"You shouldn't have done that," Sardâr reprimanded him.

Jack shrugged. "We couldn't just stay in there

and do nothing. What have the last three weeks been for? Besides, it was Lucy's idea."

She pushed him in mock anger. Her broadsword had stopped glowing too.

"And what are *you* doing here?" he directed at Ruth.

"Helping out, of course," she replied, grinning. It took Jack a moment to notice that she and all her crew looked suspiciously elf-like now: Middle Eastern complexion and hair, and significantly taller.

"But how did you know to come?"

"I called them," Sardâr answered for Ruth, holding up the alchemy-powered golden egg Adâ had used to transform Jack and Lucy into the likeness of elves.

Ruth dug into a pouch on her belt and pulled out an identical egg. "Such a good investment," she said, regarding it proudly. "Oh, and I thought you might want these . . ." She beckoned to one of her crew members, who had a large bag slung over his shoulder, and took out two rapier-style swords, handing them to Jack and Lucy.

They discarded their medieval broadswords with

relief and weighed their new weapons. The rapiers were much lighter and easier to handle.

"Well, this is odd," Adâ remarked, glancing between the dwarves and goblins.

"Nothing like a common enemy to unite old foes," Hakim commented.

Sardâr was exchanging notes on the course of the battle with Bál, as the most senior commander present. Then, as they shook hands as a gesture of respect, something began to glow. Jack immediately thought it was the weapons lighting up again but turned to see something on Sardâr's chest shining with fiery red light. As it unstrapped itself from around his neck, Jack saw that it was the other Shard, almost identical to his. Even as he watched, it glided smoothly across to connect around Bál's neck.

This had attracted the attention of most of the band of warriors. All of them, including Sardâr, looked nonplussed as to what had happened. Bál looked the most surprised; he had evidently done nothing out of the ordinary to cause this to happen.

the white fox

"What in the sacred name of Rofhæle—?"

But his words were cut short by a cry from one of the goblins. They turned to look back the way they had come. The demons were much closer, gushing down the bridge like a tightly packed swarm of locusts, their crimson eye maws fixed unflinchingly on their victims like a single collective being.

the white fox

Chapter XIII
sealing the door

"We can still run," Ruth called out over the noise of the impending storm of Darkness.

"No," Sardâr replied, drawing his blade. "We need to fight this out. There are people in that fortress who we have a duty not to abandon."

Jack, Lucy, Adâ, Hakim, and Bál all nodded. Vodnik, meanwhile, seemed to have assumed command of all the goblin troops. He ordered them to draw their weapons and keep their ground, then took to the front line with the elves and dwarves. *The Golden Turtle* crew seemed remarkably unperturbed by the apparent wave of death that was washing towards them. They produced similar rapiers to the ones Jack and Lucy had been given. Ruth took her place between Hakim and Bál, her sword held

ready in front of her.

"Just worry about your own weapon this time," Sardâr muttered to Jack, standing next to him. As he did so, with no apparent effort, every axe, scimitar, and rapier around them flared up with the same white light as before.

Once again, Jack calmed his breathing and focussed his mind. It took a lot less doing this time. Within seconds his new sword was shining with the same light as everyone else's.

They steeled themselves, and soon the demon horde was upon them.

Jack was only dimly aware of what was going on around him. He could see Adâ ahead, carving swathes through the darkness with her shimmering blades. The very sky seemed to be obscured by rushing black smoke as demons materialized everywhere. Jack took a swipe at one in front of him, slicing through it successfully, and it dissolved with a shriek.

He hit out at another demon, and an idea occurred to him. Summoning a core of Light energy in his right hand, he raised it above his head and tossed it like a tennis ball. The effect was like a grenade—an explosion and a surge of light as the demons in the immediate areas were extinguished. He jumped backwards, and, remembering what Alex had done, conjured five star-shaped shruriken in his hand, hurling them towards an oncoming group of bat-like flyers. Only two hit, but they hit well, sending the demons tumbling into the abyss below.

After a few minutes of frantic fighting, the wave of Darkness retreated, and the mortals regrouped, all breathing heavily. Two dwarves and a goblin were missing, either flung over the side of the bridge or dragged off amongst the horde.

"What are they doing?" Ruth hissed, but no one seemed to know. The demons were not only withdrawing but issuing back into a mass of obsidian smoke, which was pouring over the edge of the gorge into the pit below.

Sardâr turned to look out over the edge and shouted out in horror.

The gorge was no longer a deep, dull pit but a seething lake of dark energy, frothing and boiling

the white fox

like lava. Waves cascaded on the rocks around, disintegrating them. There was a deep rumbling sound. A column of dark energy, burning with the ferocity of a raging furnace, blasted upwards towards the broken sky. It was spinning together, the horde of demons dissolving their physical forms and amalgamating themselves into a single monstrous entity. A gigantic pincer, the size of a car, whipped out of the black tornado and clamped onto the side of the bridge, forcing them all to jump back. In its wake, charred exoskeleton pulsating with flames, its body no longer anchored in rock but free to move in the lake, rose the giant demon of the volcano.

The massive crustacean demon towered over them, its eyes burning with that demonic light that seemed simultaneously to be both darkness visible and an incandescent glow. *"Little mortals,"* it roared in the same mind voice as Inari but with a repulsive taste, *"We admire your perseverance. You would make good servants. Join the right side: only death awaits you here. We can give you power beyond your wildest dreams. You can become lords of this world, conquer many others, if you align yourselves with the Darkness . . ."*

The voice seemed to be moving from addressing all of them to speaking to Jack individually. He felt the pressure of the creature as it entered his mind.

"Do not make the mistake of your friend. Put away your weak little Light, and step into the Dark. That Light cannot help you, but we can make everything you could possibly wish for come to pass. You will return home. Your friends will be unharmed and waiting for you. All very easy. All you need to do is put away the Light. Put away the Light . . ."

The world around Jack seemed to fade into monochrome, a great weight compressing his mind. His head was so heavy, he couldn't think straight. If he gave in it would all be over, and he could sleep. He was *so* very tired. It would be so easy to hand over the Shard, and his troubles would be gone. He could take Lucy with him and find Alex. Leave these fools to their petty conceits . . .

Then he could just sleep.

Then he could just . . .

"Jack!" shouted Lucy.

His eyes snapped open, and he realized he had

sunk into a kneeling position. The monstrosity was still above him, the twin cores of ethereal glow fixed upon him, but he forced himself not to look at them. To his left, Lucy, Sardâr, and Ruth were flattened against the bridge, compressed onto the stone by the weight of the multitude of thick, sinuous tendrils projected from the demon's pincer. On his right, he saw some goblins and dwarves disappearing under the other pincer. And right next to him was Bál, still standing but lulled into the same half sleep as he had been. He wondered why the creature had not captured either of them, but he found the answer almost immediately. At his and Bál's necks, shining with bright white and red light respectively, were the Shards of the Risa Star.

Bál's eyes flashed open. Jack could only imagine what the demon had whispered to him inside his head, but he could tell it had severely shaken him. He spun around, obviously shocked at his surroundings, until his gaze fell on Jack, on the Seventh Shard, and then on his own.

"Put away the Light," repeated the demon.

Jack's and Bál's eyes locked, and in an instant of simultaneous realization, they knew what they had to do. With the smallest head motion possible, they nodded at each other.

"Not a chance in hell," the dwarf said calmly, turning to face the demon.

Jack did the same. His mind was oddly clear now; he could see straight ahead, and he could feel his brain pushing away the parasitical influence of those twin cores, like fog ripped apart by sunlight. The Seventh Shard was shining at his throat. He unsheathed his sword in a flash and held it aloft, crossing it with Bál's drawn axe in an *X* between them.

From deep within the Seventh Shard, he felt the power engulf him. White light surged up his rapier, just as a corona of crimson flames blasted up Bál's axe. The two intertwined at the point of contact and launched high into the air. A shard of incandescent crystal light, encircled by a thick coil of inferno, bolted towards the demon—a white fox and a red ram charging as one. It struck the creature squarely in the chest, ripping a gigantic breach through its core.

the white fox

The demon shrieked, the noise recoiling off every boulder and mountain in the surrounding valley, as its essence was rent apart. The last image of the infernal lobster was its writhing form before it imploded in a tsunami of black smoke, its remnants dissipating into the dark lake below.

Jack and Bál stood, stunned, trying to get a hold of what had just happened.

Around them, a ragged combination of elves, pretend elves, dwarves, and goblins clambered to their feet, attempting to extricate the remaining black slime from their clothes and hair. The combination of light and fire had gone, the Shards were no longer glowing, and there was no sign whatsoever of any demons.

Sardâr was the first to speak. "Jack, Bál, one of you needs to seal that Door."

"What?"

"That is a Door to Darkness," the elf replied, his arm raised above his head to indicate the dark maw

Sealing the Door

in the fabric of the sky.

They all looked up, and Jack received the same heady feeling of sickness as when sensing a demon.

"It's a remaining passageway between Light and Darkness, just like the one on Earth. *That's* why I went searching in Mount Fafnir in the first place. I thought I might find the entry point. As long as that's left open, Darkness will continue to seep into this world. You need to use a Shard to seal it. Either of you."

Jack unlooped the Seventh Shard from around his neck.

He was interrupted, however, by Bál speaking. "I'll do it." Jack looked at him quizzically for a moment, then shrugged and stood back.

Bál raised his Shard above his head and pointed the jagged edge towards the sky. The thinnest possible beam of scarlet light shot upwards from the point like an arrowhead, shooting vertically into the air. It struck the dark mass at its very heart.

Instantly, the earth began to rumble, the debris around them bouncing off the bridge, as the black typhoon retracted. It coiled inwards, as if being sucked down a drain, compressed into the smallest imaginable space at the point of the red beam. Then as the rumbling ceased, it vanished with a crackle of air, and was gone.

Dawn broke over the peak of Mount Fafnir, the golden light surging across the valley.

Sealing the Door

Chapter XIV
the black mirror

The following hours passed like a haze to Jack. He barely had time to exchange a few words with Ruth before they bundled back into the fortress and the all clear sounded.

Dwarves began to emerge from every guarded room and declaim the wreckage of their valley. Whilst soldiers—assured multiple times that there would be no lurking demons on the battlefield—searched for the dead and any survivors and miners started the arduous task of clearing the rubble away, refugees began flooding back into the main chambers of the colony.

Jack, Lucy, and the crew of *The Golden Turtle* were immediately put to work distributing rations to all members of the population. The goblins, meanwhile, were escorted secretly into a hidden chamber by Sardâr, Adâ,

Hakim, and the king. Jack understood the reasoning. The vast majority of the civilian dwarves, hidden underground, would not have been aware of the Door to Darkness being opened, and so they were still under the impression that the goblin army had caused the ravaging of their homes. It would have been hard to keep the surviving goblins being lynched by the angry mob, even though they had lost many more of their fellows in the battle than the dwarves had.

Finally, just after midday and a long council with Sardâr, the king emerged from his throne room and proclaimed that he had a speech to make to his subjects. Every dwarf in the fortress was to assemble in the now partially cleared valley to hear these very important words.

It took an entire hour and a half to marshal the dwarf populace outside—for many of them, the first glimpse of the havoc that had been wreaked. Once this was done and the fortress had been completely emptied, the king climbed on top of a large piece of rubble as a makeshift podium. Jack, Lucy, and all the real and pretend elves were told to come up and stand beside him.

It struck Jack for the first time just how many people there were here—the uniformed guards, tunic-wearing miners, administrative scribes, peasant refugees, and forge blacksmiths clad in their thick overalls—at least a thousand denizens or visitors to this battered colony-city-fortress. He could tell he was not the only one who noticed too late that the king was now the shortest on the podium.

This did not seem to deter him, however, as he began. "Last night," he declared in a voice much louder than his usual one, which carried right to the back of the crowd, "we, the people of Thorin Salr and the surrounding localities and villages, suffered a merciless and unprovoked attack by external enemies. There are many amongst the citizens I see before me who would have me blame the goblin tribes and have done with it. There are even those who would want me to marshal our soldiers and launch a counterattack into the Wastes."

There was a cry of consent from a large minority of dwarves in the crowd.

"That, however, would be an injustice and a travesty."

Widespread murmurings.

"We were not the victim of a malicious attack from goblins, though that has not been unknown in the past. The attacks on your villages and on this city were indeed perpetrated by goblins—but goblins manipulated by a malevolent force behind them. A force, moreover, that used Dark alchemy to attempt to destroy our kingdom. I have communicated with the kings of our neighboring states, all who attest to having been the victims of similar attacks. These attacks were masterminded by an organization of sorcerers who call themselves the Cult of Dionysus."

There was a general cry of outrage at this. Thorin was clearly right in that there were elements amongst his inhabitants who were pushing for a counterattack.

"Yet we repelled them," shouted the king, overcoming the cries of outrage. "We repelled them through our belief in the righteous defense of our homeland!"

The cries of outrage morphed into cheers at this change of tack.

"However, this victory does not belong to dwarves

alone. The small force of heroic warriors that has ensured the safety of our kingdom was made up of dwarves and elves"—he gestured to those either side of him—"and goblins."

Shocked silence dissolved into whispers, as, at Thorin's beckoning, Vodnik and the surviving goblins climbed the rubble from out of sight to stand next to the king. They looked very awkward before a crowd of a thousand dwarves and did not seem to know what to do with their hands. The one with the bleeding shoulder was heavily bandaged now, though he still looked drawn and pale.

"These goblins," Thorin continued, "lost far more of their fellows than we did of ours. Yet when a brave regiment of dwarves and two elves left the fortress to assist their surrounded companions, these goblins chose to fight on our side rather than to flee. Together they repelled the forces of Dark alchemy that threatened us and allowed us to be standing once more in this valley today. For their utmost bravery in the face of adversity, I have chosen to award all these warriors honorary citizenship of our kingdom."

the white fox

There was a pause once the king finished speaking, in which the mood of the crowd was unreadable. Jack stood next to Lucy, feeling extremely tense. If the dwarves decided they didn't like this idea, there were easily enough of them to overrun the podium and probably crush all those standing on it in the process.

But his fears were unfounded. It was only a few seconds before the first claps sounded, and within a few more cheers were resounding around the valley as Thorin crossed the podium, shaking the hands—and cracking the knuckles—of each of them in turn.

Once he had finished and the cheering finally ceased, he began again. "This experience, trying as it has been, has certainly taught me a very valuable lesson. The feud between dwarves and goblins, not only in this kingdom but across this continent, is absurd. Last night showed that when we cooperate, we can achieve much more than when we fight amongst ourselves. I therefore propose that friendly relations begin from today with the goblin tribes of the Wastes, and at the first opportunity, I will call together the other dwarf kings and goblin chieftains in the first

The Black Mirror

Dwarf-Goblin Conference of the Stórr Mountains."

Bál stepped forward to speak, clearing his throat.

Jack could tell the strong political position he held even by the silence that descended upon the crowd again. As the head of a potential resistance to this new stance, his view was very important.

"I second this proposal," he said loudly. "My experiences in the last hours have led me to reevaluate my position. Early this morning I fought alongside some of the bravest soldiers I have ever met, and many of those were not dwarves. I welcome this new opportunity for good relations."

Another cheer began, intensifying even more as he too cracked knuckles with the goblins on the podium.

The late afternoon was passed in much the same manner as earlier in the day but with a more elated sense of purpose. The goblins, no longer under threat, assisted in shifting the rubble and recovering the bodies of the dead. In accordance with their tradition, a pyre was constructed away from the fortress, on which the bodies were cremated. Meanwhile, the dead dwarves were taken out of the valley to an ancestral barrow ground and laid to rest there. Neither side questioned or impinged upon the other's traditions.

Jack and Lucy spent the remainder of the day with Ruth, Adâ, and the crew of *The Golden Turtle*—the same group, in fact, that had first travelled under the ocean that lifetime of three weeks ago. Things could not be more different now. The extremes of Adâ's cool aloofness and Lucy's spoilt moodiness had gone, and all four of them laughed and joked together. As before, Jack found himself watching Ruth in idle moments and looking away hurriedly whenever she noticed.

They were helping to clear out the rubble, and now, with the assistance of alchemy, this was much easier. Lucy even managed to perform her first spell in levitating a rock, a feat that earned her praise from Hakim, who happened to be passing on an errand at the time. Jack reacquainted himself with some of the crew members he had met on their journey here, Aonair the Irishman and São the Spaniard amongst them.

At around five o'clock, just as the first hints of dusk were creeping into the sunlit sky, a messenger arrived to tell the four of them to come to the throne room.

"This was found on the battlefield an hour ago," the king informed them when they arrived. Sardâr, Hakim, and Bál were already in the torch-lit chamber. He gestured to a slab of black stone, smooth except for the symbol—an ornate black rose—carved into the center in the middle of the table. Turning it over, he showed them the other side—a sheet of glass as dark as the stone itself, completely unreflective.

"It's a dimension mirror," Sardâr said. "It's what the Cult of Dionysus use to communicate."

"How does it work?" Ruth asked.

"It would normally respond only to a member of the Cult," Sardâr replied, "but I think I can fool the alchemical protection." He placed his hand over the surface and began whispering under his breath.

Then, suddenly, with a whip crack, a black force exploded outwards from the mirror, shrouding the

427

the white fox

room in shadow. Sardâr backed away quickly. They saw lights flashing by—stars, planets, and galaxies all moving outwards. They zoomed in on one in particular. As they got closer it became a cluster, then a shape, a perfect spiral of glowing orbs—a miniature galaxy suspended at the center of the room. They continued moving closer to one of the nearer spirals. More stars flashed beside them until they reached one, a massive ball of fiery energy which, to them, took up only half the room.

The speed did not stop there. They blasted by the star and five more planets, getting closer all the time, until they reached an orb, its surface like that of a spherical stormy sky, though spinning slowly on its axis.

Farther in, it was as if they were going to hit the surface. Past many layers of clouds and they were hovering over a vast ocean, thunderous and dark. They moved sideways and over land, a mass of dark buildings and skyscrapers glowing with ghostly blue windows. Now upwards to an immense dagger shape—a castle suspended above the waves on a floating rock. Up to the third highest tower, then in through the window, down a corridor. They were about to hit the door . . . but they went straight through it into a dark chamber and finally stopped.

They were in a large circular chamber by the door. Tall, black thrones rose up in a circle around them. In each one sat a black-cloaked figure, and in pride of place, in the highest position, was someone with silver embroidery to his robes. They were all looking downwards into the center of a room, where a man knelt, shaking upon the same embossed rose emblem engraved on the dimension mirror.

Jack started towards him and cried out in pain. Though he could not see it, he had just walked into where the table had been before the mirror activated.

"It's no use," whispered Sardâr from his side. "This is just a vision of what is happening elsewhere. You can't touch any of these people, and neither can they see you. Just watch."

Jack turned back to the scene just in time to hear the man in the silver-embroidered robes speak.

"You have failed us, Iago." The voice was perfectly

the white fox

clear, as though he were actually in the room with them.

"Master," Iago moaned, shuddering. "Master, please . . ."

"Please what? You wish for mercy? I do not give mercy."

"No, master . . . the girl . . . the informant . . . that was me. I retrieved her for you."

"That is beside the point." The master's voice was shrilly cold. "Have you, amongst your many failings, forgotten the mantra of the Cult?"

In unison, the eleven other figures chanted: "The Darkness is power. We wield the Darkness. We become power itself."

Iago gave another shudder, as though the words made him gag.

"Precisely. And what have you done, Iago? Not only did you fail to retrieve that Shard of the Risa Star, but you did not even weaken that world sufficiently to absorb it into the Darkness. You have squandered the recent work of Archbishops Icarus and Tantalus."

"But, my liege, my years of service—"

"Count for nothing. You have made us suffer an

The Black Mirror

irritating setback. You have failed us, and you must suffer the consequences." The master clicked his fingers.

Instantly, something stirred in the darkness behind the throne. Jack gave an involuntary shiver, remembering Iago's own *Sleepy Hollow*–esque demon.

"Execution?" one of the other cloaked figures said, though not at all concernedly.

"No. Iago shall suffer a fate much more painful. His essence shall be wrenched from this reality and sucked into the Dark Realm. There he will traverse the Darkness for eternity, tortured by the insatiable temptation to submerge himself into the collective Dark, but with the knowledge that if he does so, he shall become a mere tool for the Darkness itself." The master's lip curled. Jack knew that he was deliberately explaining in gory detail to make Iago's fate even worse.

Below the foremost throne, only just discernable in the dark, black smoke was beginning to coil upwards from the floor. As its tendrils twisted around themselves, they formed into the shape of a tall, long-haired humanoid, completely naked, with a pair of massive dark wings extending from its shoulder blades to shadow its face.

"No, master, please!" Iago's voice rose to a scream as the creature dived. A mass of dark feathers, robes, and hair engulfed the elf, his hastily summoned Abaddon falling pathetically under the master's demon. Iago's screams rent the air around the chamber, and Jack noticed many of the others averting their eyes.

In a moment it was over. The shadowy, vaguely humanlike winged creature evaporated. Iago's lifeless form slumped, motionless, on the marble floor. A pool of congealed dark liquid began to form about it, and it sunk like a rock into the sludge until it was completely submerged. Then the pool shrunk and closed, with no sign that there had ever been a body there.

"Now that is dealt with, we have to right his mistakes. Iago's blunders, whilst dangerous, will not be fatal if we act quickly. Another Door to Darkness has been sealed by that infernal Star, so we must move onwards. Phaedra, Paethon," he addressed two figures in seats opposite, "our latest intelligence shows that the goblins of the Sveta Mountains on the planet of Yarkii are long known to have guarded the Fifth Shard. Go there and extract it from them."

They stood, bowed in unison, and disappeared into the same gusts of dark smoke Iago had used during the battle.

"Nimue, time is short. We now know that the Third Shard is hidden somewhere around the city-state of Albion in the Centauras galaxy. Obtain it by any means necessary."

The woman, one of the few with her hood down, nodded and made for the exit.

"Nimue," the master called as she opened the door, "take our informant. She may be useful in negotiations."

Nimue nodded again and left, and the door swung shut behind her.

"Now, Icarus. You have proved yourself time and time again as the prime example of a loyal servant."

The hooded figure on his right bowed his head.

Jack felt his stomach squirm. This was the man who, he now realized, he hated above all others, only meters away, and yet he could not touch him.

"We will discuss your next assignment in private—"

"Master!" A shrill voice interrupted him.

He quickly turned to the woman across the room from him. "What, Ino?"

"We are being watched."

There was a pause, and then the message sunk in. Figures all around the room began pulling their hoods over their faces. The master clapped, the noise echoing supernaturally loudly around the chamber. Dark fog rose from the floor, tentacles twisting like black serpents around the bases of the thrones and their feet, cloaking everything in deep shadow.

Jack couldn't see anything. He seemed no longer to be standing; he was falling backwards into darkness, and it was cramming into his eyes, his ears, crushing his lungs under its weight . . .

An arm grabbed the neck of his tunic and pulled. Slowly, the fog drifted away, leaving him behind. Then he crashed onto the throne room floor. Blinking furiously and rubbing his head, he stood up.

Everyone stood and moved away from the mirror.

It hovered in the air above the table, the oppressive dark smoke swirling around it.

Jack looked behind him and saw Hakim, evidently the one who had pulled him out of the fog. He became aware of chanting. Somewhere to his right, Sardâr was bellowing syllables with his hands pressed together, a blinding white light shining within them. At a last word, which seemed to shake the room itself, he released the light. It flashed across the room and exploded, imprisoning the mirror in a cube of burning energy. There was another flash, and the smoke vanished, the mirror falling to the table with a dull clunk.

Jack breathed out slowly. All around him, people were making their way cautiously towards the incarcerated mirror.

"Don't touch it! I have restrained the Dark alchemy for a time, but it is still very dangerous." Sardâr approached, and everyone backed away. "The Emperor has blocked this mirror from tapping into Nexus. It is unlikely that we will be able to access it again."

"So that was the Emperor?" Ruth asked breathlessly.

"Apparently so. And that was this mysterious planet Nexus. It must have been the Council of Thirteen, which coordinates the Cult of Dionysus."

There was silence. Everyone around the room was trying to work out the intricacies and implications of what they had just seen.

Eventually, Sardâr let out a long breath. "I think it would be best if everyone went to bed. There's nothing we can do about that now, and I need some time to compose my thoughts. I suggest we meet back here tomorrow morning."

They all nodded and departed for their rooms.

Chapter XV
the two-pronged attack

Jack and Lucy headed to their rooms on Sardâr's request. The fortress was quiet now, quieter than it had been all the time they had been here. Earlier in the day, a decree had been issued granting refugee peasants permission to return to their villages. Eager for the space and comfort, many had moved out immediately, hoping to arrive at their homes before sunset. The miscellaneous barrels, carts, and sacks that had adorned the hallways almost like festive decorations were diminishing, swept away by the rush of relieved travellers.

Jack bid Lucy good-night, and after seeing her into her room, he opened the door to his own. He was only mildly surprised to see the glimmering, white-furred form of Inari sitting on his bed. "I haven't seen you for a

while," he remarked, taking off his boots.

"*You haven't needed me for a while,*" Inari replied, hopping off the bed to let Jack sit down. The fox spirit positioned himself on the floor, looking up at the human elf.

"Where do you go when you're not here?" Jack asked.

"*Now, that would be telling,*" the fox said, echoing his reply the last time they had spoken in this room. "*Around and about. Lots of different worlds. I'm always pulled back to the same place in the end, though.*"

"You don't know anything more about Alex, then?"

"*Sorry, but no.*" Inari stretched out, yawning. "*You've become quite the hero since we first spoke. An alchemist. Who would have thought it? And a fairly competent swordsman, if you don't mind me saying so. You're almost unrecognizable.*"

Jack glanced down at himself. He knew he looked different, thanks to that alchemical egg. But he felt different too. He felt braver, as if he had proved to himself as well as everyone else that he could hold his own in a difficult situation. He did not hear Inari's words without a slight flicker of pride within.

"We've spoken four times. The first time you gave

The Two-Pronged Attack

me the Shard. The second time you gave me some answers, and the third time you saved my life. So why are you here now?"

The fox turned his head slightly, as if trying to look at Jack from a different angle. *"Tomorrow morning you're going to be faced with a choice that will have repercussions much more far-reaching for you and your friends than you can possibly see now. You will be made an offer, and I would urge you to accept it. If you do, then I'll be seeing you again very soon."*

"Do you have a setting that talks in something other than riddles?" Jack asked exasperatedly.

The fox gave the closest thing a fox could give to a smirk.

It was then that Jack noticed something. "You've got two tails. I'm sure you had only one last time."

Inari turned to look at his own rump. *"So I have. You learn something new every day."*

Early the following morning, Jack, Lucy, Sardâr, Adâ, Hakim, Ruth, Bál, and King Thorin were seated in the throne room. Golden sunlight slanted through the arched windows, throwing one half of the central table into bright light and the other into dim shadow. No one had spoken beyond curt greetings. They knew the seriousness of the situation, and Sardâr's grim expression only emphasized this as he got to his feet.

"You are all here because what happens next will affect you, whether you like it or not. With the events of yesterday, we have entered a transitional phase between secret guerrilla combat and open warfare." Sardâr reached into his tunic and pulled out a folded piece of paper. "This is a letter from Isaac. I believe the last one that he sent before his disappearance. I apologize; I did not maliciously withhold its contents from you. The reason I came here some weeks ago was to try to prevent this outcome, but now we are firmly set on this course and must make informed choices based on these facts."

He unfolded the letter and began to read.

Sardâr,

As you know, I have found my way to Chthonia, a world on the very edge of the Darkness. I have made a drastic new discovery the Apollonians need to be aware of. There is little time, and I fear that my presence here has not gone unnoticed.

There is a new part of the legend of the Risa Star I have uncovered in an ancient document in this world. It speaks of one who led the bearers of the Shards of the Risa Star and reassembled it into a single device two thousand years ago. He was the Übermensch—the Great Mortal—the only one with the ability to wield the Risa Star in its entirety.

We can guard the Shards from the Cult to the best of our ability, but that will only result in a stalemate. Without the Übermensch we are powerless to unify them. So, our attack must be two-pronged; we must continue with our thwarting of the Cult's ambitions to create a superweapon and continue searching for the Risa Star but also find the Übermensch.

Time is running out. Beware the white fox: he is not what he appears to be.

Isaac

443

the white fox

Sardâr looked up, his expression, if possible, even grimmer.

No one spoke. As with the vision into the Cult's plans the previous evening, everyone was running over what they had just heard, trying to make sense of it.

"So, not as easy as we thought," Ruth remarked eventually, grimacing.

"No, it is not," Sardâr agreed, replacing the letter in his tunic and beginning to pace around the room in his usual way. Then he stopped and stared at those gathered around the table, the same resolved glint in his eye that Jack had seen in the midst of the battle. "I think we need to reconsider our operations. We currently have possession of two Shards of the Risa Star, and the Cult definitely has one, possibly more, if we presume that Alex is indeed held captive by them. That timely insight into the Cult's plans revealed two more locations where they expect to find them: Albion and Yarkii. I suggest that we dispatch a group of agents—small, so as to not attract suspicion—to each of these and try to acquire the Shard before the

The Two-Pronged Attack

Cult does. Then we redeploy agents working against minor Cult insurgencies to redouble our search for the world of Nexus. If this is where the Aterosa is to be found, then we must, as Isaac says, sabotage it as soon as possible."

It was a mark of Sardâr's leadership that the entire assembled group was nodding along to this.

"What about this Übermensch?" Hakim asked.

Sardâr glanced at Jack before answering. "As of yet, we have no way of knowing who this might be or where he or she might be found. I recommend that we focus on our first objective and trust that this path will be revealed to us as we progress." He stood up straight, scanning the listeners intently. "Are there any objections in principle to this course of action?"

Everyone shook their heads, including Jack and Lucy. Given the evidence, Sardâr seemed to have made some perfectly intelligent judgements.

"What is the white fox?" Hakim asked.

Sardâr shook his head. "I'm not yet sure."

Jack looked down to avoid catching anyone's eye. He supposed he should tell everyone about Inari at some point, but something made him bite his tongue. The fox spirit hadn't led him astray so far, and the Apollonians didn't need to know *right* now that he'd been keeping something from them all along. He'd thought he could trust Inari, despite his sporadic appearances and disappearances. He resolved to ask the fox about it when they next had a chance to speak.

Sardâr turned to Jack and Lucy. "You two have a choice. One option is for you to return to Earth. I cannot pretend that your hometown will be any safer than when you left it. We thought that with the focus of events here, you could return within weeks. But now that *this* Door to Darkness has been sealed, it is likely that the Cult will renew their efforts to reaccess the one on Earth.

"The other option—and I have discussed it with everyone in this room, bar Bál—is for you to join the Apollonians. You have both proved very brave in yesterday's battle, and you are now more than capable of defending yourselves. We would feel honored if you joined us; you would be fighting for the defense of your home world and all others in the Light. And

The Two-Pronged Attack

when we finally defeat the Cult once and for all, your home would be a much safer place."

Jack became aware that everyone in the room was staring at them. He looked at Lucy and was reminded vividly of the two previous times they had faced this choice: in the library of the manor back on Earth and in Sardâr's study after the volcano incident. The girl he was looking at now, though, was different than the one he had left Earth with. Her face was flushed with color from exercise and fresh air, and her hair was pinned back rather than arranged in a delicate style. She was changed—no, not changed; she had become the girl she truly was, as she might never have done if she'd stayed on Earth. He saw in her eyes the same sense of purpose that was now implanted at his core.

They both had an obligation to those they cared about. For Lucy, it was the ongoing well-being of her family and friends. For Jack, there were only two people who had really cared about him back at home, and one was at his side whilst the other was currently imprisoned by the Cult of Dionysus for trying to protect him. They had both enjoyed the protection of the

Apollonians. It was now time for the rights and safety they enjoyed to be repaid in the duties they owed.

In unison, they turned to face the room and nodded.

Sardâr, Adâ, Hakim, Ruth, and Thorin nodded back at them. Their path was set.

Only Bál looked uncertain. He hesitated, then stood up.

Everyone looked at him, surprised—all except Sardâr, who stepped backwards out of the circle, smiling knowingly.

"I know I haven't been the most inviting to you all," Bál began hesitantly, "but in the last twenty-four hours my eyes have been opened. I don't know exactly what this means"—he pulled the First Shard out from beneath his tunic—"but I know I want to find out. There's much more of the world outside these mountains than I ever thought there could be. I want to join the Apollonians. I want to go with you, wherever that may take me, to help put an end to these sorcerers' filthy schemes."

The king looked surprised at his nephew's change of heart, but none of the elves now looked

The Two-Pronged Attack

particularly so.

Just as Jack had seen a new force within Lucy, he saw in Bál a warrior who had ruled his small world, now humbled before the breadth of his new experiences. He smiled involuntarily, and the dwarf seemed to take encouragement from this.

"I think," Sardâr said to the room at large, "that Thengel and Bál need some time to discuss this." He strode over to the door and held it open.

Jack, Lucy, and the elves issued out in a line, leaving the king and his nephew on opposite sides of the table.

They walked down the sun-dripped hallway, through bands of light and shadow. Jack was at the back, Sardâr far in front, and Hakim, Lucy, and Adâ talking amongst themselves. He caught a flicker of white on the edge of his vision. He turned instinctively, but it was already gone.

That didn't stop him from hearing the low comment in the BBC accent. *"Good choice."*

Chapter XVI
journey's beginning

Jack and Lucy packed their meagre possessions. They had little to take; their mangled school uniforms had been disposed of, so their only clothes were three additional sets of tunics and one more cloak. They also kept hold of their swords, sheathed firmly in scabbards designed to be worn diagonally over the shoulder, but on Sardâr's advice they left the armor behind. Lucy hadn't thought twice about pushing the entire contents of the bathroom, which was not unlike complimentary hotel toiletries, into her leather rucksack. Jack did not need much convincing to do the same; he had no idea where they were going and what they might need.

All the time they were packing, Sardâr's words to them as they walked back through the fortress echoed

in his head like a repetitive song. "If Bál elicits permission for travel from the king, which I'm sure he will, then there shall be six of us to begin dealing with this preemptive strike. Thengel is needed here to carry through the peace process, so we cannot rely on his help for the time being. From that snapshot of the Cult's plans we know that they intend to infiltrate Albion and Yarkii.

"I will inform our other agents, including Charles's group on Earth, that they should be especially on their guard and should redouble their efforts to discover the whereabouts of the planet of Nexus. Then I suggest we split into two groups and each one travel to a different world. As there are so few of us, it would be safest for Jack and Lucy to split up and be accompanied by two able guardians each. Jack, Bál, and I shall go to Albion, whilst Lucy, Adâ, and Hakim will go to Yarkii."

They finished packing, and, after a last check of their rooms, they made their way down to the entrance in silence.

As agreed, they met outside the gate. The sun

was still rising—a mark of just how early Sardâr had called them to the meeting. The rubble was beginning to be dispersed to the sides of the valley; some had been piled as far as possible against the surrounding cliff faces, others pushed into the large gorge that spanned across the valley.

When they arrived, they found a small send-off party awaiting them: Sardâr, Hakim, Adâ, King Thorin, Bál, and the small group of goblins who had survived the battle.

Vodnik flashed a toothy grin at them as they strode up.

"How are you doing?" Jack asked, smiling back.

The goblin looked tired but well; moreover, without his battle armor on, he looked positively amiable. "Good. I've been elected new chieftain," he replied proudly, indicating a shiny metal bracelet on his wrist. "We owe you majorly, human. We want you to take this—both of you."

One of the other goblins produced two more bracelets.

Jack noticed that they were all wearing them—

the white fox

a thick line of decorative jewelry up their left arms. He supposed it was the equivalent of tribal tattoos or military epaulettes.

The bracelets were passed to Vodnik, and he clasped them around Jack's and Lucy's left wrists on the same arm as the glowing language rings. They appeared to be something like burnished steel, curved in a wavelike spiked pattern with a glimmering jewel set in each. "It ain't much, but you're honorary goblins as well as dwarves now."

Jack and Lucy smiled in gratitude, cracking their knuckles with each goblin in turn.

Then something occurred to Jack, and he said in a lowered voice in case anyone else was listening, "How did you know we're not elves? None of the dwarves worked that out at all."

Vodnik grinned slyly at him. "We ain't *completely* stupid."

The king in full regal clothing was next, and he nodded at them, smiling slightly. "It would not be too much of an exaggeration to say that your stay here was enjoyable?"

"Well, I wouldn't go *that* far," Lucy said, smirking.

The two of them shook hands with Thorin and bowed their heads. "Bál's coming with us, then?"

The king and his nephew exchanged looks. Bál looked slightly odd out of his ceremonial guard uniform or armor. He wore a deep red tunic, not unlike that of the miners', with a backpack and a large cluster of pouches clamped close to him by leather belts. He looked almost like an American pioneer with his ruddy complexion and a wide-brimmed hat on his strawberry-blond crown.

"Yes, I am," he said. "I have been granted leave until this threat is sated. It is to be presented as a matter of international security to the public."

"Have you got everything?" Sardâr asked.

"Yep. Clothes, boots"—Jack glanced at Lucy—"and any complimentary stuff we could grab from our rooms."

Everyone laughed.

"Good. We're going to be travelling for a while."

"How're we getting to this Yarkii place, anyway?" Lucy asked, looking at Hakim and Adâ.

"Vince is coming to pick us up in the dimension ship," Adâ replied, not without a hint of her old disdain.

Lucy cleared her throat slightly; the memories of their last little adventure obviously still turned her stomach.

"And what about us?" Jack put in, gesturing at Sardâr and Bál.

"That's where we come in," Ruth said.

He turned to see her and a select group of her crew emerging out of the shadows of the entrance chamber into the sunlit valley. The majority of the crew had already returned to *The Golden Turtle*, but a few of the heavy lifters had remained to help clear the valley. They were now all carrying a variety of crates and baskets.

"Supplies," Ruth answered to Jack's quizzical look. "We wouldn't want to be going hungry on our jump through space, would we?"

He grinned awkwardly. He was struck again by how stunning she looked—her jet-black wavy hair and deep brown eyes. He caught himself staring and focussed on a boulder somewhere to her right, conscious of his blushing cheeks.

"We need to go," Sardâr prompted, gazing across the valley at the entrance to the tunnel.

Adâ was the first to make her way round the dwarf king and all the goblins, shaking hands and cracking knuckles as appropriate. Hakim followed her, then Sardâr, then Lucy, then Ruth, and finally Jack. The goblins grinned at him as he passed, and the king responded with his usual solemn nod.

Amidst waves and good-byes, they departed, striding out across the valley in a trace of the route they had trod during the battle. They reached the bridge and crossed it, beginning the shallow incline to the mouth of the tunnel. They passed the pyre of goblin dead, now little more than grey ash and commemorative banners fluttering in the breeze. As they reached the top of the rise, with the torch-lit entrance to the tunnel looming before them, they turned back.

They stood in silence, surveying the valley before them. The plateaued cliffs and boulders, rust red in the dusk that had so permeated the rocks in their experience, now shone metallic golden grey in the morning sun. The rock formation of the fortress rose like a resolute beast, its many horns of metal chimneys and gangways glinting in the light. It was the glow of a kingdom that had come to the very brink of destruction, whose enemies had come right to the gates, and had stood steadfast against invasion and now xenophobia.

Jack saw Bál's expression. It was one of mingled pride and sadness. With a start, Jack realized that the dwarf was probably facing exactly the same experience that he and Lucy had only weeks before. Bál had spent his entire life cushioned within these mountains—this fortress was his workplace, social life, and home—and now he was duty bound to protect it by travelling far away from it.

Bál lingered there on the edge of the precipice for a few seconds. Then he turned, and, nodding at Jack in recognition, marched past him into the deep shadow of the tunnel.

Jack waited a moment longer and followed.

It did not take them long to return to the lake where *The Golden Turtle* was again moored. The dome of shiny metal, the size of a small jet, bobbed above the water, the artificial flippers glistening under it at the four compass points. The hatch on the top of the shell was hauled open as they arrived, and the crew began storing their baskets and crates within. The unlikely platoon—three elves, two humans, and one dwarf—stood by the water's edge, watching the process silently.

"Right, we're sorted," Ruth called from the hatch after the last of the boxes had been stowed securely below deck. "Ready to go."

Jack breathed out long and low. The sun had just risen over the crest of rock behind them, showering the bright irradiance of an autumn morning over their mountainous basin. Sparkles of silver crystal shimmered over the surface of the small lake, and the dome of the turtle shell looked almost as if it belonged to a real-life amphibian. The solitary tree, hanging over the face of the water and so slate dead before, rustled with new life as every one of its myriad leaves became a dancing platinum gem.

He turned to Lucy. Sardâr and Adâ had already withdrawn to walk around the lake, facing each other and conversing in low voices. Hakim and Bál had tactfully given them space and were engaged in the awkward farewell of two who had to respect one another.

Lucy's gaze was fixed firmly on the water, determinedly not looking at him.

Jack cleared his throat. This was the moment he'd been dreading.

There was a long, long silence.

"Look ... take care of yourself ... We'll ... we'll be seeing each other ..." He gave up. He was frantically running over all the emotional good-byes he'd seen in films, but the best he could come up with was Rachel Dawes's final letter to Bruce Wayne in *The Dark Knight*, and this was an awful source as the character had died within hours of writing it. Not very reassuring.

She looked at him. Her eyes were slightly red and glimmering with the evidence of blinked-back tears. She didn't try to speak. She just pulled him into a hug and pressed her head into his neck.

Jack put one arm around her and stroked her hair gently with his other hand. He could feel her tears streaming down his tunic. He didn't care that Ruth was watching, that Sardâr and Adâ had returned to their side, that Hakim and Bál had lapsed into silence. He only cared that Lucy would be okay.

Finally, after what must have been minutes, they broke apart, Lucy dabbing her eyes crudely with her palm.

"Look after yourself, won't you?" she said eventually, her voice soft but steady.

"Of course I will. It's you I'm worried about."

"Don't be stupid. I'm the Karate Kid." She grinned. "And you're Gandalf the wizard. But I'm ready to leave this world, I think. I've had enough of living inside *The Lord of the Rings*."

Jack stopped himself from saying, "What could possibly go wrong?" He knew it would have reassured her, but given where they were going, he didn't want to tempt fate.

Sardâr, seeing an opportunity, interjected. "I'm sorry, but we really should be going." He exchanged

461

a few friendly words with Hakim. The latter turned to Jack and wished him well.

Adâ was next, and she pulled Jack into a brief hug as well. "You'll be fine. Look out for Sardâr. You're good at that."

Jack smiled. He, Sardâr, and Bál moved up the gangway.

Ruth was standing by the hatch, looking jokingly exasperated. "You took your time."

"Shush," Jack hissed, pushing her lightly into the hatch.

Her laughter echoed around the metallic chamber below.

Bál descended next, sliding in easily despite his stockiness, and Sardâr after that.

Jack was left standing alone on the top of the shell. He took a moment to savour his last experience of the Stórr Mountains, the magnificent grey rock guardians on all sides, the fresh scent of the mountain air, the slight tanginess of volcanic wind that he'd become too accustomed to. The sun burnt in the blue heavens—a different sun, he realized, to his own and to the one he would next be seeing.

And he saw the three figures under the glistening trees—two women, one man; two real elves, one false one. They were all smiling up at him. He raised his arm to wave, and they did so too. Grinning, his arm clinking with the language ring and the goblin bracelet, he descended into *The Golden Turtle* as the falcon-like bird circled and cawed high above.

the white fox

Chapter XVII
the offer

The grey energy subsided, and the Emperor stepped out of the doorway.

He strode across the bridge, his boots snapping harshly on the stone. The entire city of Nexus splayed out before him, chaotically regimented into an intricate weave of closely cut alleyways and wide open roads. Out to each side in the distance was the mirror black surface of the endless ocean. The white-crested waves were highlighted in the perpetual moonlight, making each look like individual, wrathful sea beasts.

The exposed walkway between the Cathedral and the Precinct of Despair was completely deserted, save for him. His typical black and silver cloak fluttered eerily in the marine wind. It gave the right impression,

he thought, where he was going.

He reached the end of the walkway and stopped, looking down. The Precinct of Despair certainly lived up to its name: a raw, undecorated spike of obsidian stone, shooting upwards into the sky. Each level was a concentric ring, with circular, alchemically protected and barred windows set into it. The spike ran all the way down to the top of the buildings below, where its structure thinned to an impossible diameter. Four elevators operated up and down the very core. Three were used by guards, but one was reserved for the Council of Thirteen.

The Emperor stepped into the Precinct doorway. As he passed under the worn archway, the twin statues on either side reacted. The sinister demonic dragon-like creatures were also carved out of black stone. Their feral eyes lit like will-o'-the-wisps as the Emperor moved between them, and there was the harsh noise of stone on stone as they began to extricate themselves from the walls. A pacifying flick of his hand, and they skulked back into their positions, their eyes dimming.

Four doors were before him, three lit with blue, one with red light. He took the red one. Standing in front of it, he looked straight into the heart of the black rose that was the symbol of the Cult. It scanned his optical profile, then the door slid open. He walked in, and it closed silently behind him. He entered an access code into the keyboard on his right, then the floor. The elevator began to sink into the floor, and then, gathering speed, plunged into the dark abyss.

The wind swirled his cloak around him, threatening to blow his hood down. Clutching it with one hand, he tapped another key on the board. A glass visor rose on all sides, blocking out the worst of the dimensional gale. As he descended, the Emperor looked at the dial on the wall in front of him. The needle swung steadily from the left to the right, each number lighting up in red as it passed. The last number was 52. This floor was reserved for the most high-profile criminals: heretics, unauthorized murderers, and enemies of the state.

Finally, the elevator screeched to a halt and sank slowly into its bottom position. The two layers of

the white fox

doors creaked open, and the Emperor stepped out, his robes rippling slightly in the cold breeze from the shaft. The hallway led away on both sides, only a slight curve showing the shape and size of the Precinct. Metal doors lined the walls, each engraved with numbers. The Emperor strode off to the right, following the plasma lighting on the walls. Despite this, the corridor was still dim, and the ceiling was shrouded in darkness. He stopped in front of the door numbered Genesis III. He had come all this way to find the convict. He only hoped it was worthwhile.

Reaching into his pocket, he drew out a rusted key. These doors could not be opened by alchemy, as sorcery-powered blocking stones lined the inside of the walls to prevent the prisoners escaping. Archaic but effective. He waved his hands over the engraved number, and the illusion was replaced by a keyhole. Inserting it into the lock, he turned it three times. The dials clicked into place, and with a cracking sound it split in half. The two halves slid backwards and parted, revealing the cell beyond.

It was very small and entirely occupied by a

figure restrained and suspended by the arms, legs, and neck. His head was slumped forward, so only a hedge of unkempt and filthy hair was visible, framed against the little window. His ripped and dirty clothes hung off him like ragged wings, and his shoes had completely gone.

"Mr. Steele. It's been a while." The Emperor received no reply, but the boy did glance up. He was in his late teens, very thin and tall for his age. His skin was barely distinguishable from his dirt-encrusted clothes, but his green eyes were alert and fierce. "How are you?"

This time the boy answered, spitting the words out in a hoarse gasp. "What do you want?"

"Merely to talk to you. A cooperative chat could serve us both well."

"Don't patronize me. Why are you here?"

"Well," replied the Emperor with a mirthless

the white fox

chuckle, "we are in my prison cell, in my dungeons, in my fortress, on my planet . . ."

"But what could you possibly want with me?" Alex's reply was edged with sarcasm.

"As I said before, a *cooperative* chat." The Emperor stared into Alex's fiery emerald eyes.

Alex stared back into the darkness of the hood. "I don't trust you."

"Perhaps a gesture of goodwill. I am not what I appear to be." The Emperor pulled the hood off his head. A fairly young man, skin midnight blue, stood before him, one side of his bald head etched with a series of archaic symbols. The eyes, however, were the most striking—set like twin globes in hoods of deep space, they blazed molten gold with the heat of a thousand stars.

And he told Alex something that Alex himself had told no one—something that no one but Alex could possibly have known.

Alex was petrified by the knowledge of what was really standing before him and the cataclysmic implications of it. "B-but," he stuttered, "that's impossible . . .

The Offer

How could you know? You can't possibly be . . ."

"I know what I am not very well," snapped the being, glancing down the corridor. For the first time animosity and—was it possible?—panic were clear in his voice. "But that is not the point. You have something you may use against me if you so wish, and I have you imprisoned. We are now on equal footing."

Alex said nothing. He was trapped in a loop, reeling over what had just been revealed.

"So, what do you say?" The Emperor looked intently at Alex, who avoided his gaze. "You accept the terms? You will, if nothing else, cooperate?"

"Yes," Alex said finally, uncertainly.

"Excellent," replied the Emperor, replacing the hood over his face. Reaching to the wall on his right, he turned the key back twice. The chains around Alex instantly loosened, clanking to the stone floor. Shrugging them off, he stood up straight, wincing and massaging his wrists and neck.

"Come up to the Cathedral, and I can get you some new clothes. We can then discuss your fate." He turned and stalked out of the cell, Alex in tow. He

the white fox

strode down the corridor.

Alex paused. Now was his chance. Checking he was out of the cell so as to not activate the alchemical restraints, he gathered the last of his strength and pointed at the Emperor's back with his two forefingers. Two bolts of silver lightning sprung from his fingertips towards the black-cloaked figure. They diverged, about to strike . . .

Alex didn't know how it happened, but the Emperor turned at the last possible millisecond. Raising his arm in one swift motion, he reached out for the lightning bolts. They deflected off the black orb he had conjured around his fist and were flung back at Alex. They clutched at him like claws, hugging him with their torturous embrace. He gasped and collapsed to his knees, hundreds of volts running through every fiber of his body.

"In the future," said the Emperor, "I don't expect to have to defend myself from *you*." He marched down the hallway, leaving Alex to stagger to his feet and follow.

MEDALLION
P R E S S

Want to know what's going on with
your favorite author or what new releases
are coming from Medallion Press?

Now you can receive breaking news,
updates, and more from Medallion Press
straight to your cell phone, e-mail,
instant messenger, or Facebook!

Sign up now at
www.twitter.com/MedallionPress
to stay on top of all the happenings in and
around Medallion Press.

For more information
about other great titles from
Medallion Press, visit
m e d a l l i o n p r e s s . c o m